SPECIAL MESSAGE TO READERS

This book is published under the auspices of

THE ULVERSCROFT FOUNDATION

(registered charity No. 264873 UK)

Established in 1972 to provide funds for research, diagnosis and treatment of eye diseases. Examples of contributions made are: —

A Children's Assessment Unit at Moorfield's Hospital, London.

•

Twin operating theatres at the Western Ophthalmic Hospital, London.

•

A Chair of Ophthalmology at the Royal Australian College of Ophthalmologists.

•

The Ulverscroft Children's Eye Unit at the Great Ormond Street Hospital For Sick Children, London.

You can help further the work of the Foundation by making a donation or leaving a legacy. Every contribution, no matter how small, is received with gratitude. Please write for details to:

THE ULVERSCROFT FOUNDATION,
The Green, Bradgate Road, Anstey, Leicester LE7 7FU, England. Telephone: (0116) 236 4325

In Australia write to:
THE ULVERSCROFT FOUNDATION,
c/o The Royal Australian and New Zealand College of Ophthalmologists, 94-98 Chalmers Street, Surry Hills, N.S.W. 2010, Australia

Anna Jacobs was born in Lancashire, but now divides her time between England and Australia, thus avoiding winters totally, which she doesn't mind at all! She has worked as a teacher, lecturer and human resources officer, but finds writing novels much more fun. In fact she's addicted to storytelling. She and her husband have two grown-up daughters. She is the author of over forty novels — including the acclaimed Gibson Family saga.

Anna Jacobs is also the author of *Family Connections*, *Kirsty's Vineyard*, *Chestnut Lane* and *Saving Willowbrook*.

IN FOCUS

When a new feature on Pete Newbury's TV programme shows his adult image digitally transformed to that of a young child, Beth is shocked to realise that he's her 'baby' brother, who vanished without trace thirty-eight years ago. Her mother, never having recovered from the loss, desperately needs closure, but Pete is emphatic in not wanting to know his birth family. To further complicate matters, Beth finds herself falling in love with Pete's cousin and manager, Edward. At the same time Beth's runaway daughter reappears, complete with child, and Beth is terrified of losing her again. It's not easy to build bridges and bring families together after so many years and so much heartache, and she may lose the man she loves in the process . . .

Books by Anna Jacobs
Published by The House of Ulverscroft:

OUR LIZZIE
OUR POLLY
OUR EVA
CALICO ROAD
PRIDE OF LANCASHIRE
STAR OF THE NORTH
BRIGHT DAY DAWNING
HEART OF THE TOWN
FAMILY CONNECTIONS
TOMORROW'S PROMISES
KIRSTY'S VINEYARD
YESTERDAY'S GIRL
CHESTNUT LANE
SAVING WILLOWBROOK
FREEDOM'S LAND
FAREWELL TO LANCASHIRE

ANNA JACOBS

IN FOCUS

Complete and Unabridged

CHARNWOOD
Leicester

First published in Great Britain in 2009 by
Severn House Publishers Ltd.
Surrey

NORFOLK LIBRARY AND
INFORMATION SERVICE

SUPPLIER	ULVE
INVOICE No.	
ORDER DATE	8 8 16
COPY No.	

First Charnwood Edition
published 2010
by arrangement with
Severn House Publishers Ltd.
Surrey

The moral right of the author has been asserted

Copyright © 2009 by Anna Jacobs
All rights reserved

British Library CIP Data

Jacobs, Anna.
In focus.
1. Television peronalities- -Fiction. 2. Missing children- -
Fiction. 3. Adoptees- -Fiction. 4. Love stories.
5. Large type books.
I. Title
823.9'14–dc22

ISBN 978–1–44480–429–4

Published by
F. A. Thorpe (Publishing)
Anstey, Leicestershire

Set by Words & Graphics Ltd.
Anstey, Leicestershire
Printed and bound in Great Britain by
T. J. International Ltd., Padstow, Cornwall

This book is printed on acid-free paper

This book is for Donna Hay of Western Australia, who's been a dear friend for more years than we both care to remember.

Prologue

It seemed a day like any other. Beth Harding got up at six o'clock and stared out of the window. Another grey London day. Would spring never come? She made a mug of tea and went to check her emails before work. Living alone meant she could do as she pleased in the mornings.

Today there was an email from someone called 'lostgirl'. She nearly deleted it, then previewed it and choked on a mouthful of tea.

> Hi, Mum
> I'm all right. I know you've been worrying but I had to get my head together. Give my love to Gran.
> Jo
> PS In case you think this is a joke, I still remember my dog, Libby.

Beth read it again, printed it out and carried the piece of paper into the kitchen, pressing it against her cheek as if that would bring her closer to the daughter who had run away from home at the tender age of sixteen. She'd heard nothing from Jo since.

Three whole years of worrying!

Tears welled in her eyes and everything around her turned into a blur. Suddenly she was sobbing, a harsh ragged sound that seemed to echo through the flat.

1

By the time she'd calmed down a little, the message she'd printed out was bubbled and blotched with her tears.

Her daughter was alive! Alive!

Until this moment Beth hadn't even known that, though she'd hoped. You had to hope. Three years ago Jo had gone out one day and not returned. She'd taken a few of her possessions, but left most of them behind. The police investigations had got nowhere and none of Jo's friends had seen or heard from her since.

Beth's marriage had broken up the year before Jo vanished, but Shane had joined her in night watches for their daughter, searching places where down-and-outs congregated, visiting hostels. They had both been desperate for anything that might give them a clue, anything at all. They'd even forgotten their differences and grown to be almost friends again.

Shane now lived in Canada, was married to a much younger woman and had two young children. Beth was still on her own and at forty-three she had no intention of risking another relationship.

As she made a second mug of tea, she murmured her daughter's name like a mantra. 'Jo, Jo.' More tears welled in her eyes, leaving cool trails down her cheeks. It was wonderful news, but painful. She didn't doubt that the email was genuine because of the dog's name. Jo had loved that dog, been desolate when Libby died.

Beth hadn't realized how passionate teenage rebellion could be, because she'd never been free to rebel, had always had to be sensible. Maybe she should have gone a bit easier on Jo after the divorce. Or maybe not. She could live with an untidy home, but not a dirty one. And though she could also live with Jo being sexually active from an early age, however much she disapproved, she didn't want a series of randy young guys bedding down in her flat. She'd freaked out the first time she bumped into a strange man in the corridor. She and Jo had had the first of their bad quarrels over that.

She sighed. What use was there in agonizing over the past? It was another country. She wasn't sure who had said that, but it fitted her situation.

Although she knew the email off by heart, she read it again anyway. The message was painfully short. There was no clue as to where her daughter was, or if she was ever coming back.

She'd thought it would be enough simply to know Jo was alive, but it wasn't. She ached to see her only child again, be with her.

After a quick check of the time, she rang Shane. He'd not received an email from their daughter, but he sobbed at the other end of the line when she told him Jo was still alive.

1

Normally the six-storey building was deserted when the cleaning team came in, but Beth was surprised to see lights at one end of the top floor even though it was ten o'clock at night. She waited in the basement car park, only getting out of her car when the two other cleaners arrived, because she always felt nervous if she had to be out alone late at night.

One of them greeted her with a friendly grin. 'Hi, boss! Coming to keep an eye on us, are you?'

Beth smiled back. 'Pam couldn't make it tonight and all my relief staff are busy.' She occasionally filled in when someone called in sick. It kept her in touch with her staff and she knew they respected her for not being afraid to get her hands dirty. 'Which floors shall I take?'

'Pam always did the top two.'

They walked in together, setting more lights blazing.

On the sixth floor, Beth checked the large, cluttered room in the small corner suite belonging to the IT company Aldeb, since this was where she'd seen lights. It had even more computers and pieces of equipment crammed in than last time she'd been here. The two young owners, Al and Debbie, were hunched over their

5

computers to one side. A guy in a suit was sitting in the corner, drumming his fingers on the desk and looking bored.

The woman turned to smile at Beth. 'Sorry. We've got a glitch in the new program and we're still trying to sort it out. Can you clean round us? We don't mind the noise and it won't hurt to leave a few metres of floor untouched for one night.'

'No worries. I'm doing the top two floors, so I can start on the fifth and come up here last.'

Just as she was about to tackle their part of the sixth floor, she heard a yell of triumph from the corner and turned to smile at the joyful faces.

The woman beckoned to her. 'We think we've fixed it but we need to test it out. Would you mind helping us? It'll only take a few minutes.'

'I'm no expert on computers.'

'We don't need your expertise; we need your face.' She chuckled at Beth's puzzlement. 'This program turns older faces back to children's, or vice versa — and it can be about eighty per cent accurate, as far as we can work out, unless someone's had plastic surgery, of course.' She brandished a camera. 'If we take a photo of you and turn it into you as a child, you'll know whether it's a good likeness, won't you?'

'Yes, of course.' Beth had intended to refuse because she was exhausted, but was intrigued by the idea. 'Oh, OK. But we usually go out to our cars together for security reasons and the others won't want to hang around after their shift is over. Could one of you walk me out to my car afterwards?'

The man in the corner spoke. 'I'll do that.'

She studied him: tall and looked a capable sort. Yes, she'd feel safe with him. 'Thanks.'

They photographed her and asked her a couple of questions about herself as a child.

'I had blonde hair, a little lighter than now, and I was scrawny.'

As they fiddled around with the computer, the man sitting by the window continued to watch. He was good-looking in a quiet way, wearing a smart business suit with his tie loosened. The other two were dressed extremely casually, and the younger man had dreadlocks tied in a bunch at the back of his head.

Beth was suddenly conscious that it was the end of a long, hard day. What a time to have a photo taken! She must look a real mess. Then she shrugged. As if that mattered!

But when she sneaked a look at her reflection in the big glass windows, she realized she looked haggard as well as untidy. And for the first time in ages, that did matter, for some reason.

* * *

Edward watched the woman lean against a cupboard and study the two programmers. She was gaunt, looked weary and her clothes were crumpled beneath the cleaning company overall. He'd not have given her a second glance if it hadn't been for her eyes: big, brown and surprisingly beautiful in a face that was bleached bone-white with exhaustion.

He was tired too. Managing his celebrity

cousin wasn't the easiest job on earth, though it did pay well and — just as important to him — led him into some interesting experiences. This wasn't one of them. He'd been marking time here all evening while Al and Debbie fiddled around with their computers.

He'd read the newspaper from cover to cover, done the crossword, grimaced at the foul taste of coffee from the machine in the corridor and settled for chilled water from the dispenser. He didn't want to get on his mobile phone and chat to anyone, or even go on the Internet. Given a choice, he'd be sound asleep in bed by now, and was hoping these two would get the problem sorted out soon.

If their software didn't have potential for a new segment on Pete's show, he'd have gone home hours ago and left them to it, but it did. And once his cousin got word of something promising, he didn't let go. Trouble was, Pete sometimes went overboard over unsuitable ideas, so Edward always checked them out and made sure his cousin didn't rush into things he'd regret. This more cautious approach had saved the show from a couple of major problems in the past year or two.

He moved his body again, trying in vain to get comfortable in a typing chair designed for a midget, and ran his fingers through his hair, deciding it was too long and needed trimming.

Then Al and Debbie got the woman's photo up on the screen and he forgot his discomfort, leaning forward to watch what happened.

* * *

Beth looked at her image in dismay. She looked far worse than she'd expected. Well, anyone would be tired if they'd been working since five o'clock that morning, first doing the early shift at the office, then filling in for people this evening. The current flu virus had hit the cleaning company badly.

She watched what was happening, not really believing they could get close to what she'd looked like as a child.

'Here, sit down. You look tired out.'

She looked up in surprise as the man from the corner rolled a chair towards her. 'Thanks. It's been a long day.'

'I don't think Debbie and Al will be long.'

Then the program started to change her face and they both turned to watch. Amazed, she saw herself morph into a teenager.

When the lines of pixels had stopped rippling and changing, Debbie turned round. 'Well? Does it look like you at about fifteen?'

'Yes.'

'How like you?' Al prompted.

'Very. I wore my hair long, though, tied back.'

They adjusted the image. 'How's that?'

'Amazing.'

'Give me a percentage.'

'Ninety per cent at least.'

Al punched the air with one fist and turned back to the keyboard.

'You're sure of that?' the man in the suit asked.

She was surprised by the intensity of his gaze. 'Of course I am. I should know my own face.'

Gradually the image changed again, this time turning her into a child.

'Hair?' Debbie asked.

'Short, just below my ears, parted on the right.' She watched them adjust that, then sucked in her breath in astonishment. This could have been one of the old family photos. She realized all three of them were looking at her enquiringly, waiting for her reaction, and made an effort to gather her wandering thoughts.

'Well?' Al prompted.

'I can't believe it. That's so like me as a child. How do you *do* it?'

The young woman ignored the question. 'How close is it this time?'

'Ninety per cent again.'

Debbie beamed at her. 'We daren't claim that, of course, because it doesn't always happen. But sometimes it can be amazingly accurate, as long as we don't try to make the images too detailed. It's a fine line to tread.'

'Do you want to see what you'll be like when you're sixty?' Al asked.

Beth shuddered. 'No, thanks.'

Debbie chuckled and dug Al in the ribs. 'Not many women would want to see that, you dope.'

'What do you use a program like this for?'

The man in the suit cut across what Al had been going to say. 'That's confidential information, I'm afraid.'

The younger man rolled his eyes at her.

'Well, your program works brilliantly.' She

glanced once more at the screen, shaking her head in disbelief.

'How old were you then?'

'About six.' She closed her eyes for a moment as memories flooded back. Not a good year, that. Her little brother had vanished while on holiday, kidnapped or murdered, or else he'd simply wandered away and fallen into the sea. Her mother had been distraught.

Afterwards Beth had been passed from one relative to another for months while the police searched desperately for little Greg and her father nursed her mother through a breakdown.

But there had been no further sign of the child, no ransom notes, no body, nothing. It was as if the boy had simply vanished off the face of the earth a week before his third birthday.

The family had never settled down again. Her father and mother had started arguing a lot. She'd known, even though they tried to keep their voices low. You couldn't mistake that tone of voice. In the end, her father had left and hadn't come back. He had a new family now, living in the north of England. She saw him sometimes, but they weren't close. She was much closer to her mother, had had to be because without her support, her mother might have collapsed again.

Beth pushed the painful memories away and forced her tired, aching body upright. No way was she going down into that dark basement car park on her own. She looked at the man in the suit. 'Well, if that's all you need me for, I'll go home to bed.'

'Have you much more to do to the program?' he asked the two at the computers.

'Two or three hours of fiddling, probably.'

'Then I'll come back tomorrow. Give me a ring when you're ready to roll again. I'll need to see a few more successful regressions before we take it any further.' He turned to Beth. 'I'll walk you to your car. Here, let me carry that.'

'I can manage.'

He ignored her and took the cleaning equipment out of her hands. Clearly, the masterful type, but with beautiful manners.

As they stood waiting for the lift, he said, 'We haven't been introduced. I'm Edward Newbury.'

'Same surname as the talk show host,' she said without thinking. Pete Newbury had hit the headlines several times lately.

'He's my cousin, actually. Do you watch his show?'

'Not often. *In Focus* was on a bit early in the evening for me last season. I'm usually busy at that time of day.'

'And you're . . . ?'

'Beth Harding.' She didn't give him any further information about herself. What was the point? They'd probably never meet again.

'Have you worked here long?'

'I've been with Sherbright Cleaning Services for a few years now,' she said carefully. She never told strangers much about herself, if she could help it.

'Good employer?'

'Most people think so.'

The lift stopped at the basement car park and she shivered involuntarily. Of course, he noticed.

'Can you not find a job that doesn't involve night work?'

'I'm just filling in for someone who's sick. Normally I — um, work in the office. Our cleaners always go in and out of buildings in groups at night. Company policy. What do you do for a living?'

'I'm my cousin's manager.'

She might have asked him more about what that involved but they'd reached her car.

She zapped the locks, watched him put her equipment into the rear and got in. 'Thanks for coming with me to the car. I appreciate that.'

'No problem. You can't be too careful these days.'

She saw in the rear-view mirror that he stood watching her drive away. She wondered what it was like to manage a celebrity, and what they wanted the computer program for, then yawned and dismissed Edward Newbury from her mind. She'd probably never see him again. Pity. He was rather attractive. But she wasn't on the hunt for a man, didn't have the time or the inclination these days.

★   ★   ★

When she got back to her flat, Beth hesitated, then went into the third bedroom, a place she usually avoided. It'd been five years since her daughter had run away, but Beth had kept all Jo's things — just as her mother had kept little Greg's things, still had them tucked away somewhere.

13

Seeing that picture of herself as a child had stirred up a hornet's nest of old memories. No one had seen or heard of her little brother since the day he vanished. There had been no closure and that mattered more than people realized.

She still had photos of Greg somewhere and could remember playing with him as a child, but he didn't feel like part of her family any longer. He was just a legend, a ghost at every feast, especially if her mother was present, though for the past few years her mother had been a lot better, thank goodness.

With a sigh, Beth picked up one of the last photos of her daughter, one which resembled her own teenage self on the geeks' computer. It was ironic that Jo too had vanished. Was she destined to lose everyone she loved? Beth wondered.

But Jo was alive, at least. She had that to comfort her, and her daughter now sent emails every month or so, always from an Internet café, never giving any clue as to where she was or what she was doing. *Still alive, Mum.* Or: *Things going well, got a new job.*

Beth sent equally brief replies, not sure what she dared say, terrified of upsetting her daughter by asking to meet.

Surely the messages were genuine? She had to believe that. They were painfully sparse dribbles of information but better than nothing.

Would she ever see Jo again?

She stared round the dusty, unused bedroom. She really ought to clear it out, refurnish it perhaps, but you couldn't help hoping. And since no one else ever stayed here, it didn't matter what the room was like.

Oh, she was being silly tonight. Why revisit old pains? She had better things to do with her time. Like sleep.

An eighteen-hour day was no good for anyone. Whatever the emergency, she wasn't doing any extra shifts tomorrow.

She went into her own bedroom, intending to take a shower, but was so tired she simply fell on the bed for a moment's rest. As she reached up to release her long hair from its ponytail, she closed her eyes.

At three o'clock in the morning she woke, shivering, switched off the light, climbed under the covers and went back to sleep again.

* * *

In his comfortable flat in Hampstead Edward Newbury was woken in the middle of the night. He cursed the phone, letting it ring out. He needed to sleep, dammit.

But the noise started again, almost immediately. Two rings, then it stopped. Two more rings, then it stopped again. He groaned but when it rang a third time he picked it up. This was a special signal between himself and Pete, used only when one or the other of them was in trouble.

Or more accurately, when Pete was in trouble.

'What's the matter now?' Edward growled.

'Just had a quarrel with Fran. The bitch has locked me out and all my keys are inside the flat. Is your spare bedroom free?'

15

'Yes. Come on over.'

'I'll get the concierge to phone for a taxi.'

'Couldn't he let you into the flat?'

'I'd as soon walk through the fires of hell as face that bitch again tonight. Oh — you haven't got company there, have you?'

'No.' Edward hadn't had company of the female sort for a while, had been working too hard. Or perhaps he was getting more picky as he grew older. Though forty wasn't old and he kept himself fit. But he wasn't out to remarry and had always needed more than a willing female body to turn him on.

'You'll have to come down and pay for the taxi, Ed. I haven't got my wallet.'

It was the second time this month Pete had woken him. And actually, Edward didn't blame Fran for getting angry at him. Since his TV show had started getting top ratings, his cousin had turned into a bit of a prima donna, wanting others to dance to his whims.

Edward made his way to the kitchen for a drink of water and went to stand on the balcony. It was a mild night and at this hour the nearby buildings were mainly dark, so you could actually see the stars.

Just over ten minutes later headlights played along the dark street below and a taxi stopped in the visitors' parking area. He went down to pay for the ride.

After the taxi drove off, Pete wove his way unsteadily across the car park beside him.

Drunk again. That explained why Fran had locked him out.

16

When his cousin began to talk loudly in the foyer, Edward grabbed his arm and gave it a shake. 'Shut up, you fool. Other people are sleeping.'

Pete laid a mocking finger on his lips and pretended to tiptoe. Once inside the flat he leaned against the wall and grinned. 'Good old Edward. Always there to rescue me. Got any cognac to drown my sorrows with?'

'No. Go to bed and sleep it off. You've work to do tomorrow.'

'What time is it?'

'Two o'clock in the morning and I'm sleepy, even if you aren't.'

'Y'know, you've turned into a party pooper lately.'

'It's called growing up. And if you want to keep earning good money, you should do less partying and more sleeping. Here.' He pulled Pete along the corridor and opened the door of the spare bedroom. 'Be my guest. Do you need any pyjamas?'

Pete snickered. 'I'm hot enough without.' Then he frowned and peered at himself in the mirror. 'Hmm. Perhaps you're right. Sleep it is. I'll need to get up at six o'clock, so I can go home and change. Wake me then, will you?'

Edward walked across and set the bedside alarm for six, knowing he'd still have to come and drag Pete out of bed, by which time he'd be wide awake himself.

'And if Fran doesn't let me back in, I'll break the bloody door down. That'll teach her.'

'That'd be stupid. Get the concierge to use his master key.'

'It's my door. I can do what I want with it.'

Even before he left the room, Edward heard deep breathing. His cousin had always had the capacity to fall asleep within seconds of putting his head on the pillow. He only wished he shared the same gift. It was half an hour before the glowing numerals on the bedside clock began to blur.

He woke to the sound of the alarm beeping in the next bedroom and went to drag his cousin out of bed then put on some coffee.

By the time it was ready, Pete had dressed and joined him. He poured a cup of black coffee and took a long gulp, hot as it was. 'Thanks.'

'Considering how drunk you were when you arrived here, you look amazingly fresh and alert.'

'Yeah. I never get that morning-after stuff.'

He gave Pete money for the taxi and breathed a sigh of relief when he had the place to himself again. It was still too early to go into the office, so after clearing up the kitchen, he went down to the excellent basement gym that went with these prestigious apartments.

He doubted Fran would have kept Pete locked out for more than a few minutes last night. She knew which side her bread was buttered on.

And Pete knew that too. So what sort of statement was he making to her by spending the night elsewhere? The games those two played lately did Edward's head in.

He got on the treadmill and started his exercise programme. Other people were working out but to his relief no one wanted to chat.

2

The following week Beth had to fill in again for the same cleaner.

There was no one in the IT suite this time, so presumably the computer program had been fixed and they'd gone home like everyone else. She wondered what the software would be used for that was so hush-hush. Pete Newbury's show was very popular. The problem of what they'd do with all those faces niggled away at her as she cleaned that floor of the building.

Jo would have said, 'Get a life, Mum.' Her daughter had certainly gone after a life more to her taste, but it wasn't the sort of life Beth would have wanted. She enjoyed her peace and quiet. Well, she usually enjoyed it.

Tonight she felt restless. Tired, of course, but not ready to fall into bed yet. She switched on her computer and her heart did a flip when she saw a message from Jo. They always upset her and yet she needed to see them regularly, yearned for them.

Things are OK, Mum. Stop worrying. Shall I come and visit you one day? Would you like that?
Jo the Wanderer

Tears filled Beth's eyes. Couldn't Jo send longer messages than this? But it was the first time her

19

daughter had ever hinted at them seeing one another again. Scrubbing her eyes, she told herself not to be stupid. This was good news, wasn't it? Of course Jo would come back to see her one day. She had to believe that. She sent a message straight back.

Hi Jo
Always lovely to hear from you. Come any time. Longing to see you again.
Mum

Beth wanted to write more, but couldn't think of anything else to say. Anxiously she re-read her message. Was it all right to say 'longing to see you'? Would that worry Jo? She had to be so careful.

As she clicked on the send button, she suddenly realized why Jo's messages were so short. Her daughter must also be treading warily. That was a good sign — wasn't it?

The rest of the emails were mainly to do with business. The only other one she really welcomed was from her friend Renée. Smiling, she opened it.

Don't forget you're coming to dinner on Saturday. No excuses. Renée

Beth had forgotten about it, because it'd been a hell of a week, but she was more than ready for a bit of socializing. Renée threw great dinner parties and knew some interesting people. And her partner Sergio was an excellent cook. Of course, there was always the risk that Renée might try to pair Beth up with some guy, which had happened a few times, but Beth was more than capable of saying no.

She had to go into the office on Saturday morning, but spent the afternoon pampering herself. Renée wouldn't have called a hasty manicure and hair wash 'pampering' but that, together with a bit of eye make-up and a dab of lipstick was as far as Beth usually went in the beauty stakes these days.

She frowned at her reflection in the mirror when she was ready. She should do something about her hair, have it cut at least. And the dress which had been a perfect fit last year now hung loosely. She'd known she'd lost some more weight but hadn't realized how much. Renée would tell her off for that. Her friend had marked views about what magazine pictures of scrawny girls were doing to the female body image, and how women owed it to the younger generation to stay looking like real women rather than pre-pubescent teenagers.

But Beth had the opposite problem to most women she knew: she found it difficult to keep her weight up, and she'd got even thinner since Jo had left home.

Oh, what the hell! This was what she was like — scrawny — and other people could like it or lump it. She was her own person these days, not dependent on anyone, and she intended to keep it that way.

The dinner party was fun. Beth could feel herself relaxing, not because of the alcohol that was flowing freely, but because of the pleasant company. She enjoyed a drink, two if the wine was a good one, but that was it. She didn't have much tolerance for alcohol and hated feeling hungover the next day.

Renée had tried to match-make, but the guy was better than usual, not good-looking and slightly shorter than Beth, but fun to talk to. She guessed Daniel was a little younger than her, but he was old enough to be of interest. She found herself agreeing to have dinner with him the following week.

But she didn't let him take her home after the dinner party and would only give him her mobile number, arranging to meet him at the restaurant.

'Are you always this cautious?' he asked with a smile.

'Yes, I am.'

'Should I provide references?'

'How long have you known Renée?'

'A few months.'

'That'll do. And it's not you. I'm always cautious with new people, while Renée sees the best in everyone.'

'And do you always see the worst, Beth?'

She frowned, not sure what to say to that, then shrugged. 'I'm not good at choosing men to date. I've had a couple of bad experiences since my husband and I divorced.' She smiled suddenly. 'But you don't need to worry. It was an amicable split in the end and I won't bore you with tales of how rotten my ex was.'

He inclined his head. 'Neither will I because I've never actually got as far as marriage.'

She was surprised at that. Was he gay? He didn't seem gay, just very relaxed in his skin, as Jo would have said.

Daniel walked her out to her car without needing to be asked, which was another mark in his favour.

By the time she got home, she was wondering if she really wanted to bother dating anyone but knew if she backed out now, Renée would kill her. Anyway, she'd probably have a pleasant evening with Daniel and it could end there if she chose, which she probably would.

She backed into her parking bay, checked there was no one else around and hurried to the lift, relieved as always when it arrived quickly. This was supposed to be a safe area, accessible only by residents who had the remotes that controlled the wire mesh barrier gate, but you never knew who could break the code and get in.

It irked her that she was always so nervous after dark, but she wasn't going to any counsellor over something so minor, whatever Renée said. She was doing all right — more than all right — and didn't intend to rock the boat. She had a good job, a nice flat and a few close friends she really cared about.

It was enough.

★　★　★

Edward took Pete along to a demonstration of the finished computer program the following week. Al and Debbie had prepared regressions of themselves to start off with, then one of Edward.

'Do one of me now!' Pete said. 'We could start off with that on the show.'

They watched as the photo of Pete the man was regressed into a teenager.

'That's me!' he crowed. 'That's just what I was like! Go on. Make me younger.'

They obligingly turned him into a child of about eight.

'Can you turn me into a baby?'

'It's not very accurate with babies. They change too much. The lowest we can get with any accuracy is about two or three, and even at that age the success rate is markedly lower.'

'Do a three-year-old, then.'

He studied the resultant photo, head on one side. 'That's great! It's actually very like me. We'll use it on the first show to give people a taste of what your software can do.'

Edward watched the two youngsters — well, they seemed young to him — nudge one another and exchange quick, delighted glances.

'Do you want to see what you'll look like when you're older?' Al asked.

'Hell, no! I don't even want to think about that.' Pete glanced at his watch. 'Got to go now. Fran will kill me if I'm late. Edward, will you see to all this?' He waved one hand at the computer screen.

'Yes.' Naturally Pete didn't pick up on his annoyed tone of voice. Lately his cousin only seemed to see himself — a self-image more influenced by his publicity than by reality — and he'd always been a bit lazy about details like the legalities and financial arrangements for using the program.

To Edward's surprise, the two developers would only agree to lease the software, not sell it to him. They were more business savvy than he'd expected, for all they looked like refugees from a Sixties hippy commune. He didn't want to cheat them but he did want to make sure no one else in the entertainment industry could use their software while Pete wanted it, because if things went well, the new segment might have the potential to be franchised across the world, which would benefit all of them.

It took a while to sort everything out, and of course it then had to go to the various lawyers, but he was happy with the ground rules they'd established.

Since he'd come in Pete's car, Edward decided to stroll back to the office to pick up his own vehicle. He'd welcome a brisk walk after a day spent mainly in meetings.

He took a roundabout route and when he got there saw the cleaners going in. It wasn't Sherbright Cleaning, though.

Why did he keep thinking about the woman he'd escorted to her car? Was she any less tired this week? She must be really short of money to take on extra work in the evenings. She had the sort of face it was hard to forget — not pretty, she'd never be pretty, but strong. And she looked at you directly with those beautiful eyes, had an honest gaze, if there was such a thing. He was a sucker for eyes.

His ex had beautiful eyes. He was still fond of

her but she'd hated the long hours he worked. When they'd spent two years trying in vain for a baby, they'd found he could never get her pregnant due to a childhood illness.

A year later she'd left him for a guy who already had two children and worked regular hours, even if he didn't bring home nearly as much money. She'd had a baby within the year and another two years later, and seemed much happier now. Edward rang her sometimes or she rang him, just to catch up.

It didn't worry him that he had no children — well, most of the time it didn't — but he didn't want to spend the rest of his life alone.

Tonight his flat seemed to echo around him. He frowned as he studied it. As far as he was concerned, minimalism sucked big time as a decorating style. The place had been like this when he bought it two years ago and he'd intended to have it redecorated, but hadn't got around to it. Maybe it was time to take that in hand. He'd prefer something more cosy, with big comfortable armchairs.

But achieving that would mean a lot of fuss and upheaval. It would have to wait until he wasn't as busy, until the rest of his life was more to his liking.

He hadn't said a word to Pete, but he didn't intend to work as his cousin's business manager for more than another year at most. He needed new challenges, was tired of the role of minder. In fact, he'd been feeling restless for a while now.

★　★　★

26

The dinner date with Daniel was pleasant enough but there was no chemistry between them, even though Beth once again enjoyed his company.

He smiled at her as they sat over their final cups of coffee at the restaurant. 'No sparks flying between us, eh?'

She blushed. Just what she'd been thinking, though she'd not have put it so bluntly.

He patted her arm. 'I've come to the conclusion that I'm simply not highly sexed. I'm not gay, definitely not. But I don't seem to rouse that special feeling in women, and they don't go for me big time, either. I do make a good friend, though, if you're interested.'

'You're very frank.'

He shrugged. 'I'm comfortable with myself. I find you interesting to talk to and one can't have too many friends. We could meet occasionally for the pleasure of a chat. You may need an escort to a function or I may. You know what it's like when you're single and everyone else has a partner. Or you may just fancy going out for dinner, seeing a movie. What do you think?'

'Sounds good to me.' She could definitely do with an occasional escort to formal functions and she didn't want a permanent relationship. She had enough on her plate without that.

'I'll drive you home.'

'I live on the other side of town. It'd be more sensible for me to take a taxi.'

He pulled out a card and presented it to her Japanese-style, in both hands. 'As you wish, but take this. It has my details and you can check me out, if you're still nervous.'

She glanced down at it and couldn't help laughing. 'Sherbright has just won a cleaning contract with your company.'

'There you are. My references are in order, then.'

He hailed a taxi, saw her into it and waved as the taxi drew away.

She leaned back, smiling. Daniel was right. There was no spark, but she'd enjoyed his company. It was good to get out every now and then. Maybe she'd invite him round to dinner with some other friends. She owed Renée, for a start.

Her friend would no doubt ring up tomorrow to find out how the date had gone, and once she found out the truth, would start producing other single guys. Well-meaning friends could be a pain sometimes. Just because they were happily partnered, they thought everyone else wanted to be.

★ ★ ★

Two weeks later the same cleaner called in sick at the last minute and Beth had no option but to fill in for her again. The flu epidemic was over and 'a cold' was not a good reason for letting people down, in her opinion. If this woman continued to be unreliable, the company would have to replace her.

Again, the top floor was lit up and Beth found Al and Debbie bent over their computers. They waved at her cheerfully.

'More problems?' she asked as she dusted round them.

'No. But we've leased the program and need to make a few adjustments for our client, who wants it, like, yesterday.'

'It is for Pete Newbury, I take it?' Who else could it be when his business manager was there watching the demo?

Debbie hesitated. 'Yes. But don't tell anyone. This is for a new segment on the Pete Newbury Show and it's still very hush-hush.'

Al grinned. 'Nice chunk of ongoing royalties for us if it takes the public's fancy.'

'How are they going to use it?'

'They're considering a mixture of heart-warming sob stories and celebrity tales. They've not decided on anything yet. Maybe they'll try a few things and see what goes down best with the public. Pete's dead keen on it, anyway, which is what matters, and it's definitely going to be part of the new series, starting in a few weeks' time.'

'I must try to watch it.'

Beth got on with the work, pleased to have some of her curiosity satisfied. It had been fascinating to see them regress her own image to childhood. Perhaps she really would watch the show, though she'd have to record it. She'd guess that Pete Newbury was on to a winner here.

It suddenly occurred to her that she could use a program like that herself, to get an idea of what Jo might look like after five years. Her daughter would be a woman of nearly twenty-two not a teenager. Should she ask them to help her?

No, that was too private a matter. And anyway,

29

if Jo really did arrange to see her, she'd find out soon enough what her grown-up daughter looked like.

But she would watch the show. She wasn't interested in celebrity gossip or scandals, but she was a sucker for family reunions engineered on TV. They'd always given her hope that she might have one too some day.

* * *

The phone rang just as Beth was going out the next morning. She hesitated then picked it up, praying it wasn't someone calling in sick. But no, it wasn't the forwarding service. It was a withheld number.

'Hello?'

There was silence, someone breathing quite heavily, but just as she was about to put it down, a voice she'd recognize anywhere said, 'Mum?'

'Jo. Oh, darling, how wonderful to hear from you!' Beth's voice hitched on the last words and she clapped one hand to her mouth to hold back sobs.

'You don't sound any different.'

'Don't I? Well, you don't, either.'

'I am different, though, Mum. I've grown up quite a bit. You're not — still mad at me?'

'What for?'

'Running away from home.'

'I've been more worried than angry. Worried sick, in fact. Are you really all right?'

'Yes. I've got my act together now, I think. When's the best time to phone you?'

30

'After nine at night. I'm working crazy hours at the moment.'

'How's Dad?'

'All right, I think. We don't contact one another very often. You have a half-brother who's three and a half-sister who's not yet one.'

'Where's he living now?'

'Canada.'

'Crazy. He always hated snow.'

'His wife's Canadian and she wanted to be near her family. I can give you his address, if you like. He's still got the same email address.'

'No, don't bother. I just want to connect with you at the moment.'

There were voices in the distance, then Jo said, 'Got to go now, Mum. I'll ring again.'

And before Beth could even say goodbye, the connection went dead. She put the phone in its cradle and leaned on the kitchen bench, breathing deeply, desperately trying not to cry. But it was no use. She did cry, good and hard.

It wasn't every day your long-lost daughter proved beyond doubt that she was still alive and, best of all, still speaking to you.

When Beth arrived at work, her friend Sandy, who ran the office with ferocious efficiency, said at once, 'What's wrong?'

'Nothing. Why?'

'You've been crying.'

'Well, I had some good news this morning, bittersweet but good.' She hesitated, then added, 'Jo phoned me.'

And began crying all over again.

31

3

Two months later Beth caught a promo on TV about an exciting new segment coming soon to the Pete Newbury Show. It didn't give details, but let drop plenty of hints which made it clear it was the photo regression program she'd seen that night. She'd thought about it a few times, she had to admit, not least because it had brought back memories of her missing brother.

This season the show was going to be on later in the evening, so in theory she'd be home at that time, but she decided to record it anyway, just to be safe. Picking up the programme guide, she found the listing, circling it in red. There. Maybe after she'd seen how tacky it all was, she'd be able to stop thinking about it.

By the day of the first show, she was tired of seeing promos about the new segment, but at least that meant she didn't forget to record it.

Work was busy and everything seemed to conspire to stop her getting home in time to watch the programme live, but in the end she made it through the door with exactly two minutes to spare.

Grabbing an apple, because she couldn't remember when she'd last eaten, she picked up the remote and tuned in, sighing with impatience at the introduction and adverts.

Pete's smiling face filled the screen and she relaxed as she watched the first part of the show.

After the adverts break, Pete said, 'And now, the surprise you've been waiting for: a new segment called *Who Am I?* Life can move people on so quickly they sometimes lose touch with their families and childhood. If they've lost the family photos they might not even know what they looked like as a child. We're going to introduce you to people from all walks of life who're in exactly that situation.'

He paused then added, 'Maybe you can get involved too, and help us to help them. If you were one of their neighbours and have photos, you could make a big difference. Or maybe you're part of the family they lost. Or you could have been a close childhood friend. Wouldn't you like to help?'

He always looked so relaxed, Beth thought. She wished she could be as open and friendly as that with the world. She studied him, head on one side. He didn't look at all like his cousin Edward, who was much leaner, with dark hair; Pete had fair hair and though he wasn't plump, he wasn't slim, either.

'To do this, we're going high tech. A few months ago I heard of a new computer program. It can take a photo of an adult face and regress it to the child's face, doing so with a fair degree of accuracy. Impossible, I thought. And yet . . . what if it really could do what it promised? So I looked into it, and guess what? It can. It can also move forward in time to show what people might look like when they're older, but who wants to know that?'

He paused again for the studio audience to

laugh. 'So . . . using this program we've got a lot of stories to investigate and people to help. We're relying on you, the viewers, and can't do anything without your help. I think you'll find it very rewarding, as I do.'

The audience applauded again. Someone was probably holding up a sign to them, Beth thought cynically.

'Before we start, I'd like you to meet Al and Debbie, the program's developers.'

He gestured with one arm and the view changed to the two, who were as weirdly dressed as ever, sitting behind a computer.

'And now, let me give you a demonstration of what our program can do.' His brilliant smile faded a little. 'I volunteered to be the first guinea pig, because I'm one of the people who don't have any photos of themselves as a young child. Our family house burned down when I was about three, you see. I really wanted to see what I was like then.'

He was openly wistful now. 'There must be other people in the same situation, or far worse. Why don't you get in touch with us? We may be able to connect you with your past or even find your families. The computer program is about eighty per cent accurate. Just think of that, four chances out of five that they've got it right. Pretty good, eh?' He turned his head slightly. 'Ready to roll, guys?'

A still photo of his head came on the screen, while in the back-ground he continued to talk them through the process. The same rippling that Beth had seen before began and gradually a much younger Pete Newbury emerged on screen, wearing a bright blue tee shirt. He looked about fifteen.

'From now on, the blue tee shirt will be the clue that this is the computer-generated image. I've brought along an actual photo of myself as a teenager. We'll see how it matches up after this advert break.'

★ ★ ★

In a waiting area behind the set Edward sat next to his aunt. He glanced up at the monitor, surprised it wasn't on, wondering how the show was going, then looked back at her.

At seventy, Sue Newbury usually radiated good health, but he was getting worried about how pale she was tonight.

'You look nervous. You don't have to go on if you don't want. I can do the segment for you, if necessary.'

'Pete would be furious if I didn't do what he wanted. You know what he's like. This show is his baby. And anyway, you couldn't do it, from what he's said. It's something to do with when he was a boy.'

'But you don't want to go on television, do you?'

Sue shook her head.

'Why did you let him persuade you?'

'I think Pete could persuade a mountain to move across to the next valley, if he really tried. And I owe him so much. He bought me that lovely house after Donald died, keeps me in comfort and — '

A young man with a clipboard came into the area. 'I'm Gerry, here to take you through. Ready, Mrs Newbury?'

Sue took a deep breath and stood up, smoothing down her skirt with a hand that trembled slightly.

'No need to be nervous,' Gerry said brightly. 'Everyone's very friendly and we have a lovely studio audience. I'll show you where to go. Oh, just a minute.' He darted across to switch on the monitor.

Edward frowned as he settled back to watch the next segment. Why had the monitor been switched off while his aunt was here? Why hadn't Pete told her exactly what they were doing?

He had a bad feeling about this. Why the hell did Pete have to involve his own mother?

★ ★ ★

Annoyed by the advert break just as it was getting interesting, Beth nipped out to make herself a cup of instant coffee. She couldn't believe how this segment had grabbed her attention. Was it just her or were other people similarly engaged by the concept of helping people to find their lost childhoods and maybe even their lost families?

When the show began again, they quickly reprised what had happened — as if you'd forget during such a short break, she thought in irritation — after which they showed the computer-generated image of Pete in a blue tee shirt.

'Now,' said Pete, 'here's a photo of me at fifteen.'

A photo of a lanky, grinning youth came up. He'd not yet got his man's breadth but was very recognizably Pete Newbury. After a moment the screen split in two to show the computer image and the real photo.

'Ninety per cent,' Beth said aloud.

The audience oohhed and aahhed.

The present-day Pete came back on the screen. 'Marvellous, isn't it? Now, let's take it a step further. Let's regress me to a child.'

More rippling, backed by music designed to build tension. Beth frowned as a younger lad appeared on the screen, again wearing a bright blue tee shirt. He reminded her of someone, she couldn't think who.

'I'm about nine now,' Pete said. 'Let's see how it compares.'

A real photo of him came up next to it and Beth said in amazement, 'Still ninety per cent. I can't believe this.'

He came back, still with that rather wistful smile, which was very unlike his usual grin. 'As I said earlier, I don't have many photos of myself as a very young child, due to a house fire. So I wondered what I'd looked like at two or three. The makers of the program don't guarantee as close a match at this age, preferring to use ReGress only to go back to about six years old. But I couldn't resist trying it anyway. After all, a man does like to know the little boy he was. Thanks to my mother, I was able to tell them my hair colour, because young children's hair can

37

change, but the rest is down to our fabulous IT team and ReGress.'

He held up his hand. 'Just one more thing before we turn our computer experts loose. We always like to verify that the images we get are true to life, so I've asked my mother to join me for this segment. She's the only one left who'll know if it really does look like me at that age.'

He gestured and stood up as they brought an older woman on to the set. Moving across, he gave her a hug then swung them both round to face the cameras. 'This is my mother, Sue. She doesn't know exactly what we've been doing, but she'll remember what I looked like at the age of three. Won't you, Mum?'

Beth saw his mother throw him a startled glance. Surely he'd told her what he was doing?

He walked her across to his seating area, with its famous dark purple armchairs. 'Come and sit down, Mum. I've got something fascinating to show you. Pity Dad couldn't have been here with us tonight, eh? But perhaps he's watching from up there.'

When he explained the details of what was going to happen, his mother stared at him in utter horror.

Beth stared too. 'Horrified' was the only word to describe Sue Newbury's expression, which seemed rather an extreme reaction to what was only light entertainment, after all.

'I don't think we should do this, Peter,' Sue quavered. 'It'll bring back too many memories.'

'Just bear with me, Mum.'

More rippling then the screen settled down to

show a little boy with white-blond hair, staring at the camera in a way Beth recognized. The image wasn't exactly like her little brother, but it was close, very close indeed. How bizarre! But then a lot of little boys looked like that at three, surely?

'How like me is it?' Pete asked.

His mother shook her head and her voice wobbled as she spoke. 'There's a — a faint resemblance, but it's not really close. You were — a bit plumper — and your hair was much shorter, and perhaps a little darker.'

The image flickered and reappeared with shorter hair and a slightly plumper face. The resemblance to Beth's little brother vanished.

'Yes, that's more like it,' Sue said.

But she still looked terrified, poor woman. Why? Beth thought.

The camera moved away from Sue to a close-up of Pete. 'So,' he said, 'the creators of this program were right when they said it wasn't accurate if we went back beyond about six years. Let's look at me around the age of six, then.'

The photo reformed and a cute little boy appeared. A real photograph of him at six came up next to it and the resemblance was quite striking.

'That's great. Gee, I was a good-looking kid, wasn't I?'

The audience laughed. His mother didn't even crack a smile and had a white-knuckled grip on the arms of her chair.

'Now, Mum, I'll let you escape.' He escorted her off the set and went back to his chair, saying, 'My mother might hate being in focus here, but our next guest enjoys it and he's the one who needs your help. Cassadee, come and join me.'

The well-known singer walked on to the stage. His lean face and shock of dark hair, streaked with grey now, were almost a trademark.

After a couple of minutes of chat, Pete's voice softened. 'Can we move now to the main reason for you being here tonight? What happened, Cassadee? How come you have no photos of your childhood?'

The singer bowed his head for a moment, then said in a harsher voice, 'I ran away from home when I was fourteen. I didn't go back for a long time and when I did, I found that my parents had been killed in a car crash and their possessions given to a charity.'

'Did you have no other relatives?'

Cassadee hesitated, then said, 'Not that I could find.'

The camera moved in to show the tears in his eyes as he continued, almost as if talking to himself, 'You think when you run away that you'll go back one day, but you can't always do that. I've regretted bitterly that I didn't keep in touch and now, well, I've nothing to show my own children, and they're keen to find out about their family background.'

Pete smiled at the pop star like a wolf about to pounce. 'OK, so your three children want to know what you looked like as a child. According to our computer experts, this is what you looked like as a teenager.' He paused to let the image form. 'About fifteen, would you say?'

'Yes. But I was quite a bit thinner. I wasn't

eating well in those days. And my hair was long, tied back — cheaper that way. No hair-cutting bills.'

The image rippled and changed slowly.

Cassadee's intake of breath could be heard very clearly. 'Yes. That's me.'

'Percentage of accuracy?'

'About ninety.'

'You took the name Cassadee and you've been adamant about not sharing your real name with anyone. But if you want people to help you . . . '

'I was born James Redwich. We lived in Victoria Terrace in a small village called East Hannerby in Hampshire. My mother and father ran the village shop. If anyone there remembers me and has a photo of me or anyone in the family, I'd be very grateful if you'd share it.'

As his voice broke on the last few words, Pete intervened. 'So there you are, folks. You've seen the image. You've seen the pain of losing your past. Details of how to contact us are on our website. Can you help Cassadee? Do you want to meet him to hand over photos? As you can see, this means a lot to him.'

Beth picked up her half-empty coffee cup and sipped it as the adverts came on. After that, she watched half-heartedly as Pete interviewed a famous soccer star. He did a good job of it, but she couldn't concentrate on what they were saying.

The segment with Cassadee had been very moving, but it was the first image of Pete as a young child that stayed with her. It had roused sleeping tigers, reminding her strongly of one of the few photos she had of her little brother Greg. Sue Newbury had been very sure it didn't look like her son, so the resemblance was mere coincidence, but it had still upset Beth.

Only when the programme ended did she realize she hadn't stopped it recording. She switched it off and on impulse went into her bedroom. Grabbing her oldest photo album, she was back within the minute. She ran the recording back to the beginning of the regressions and froze it, staring at the little boy on the screen, then flipped quickly through the album.

She didn't really need to look at the old photos, though. The image of her little brother was burned into her brain.

The first picture they'd shown of three-year-old Pete Newbury was . . . well, it was as if he were her brother's identical twin. Or Greg himself. No, that wasn't possible. She was imagining things. His mother had said very definitely that it wasn't like him, which settled it. Pure coincidence.

How weird, though! Coincidences happened all the time, but not usually to her.

She just hoped her own mother hadn't been watching the show tonight. It'd have upset her big time.

Putting the photo album away, she went to grab something to eat and decided to read in bed. She looked for one of her favourite comfort reads, a Georgette Heyer, and settled down with a banana and a few pieces of chocolate, letting the silence wrap round her like a cosy blanket.

But she dreamed of her little brother that night, dreamed she was chasing him through a wood, calling to Greg to wait for her and weeping as she fell further and further behind.

★ ★ ★

Edward went to meet his aunt as she came off the set. 'That upset you, didn't it?'

She nodded. 'Did you know what he was intending?'

'In general terms, yes. I'd have given you a hint or two if I'd known you were going to be totally unprepared. It must have been hard losing the photos and everything else, and to have this bring it all back — well, I think Pete was way out of line.'

Her voice was faint, hardly more than a whisper. 'It was terrible to be reminded . . . '

'Shall I take you home now?'

She hesitated then nodded. 'If you don't mind. Peter wanted me to stay for some party or other, but I'm not feeling well, probably coming down with a cold.'

Edward had her out of the studio in two minutes flat and drove her home. She didn't go out and about much these days, because she no longer drove, and anyway, there were plenty of group activities in her retirement complex. He visited her quite often, because she was like a second mother to him — and he knew Pete didn't go to see her as often as he might have done.

'Want me to stay for a while?' he asked.

43

She shook her head. 'No. I think I'll go straight to bed, dear.'

'I'll just see you inside, then, and make sure everything's all right.'

Of course it was, because the flat was in a gated community with inbuilt alarm systems. He'd always enjoyed visiting her former home, which had been a spacious old house lovingly restored, and he knew she missed it, but she'd not have been able to manage it these days.

How sad life was! He remembered her comforting him after his own parents were killed when he was ten and he'd gone to live with his aunt and uncle. She'd been very lively then, playing cricket with them on the lawn, doting on Pete and perhaps spoiling him. No, not perhaps, definitely spoiling him. But she'd been unable to have any more children, so her over-protectiveness didn't surprise anyone. Edward loved her dearly. His uncle had been kind, but there hadn't been the same connection because Donald had been a busy man. Edward always felt he'd worked himself to death and had decided long ago that he wasn't going down the same path.

He waited till his aunt had switched on the lights before going back to his car, returning reluctantly to the studio to attend the party to celebrate the new series, and especially the new segment, a party to which several VIPs had been invited. He didn't want to go, but it would be better to show his face. At least the party would be half over by now.

Even as he was talking to this person and that, he kept remembering his aunt's unhappy expression, her trembling hand on his arm. He hated to see her so upset.

Not kind of Pete to toss his mother into the deep end like that. Was there no limit to what his cousin was prepared to do for his precious show? Or to what he'd expect others to do?

Well, Edward had had enough of being on call twenty-four-seven.

★ ★ ★

Two days after the show, Daniel rang to ask if Beth would like to accompany him to an official company function.

'It's a ball, actually, the annual bash. I promise you'll eat well, I'm not a bad dancer, and we've got some interesting people on our table. Maybe you don't like such functions? Not everyone's into ballroom dancing these days. I won't be offended if you say no.'

'I'd like to come. I enjoy your company and I love dancing.'

'Great.' There was silence then he said hesitantly, 'Look, it's a pretty dressy affair. If you've nothing suitable, I'd be happy to buy you an outfit. I'm — um, not short of money.'

'Thanks, but I can buy my own outfit, Daniel. I'm not short of money, either. It'll be fun choosing something elegant. I'll see if Renée is free. I always find nicer clothes when I go shopping with her.'

When she phoned, Renée said, 'About time! Your clothes are so shabby you're starting to look like a bagwoman.'

45

She laughed. 'Not that bad, surely?'

'Worse than you realize, Beth.'

'Oh.'

'I know you've had some hard times these past few years, but you're out of that patch now and Jo's in touch again, so how about spending a little time and money on yourself? You ought to visit a hairdresser, too. You have lovely hair. That colour of dark, natural blond is very attractive. But you tie it back in a ratty tail, and if you've used conditioner on it regularly, then all I can say is, you're buying the wrong conditioner.'

'I ran out a week or so ago. No, it must be last month. That flu epidemic — '

Renée's voice grew firmer. 'The flu epidemic's well over now. The weather's getting brighter and so should you. No excuses, my girl. We'll go shopping on Thursday morning and do lunch afterwards, then I'll book you in with my hairdresser in the afternoon. About time you took a day off work.'

Another quick glance in the mirror and all Beth could say was, 'All right.'

★ ★ ★

She'd never enjoyed a shopping expedition more. When she'd have gone for a black velvet trouser suit, Renée pulled her away sharply and found her a wonderful skirt and top in glossy teal satin and lace.

'You've got enough black in your wardrobe, and until you put on some weight you need girly, flouncy clothes to soften your outline, not stark,

46

tailored stuff. Try this other skirt as well.'

'But it's a floaty material. Where will I wear it?'

'You could try wearing skirts to the office sometimes.'

'But what if I have to fill in for someone and — '

'Leave some older clothes at work, or wear one of those garish bright orange overalls, if you must. Best of all, let someone else do the filling in.'

Beth tried on the lilac skirt, found it flattering, chose a top to go with it and hugged Renée. 'You're good for me.'

'You helped me when I was down. Now it's my turn.'

'I'm not down!'

'Aren't you?' Renée held up one hand in a stop gesture. 'I won't pry, but I think you are, have been ever since Jo walked out. As I've said before, when you want to confide in someone, you know where to find me.'

Beth nodded, her throat suddenly thick with emotion. 'Thanks for not pushing about that. I am a bit fragile at the moment.' It had been two weeks now since the last call. Had her daughter changed her mind about meeting? Beth desperately hoped not. 'Oh, and thanks for introducing me to Daniel as well.'

'I'm surprised you're going out with him again. You said there were no sparks between you.'

'There aren't. But he's got the potential to turn into a good friend and I haven't been dancing for ages.'

'I'd be happier if you found yourself a sexy guy and had a mad, passionate affair.'

'I'm a bit old for that.'

'There! That's just what I mean. Forty-five is the new thirty-five, and you don't look anything like your age.' She eyed her friend severely. 'Or you wouldn't if you dressed better. But you act as if you're sixty. Get a life, Beth. A life that doesn't depend on Jo coming back.'

Beth let her friend run on for a minute or two longer, still smarting at being called a 'bagwoman', then found an excuse to end the conversation.

Unfortunately, her mirror agreed with Renée. Her hair did look a mess and her clothes were shabby.

* * *

Edward kept an eye on the preparations for the next TV show. To everyone's surprise, information had come in almost immediately after the appeal to help Cassadee. He'd left it to the research team to check it all and select what material they used from that offered.

It had surprised him that the singer wanted to come back on the show so quickly. 'You're not having him on two weeks running, Pete! Give it a break of a week or two.'

Pete grinned. 'Cassadee's hot stuff. He's just what I needed to start off with a bang. And the quicker we show feedback the quicker people will want to get involved.'

'His face is always in the media. I'm sick of the sight of it.'

'Get out of the bed on the wrong side this morning, did we?' his cousin teased.

'None of your business. Why are you going overboard with him, Pete?'

'You've heard his story. Well, most of it's true. He really was a street kid, lost touch with his family for years. It tugs the heart strings. We've had a huge response. This new segment is going to make our ratings soar.'

'Has it ever occurred to you that you could hurt people with this?'

'And has it ever occurred to you, Edward, that I can help people, too? Really help them. Besides, no risk, no gain. They know that.'

'*You* — wanting to help people out of altruism?'

Pete shrugged. 'Why not? It's good for my image.'

'You should stick to what you do best: interviewing celebrities.'

'You've got to change and grow, or you lose ground in this business.'

Edward was sick of his cousin's almost total focus on his career. 'You have a tendency to play with fire. Don't expect me to pull you out of the flames every time. I've got a life to lead as well, you know.'

But he could see that Pete wasn't really listening.

★ ★ ★

Feeling a little guilty at not going back to work after the visit to the hairdresser's, and taking the whole day off, Beth rang the office. Sandy assured her that everything was under control and she wasn't needed.

She put the food she'd bought in the fridge, which was better stocked than it had been for ages, and went along to her bedroom to gloat over the new outfit. It really was beautiful.

When the phone rang she glanced at the caller ID and saw it was withheld. Was it, could it be . . . ? She snatched up the phone. 'Hello.'

'Hi, Mum.'

'Jo. Oh, Jo.'

'You'll be getting tired of me if I ring you too often.'

'No, I won't. You couldn't ring too often for me.'

The silence that followed seemed louder than words. Beth held her breath, wondering if she'd been too gushy.

'Well, I might make it more often then. What have you been doing with yourself, Mum?'

'Buying some new clothes. Renée said I was looking like a bagwoman.'

Jo chuckled. 'But a very clean and tidy bagwoman, I'm sure.'

'Yes. Too clean and tidy sometimes.'

'I didn't understand then, Mum. I do now. Oh, hell, I'm crying.'

The call cut off abruptly.

Beth stared at the phone then set it gently into its cradle. Was it a good sign or a bad one that Jo had been crying? She willed the phone to ring again, but it didn't. When she went into the kitchen, she found she'd lost all appetite so

50

wandered back into the living room, unable to settle. She stared at her new self in the mirror: hair in a gleaming jaw-length bob, eye make-up — though Renée said she should get her eyeliner tattooed on to make things easier. Why hadn't she noticed before how very thin she was? She'd never been this scrawny before.

'*You've got to eat better, my girl,*' she told that gaunt figure in the mirror. Going back to the kitchen, she forced some food down, though the sandwich could have been filled with sawdust for all she tasted of the meat and salad it contained.

All the time her thoughts kept returning to Jo. As she tidied away her crockery, she found herself crying again, not sobbing but unable to hold back the tears that would trickle down her cheeks.

She had to believe she and Jo would get together again. Had to.

Her daughter was almost twenty-two now. Did she still look the same? Or was she full of studs and tattoos like some of the young women you saw in the streets?

Dammit, a mother should know what her own daughter looked like!

Suddenly Beth thought of Pete Newbury's new segment and could understand exactly why people went on it. If she'd not heard from Jo, if she never heard from her daughter again, it'd be a comfort to have a photo of what she might look like. Well, she thought it would.

Oh, she didn't know anything tonight!

4

Edward remained uneasy about the new segment of the show. If his cousin was moving beyond the light entertainment for which he was famous, he might upset some of his audience. It was such a balancing act, pleasing the public.

He went to the studio to watch the next show with the vague feeling that if something went wrong, it might be better if he were on the spot — though he couldn't imagine what he'd be able to do. What did he know about computer programs?

Ten minutes to go. He sat in the waiting area, making meaningless conversation with the first guest, a female singer whose songs left him cold and whose clothes left so little to the imagination he didn't know where to look.

Music blared forth on the set, jiggling happy music, and the guest was led away.

Pete welcomed her to the show and conducted the first interview with his usual warmth and skill, but even he found it hard to draw interesting answers out of such an airhead.

Just before the interview ended, the celebrity for the regression segment came into the waiting area. Cassadee didn't attempt to make eye contact with Edward or even sit down, just began pacing up and down, four steps each way.

He was clearly nervous about what they'd discovered about his past. Pete had decided not to tell those appearing the details, insisting there would be no drama if the segment didn't come up with a few surprises.

Edward was suspicious of surprises, especially in a public arena.

Soon after Cassadee left the waiting area to join Pete, the music changed to something Edward hadn't heard before, something softer and rather wistful.

'*Who Am I?*' It was a woman doing the voiceover now. They'd chosen an older woman, for motherly reassurance. She did a quick reprise of Cassadee's appearance on the previous week's show, then Pete took over live.

'We had an amazing response to last week's segment, so we brought Cassadee straight back, instead of waiting a week or two. He doesn't know what we've found out, though. Are you ready to face your past, Cassadee?'

'I'm here, aren't I? Bring it on.'

★ ★ ★

Beth looked at the clock. Two minutes to go. Should she watch *In Focus* tonight or not? It had upset her last week because of the coincidental resemblance to her brother. Oh, she was being silly! She was stupid to let mere chance get to her.

She pointed the remote at the TV and clicked, wondering if the new segment would continue to be as gripping.

She'd missed the intros but saw Pete smiling like a wolf about to pounce on a lamb.

53

'We've found someone from your past.'

Next to him Cassadee stiffened visibly.

'This person knew you at the age of fifteen, so will be able to verify the computer images.'

Poker-faced, Cassadee inclined his head.

Pete gestured to the side not normally used for guest entrances. 'Folks, let's welcome Stacey, another person who doesn't use a surname.'

The camera turned back to Cassadee, however, instead of going to the newcomer. At the sound of the name, his mouth fell half open, then he mouthed the word, 'Stace.'

He looked like a man in pain to Beth and not for the first time, she wondered if this segment was going to be kind to those who participated in it. It had seemed so simple when she first heard about it. Just show a computer image and get the viewers to help that person find their past. But last week, Mrs Newbury had been really upset by her son's incorrect image — and so had Beth.

The camera stayed on Cassadee as he took a deep breath and stood up, then at last it panned to the guest.

The woman who walked on to the set looked as if she'd lived a very hard life. She could have been any age from thirty to fifty. Her clothes were clearly brand new, hanging on a body thin to emaciation, and her hair hung straight and long down her back. Even the make-up couldn't give her a healthy look.

The camera caught the fact that her eyes filled with tears as she looked at Cassadee.

He went straight across to scoop her up into

his arms and give her a long hug. 'I can't believe it's you.'

'Bad pennies always turn up again,' she said in a slightly hoarse voice.

'You were never a bad penny, Stace, just a lost penny.'

Pete interrupted and got them sitting down then the programme continued, but the under-currents between Cassadee and Stacey showed in their faces and the occasional glance sideways. Once she reached out to touch him, as if she couldn't believe he was real, and the camera was on to it. He turned his head and patted her hand briefly, then looked back at his interviewer, the guarded expression slipping back into place.

The encounter had the audience riveted, as a straightforward, happy reunion could never have done.

On being questioned, Stacey too put the accuracy of the computer image at ninety per cent. 'It doesn't show his eyes properly, though,' she said thoughtfully. 'He was always kind and that showed in his eyes. He had his own troubles, but you felt he really listened to you. Helped me out a few times, he did, when I had no one else.'

When Pete judged that enough time had been spent on Stacey, he asked Al and Debbie to take the image back to six years old, and the Cassadee on the screen lost his bony, haunted look and became a lad again, with a lad's innocent smile.

'We not only had Stacey contact us but a relative of yours, who knew you as a lad,' Pete said.

Beth had already noticed that the singer's hands were white-knuckled against his jeans. When Pete mentioned a relative, the hands spasmed then lay still.

'Who is it?' Cassadee asked. 'Must be a very distant relative.'

If he'd meant to sound casual and relaxed, he'd failed, Beth thought.

Pete smiled, let the silence continue for a moment or two, then said, 'Not so distant. It's your Uncle Steven.'

'What?'

Cassadee jerked to his feet as a nervous-looking older man hesitated at the edge of the stage. As the man walked towards him, Cassadee strode quickly forward and punched the newcomer hard on the jaw, sending him flying into the first row of the audience.

Ignoring the upset this caused, Cassadee moved back to Pete and Stacey, snapping, 'Get that creature off the set or I leave. And do your research better in future. One of the reasons I left home was because of that man, who shouldn't be allowed near any innocent child.'

The programme cut abruptly to adverts and Beth leaned back in her chair, letting out a long, slow breath. Dangerous stuff, this.

She was glad she was never likely to go on this show or be interviewed by this new, harder Pete Newbury, who smiled so calmly as he tossed emotional grenades at his guests.

When the program resumed, nothing was said about the uncle. Beth watched the interview continue, heard Cassadee talk about his youth on the streets and found it gripping stuff. Stacey sat there quietly, nodding occasionally to corroborate something.

There was a grimness behind the singer's calm expression now, though, an added sharpness in his tone. But both men were professionals and knew better than to add to the gossip by quarrelling on live TV.

Then photos from neighbours were produced and Cassadee relaxed, smiling and fingering the photos, thanking the donors and promising to go and thank them in person.

Edward groaned and buried his face in his hands after Cassadee punched the older man, but looked up again almost at once. When the adverts came on, he hurried towards the set.

He met the young assistant, Gerry, shepherding the uncle out of the studio and apologising to him for the upset.

'It's all right, lad. He has good reason to be angry. I'd like to have made my peace with him before I died, though — I've got cancer — but there you are.'

Edward walked over to join them. 'We'll get you checked out by a doctor, Mr Redwich, and then — '

'No need, son. It was only a punch. Besides . . . I deserved it.'

Something inside Edward shuddered, because if this meant what he thought, he agreed that the punch was well deserved. 'Do you need a taxi?'

The old man paused to look at Edward as if he knew what he was thinking. 'Yeah. That might be best.'

'Where are you staying?'

'With friends.'

He refused to give further details and Edward watched the taxi's tail lights disappear, before going back into the studio.

The show's ratings would no doubt rocket — but at the expense of others' pain. Did he want to be involved in this sort of thing? No. Definitely not.

But he had no choice. His contract tied him to Pete for another six months. And anyway, Pete was his cousin. When something came unstuck, as it was bound to, there needed to be someone practical around to pick up the pieces. If only for his Aunt Sue's sake. No one could call Pete practical.

Luckily this uncle fellow didn't seem likely to make any claims for compensation.

When the segment ended, Edward went to the side of the set. He saw Cassadee wait till the signal was given that they were no longer on air then stand up. The singer ignored Pete's outstretched hand, put one arm round Stacey's shoulders and shepherded her off the set without a word of farewell.

Edward stepped out of the way but Cassadee, whom he'd met a few times, stopped to say, 'Better pull the reins tighter on your damned cousin and get the researchers to check things out more carefully. He's heading into danger territory.'

As if Edward wasn't all too aware of that! 'Will your uncle sue?'

The wolfish look was back. 'He wouldn't dare.'

'He told me he had cancer, wanted to make his peace with you.'

'There is no peace possible after what he did to me. If he's got cancer, then I'm glad. It means there is some justice in the world.'

Cassadee looked down at the woman standing patiently beside him. He walked out of the studio with his arm still round Stacey's shoulders, speaking gently now, the hard edge gone from his voice.

It was a moment or two before Edward returned to the waiting area, because the sight of them moved him deeply. He felt quite sure Cassadee was going to help his old friend, and equally certain she needed it desperately. So maybe some good had come out of this, after all.

The next part of the show featured a famous opera singer. Her break-up with her lover of many years had been acrimonious and had hit all the headlines. He'd trashed her home, destroying all her photos and mementoes of her youth, for which he'd been jailed. She was eager to find some photos, especially of her parents, who were dead now.

Her appeal had been filmed between performances at La Scala. The computer images showed a pretty little girl and a plump teenager.

When at last the show was over, Pete came off the set. 'It went well, didn't it?'

'As long as you don't mind hurting people.'

Pete's smile went a bit glassy. 'How can we be expected to predict such things. Sheer chance.'

'Was it?' Suddenly Edward was sure that Pete had suspected there was something amiss

59

between Cassadee and his uncle. He could bear no more tonight, so turned and walked away.

'Ed, come back. I want to ask you about — '

He kept walking, needed some fresh air.

★ ★ ★

As Beth was getting ready for the dinner dance on the Saturday, the doorbell rang. Muttering in annoyance, she went to check who it was on the intercom, then relaxed and let Renée in.

'I'm going out in half an hour. Had you forgotten?'

'Nope. I came to check that you're looking your best.'

Beth looked at her in mingled exasperation and amusement. 'Yes, Mummy.'

Renée grinned. 'You know I'm better with hair than you are.'

'I've washed and blow-dried it. It looks fine to me.'

Her friend stood back, studying her. 'Good cut, that. But it needs this for a formal affair.' She produced a small object, a jewelled hair slide. 'Get your dress on and let me fix the hair.'

Ten minutes later Beth knew she was looking her best and smiled at her reflection. 'You're right. That hair slide does look good. Subtle enough for my taste, too.'

'I know. You're definitely not a show pony. Now look, I know there's nothing fizzing between you and Daniel, but there will be other men there tonight. Don't put on your untouchable expression. Smile and enjoy yourself, and if

60

an interesting guy comes along, let nature take its course.'

'Yes, Mummy.'

Renée hugged her suddenly. 'You've been alone long enough, Beth. Life's more fun if you have a partner.'

'As long as it's the right partner.'

'I agree. All I'm saying is, don't keep the door so tightly closed or you'll never meet anyone, right or wrong.'

When the bell rang again, it was Daniel's voice on the intercom.

'I'm ready. I'll be down in a minute,' Beth said.

The two women took the lift and Renée said goodbye in the foyer.

'You look beautiful,' Daniel said to Beth.

'I think I look my best, but we both know I'll never be beautiful.'

'Lovely, then. Can you accept that word?'

She hesitated then smiled. 'Tonight, perhaps. Renée did a good job on my hair, didn't she?' And the outfit softened her figure, hinting at curves she no longer possessed.

★ ★ ★

With great reluctance Edward got ready to go out. He hadn't invited a partner to the ball and wished now that he'd bothered to ask someone, because he enjoyed dancing. But he'd been snowed under since the last show, working all hours of the day to minimize the fall-out from the Cassadee interview.

61

The uncle had committed suicide straight after the show. The old man might have been suffering from cancer, but he could have lived for quite a while yet if he'd wanted to. Luckily the press hadn't noticed the suicide.

Cassadee remained furious and rightly so. But with his uncle now out of the picture, he calmed down somewhat. Fortunately, he was hungry for more photographs of his younger self and they did him a whole series from the ReGress program, one for every year of his life from six years onwards. In addition, several former neighbours and family friends had unearthed real snaps of him as a child and contacted the show to offer them. More might still come in, because the incident had made headline news.

Another, briefer follow-up appearance was planned for a few weeks' time — with Stacey also appearing, if Cassadee agreed. He seemed to have taken his former street friend under his wing and was shielding her from the press. His agent said he'd do his best to persuade the star to appear again.

When Edward arrived at the luxury hotel where the ball was to be held, he wandered over to the cocktail area, noting that Pete and Fran, whose table he was on, were not there yet. He studied the well-dressed assembly. Who did he know that he really wanted to speak to? Ah, yes. He made his way across to a small group in the corner, not letting anyone trap him into conversation en route.

'Hi, Daniel. How are things?'

Daniel and his partner both turned round. To

Edward's astonishment he recognized the woman standing next to his old friend, but only just. She looked like a different person from the exhausted cleaner he'd escorted out to her car all those weeks ago.

'Let me introduce you.'

'Beth and I have met already. How are you?' He took her hand and awareness shimmered between them before she pulled hers back hastily. They stared at one another for a moment and he could tell she was as surprised by this reaction as he was. In fact, he was so surprised that he struggled for words and she was the first to break the silence.

'I'm well, thank you, Edward.'

'You look a lot better. You were absolutely exhausted last time I saw you.'

'The flu epidemic's over, so I'm not working as hard.'

Daniel turned to Beth. 'Perhaps you could teach Edward how to slow down a bit. He's been working such long hours this year, it's a wonder he even has time to look in the mirror at himself, let alone make new friends. His cousin Pete is a slave driver.'

'Someone has to keep the man out of mischief,' Edward said mildly.

'I wonder if you'll manage to do that with that new segment. Everyone's talking about the Cassadee incident. Is that uncle he punched going to prosecute him for assault?'

'The old guy's out of the picture, committed suicide soon afterwards. He had cancer, apparently. You have to wonder how he dared go on the show. That caused enough talk. I'm just relieved the press didn't pick up on the suicide as well.'

Hope springs eternal, Beth thought. It had sustained her for years.

'There's Pete now.' Daniel nodded towards the door.

Edward raised one hand in greeting to his cousin and his wife, but people moved quickly towards the two celebrities, presumably eager to discuss the incident on the show, so he stayed where he was and let Pete come to him.

The gong sounded for them to take their places for dinner before Pete got even halfway across the room. He was lapping up the publicity, no doubt about it. So was Fran. If you didn't know better, you'd think they were a loving couple.

But Edward did know better, had seen them quarrel only too often. He walked from the reception room into the dining and dancing area with Daniel and Beth, noting that they made no attempt to touch one another or hold hands. Daniel turned up to functions like this with various attractive women but never seemed to stick with one or show signs of a sexual connection. Perhaps he wasn't the marrying type?

And was Beth divorced? She wasn't wearing a wedding ring.

As he stopped beside his chair, Edward wondered why he'd even bothered to check her hand. He wasn't looking for a relationship with anyone at the moment.

That was another thing he'd have to think about once his life slowed down a bit: finding a life partner. Older women wouldn't be as set on having children, so he might get a happier outcome, stepchildren, even. Life could get a bit too lonely sometimes, even when you were busy.

He glanced back across the room and saw Beth talking animatedly to her neighbour at the table. She had a lovely smile and scrubbed up well. Elegant was the word he'd use to describe her tonight. Why was she doing an extra job cleaning? Surely she could find something better than that for herself?

Maybe he'd ask her for a dance later. He felt sure Daniel wouldn't mind.

★　★　★

The function was very well organized and the food tempted Beth to eat more than usual, though she put her hand across her wine glass when the waiter tried to refill it. 'Could I have a fizzy mineral water instead?'

'Certainly, madam.'

'Did anyone see the Cassadee incident on the Pete Newbury Show?' the man next to her asked, and the whole table instantly began discussing it.

'It's certainly got people stirred up, hasn't it?' Daniel said to her in a low voice. 'You couldn't pay me enough to go on that segment of his show.'

'Would you need to find something out about yourself?'

'No. I know who my family are and we've got

65

a zillion photos of everyone. And you?'

'I wouldn't like to go on the show.' But she had watched it again and kept remembering how the first attempt to show Pete as a child of three had looked like her lost brother — so incredibly like him that she hadn't been able to get the image out of her mind. Stupid, really. His mother had said it wasn't like him and Mrs Newbury should know.

But Beth still wondered sometimes where her brother was. She'd studied other children in the street when she was younger, imagining what her little brother would look like, keeping track mentally of how old he'd be. Each time his birthday came round she'd comforted her mother, similarly at Christmas.

As an adult she'd worried a few times in case she dated her brother without knowing it, and had tended to steer clear of fair-haired men. His hair might have grown darker now, of course, though hers hadn't. Silly to keep thinking of him, really. The poor kid was probably long dead.

'Would you like to dance?' Daniel asked.

'I'd love to.'

She wasn't surprised to find that he was a good dancer, not showing off but able to steer her smoothly round the smallish dance floor and maintain a conversation at the same time. She let herself move with the music and was sorry when that set ended. It was rare these days to find someone who danced as well as this.

After they got back to the table, the woman on the other side of Daniel asked his opinion of

66

something and the two of them got into a discussion. As the man on Beth's other side had got up to dance, she was left to herself, which she didn't mind in the slightest. There was enough going on around her to keep her interest.

'Would you like to dance, Beth?'

She turned sharply and saw Edward smiling down at her.

Daniel half-turned and nodded, as if to urge her to accept.

'I — um, yes, that would be nice.'

She got up and let Edward pull her into his arms. He was taller than her by several inches and led her out on the floor with an expertise that far outdid Daniel's. He didn't try to speak, but when she stole a quick glance at him, he was frowning slightly and looking down at her.

'Are you involved with Daniel?' he asked abruptly.

She swallowed. This was blunt. 'Not in the way you mean. We're friends, that's all.'

'Will you have dinner with me one night, then?'

Renée's words came back to her: *don't close the door on other men.* 'Yes. That'd be — um, nice.'

He smiled slightly. 'Good. Next Friday suit you? Since the show's midweek, Pete's usually quietened down by then.'

'Quietened down?'

'After the show there's a lot going on behind the scenes that people don't see: appearances, promotion events, planning for future shows, research. I'm not involved directly in most of it, of course, but I do have to watch Pete's interests.'

'Oh. Sounds busy.'

'It is. Too busy. A bit like your life, I think.'

She nodded.

'I'll pick you up at seven, if that's all right. You're not working that night, are you?'

'Ah . . . no.' Should she tell him she wasn't really a cleaner? No, not now. When they went out together perhaps. Actually, she thought better of him for not letting that mistaken idea stop him asking her out. People could be so snobbish.

'Give me your phone number and address when we get off the floor.'

After that he didn't speak, but he held her closer as they danced — and she let him. That wasn't like her, but he moved so well and the music was good. Why spoil it with idle chatter?

Yet one thought kept interrupting her enjoyment: why had a man as attractive as Edward Newbury asked her out? And another thought kept following it: why had she said yes so easily?

It wasn't because of what Renée had said, well only partly. It was because she found him attractive, extremely attractive. It had been a long time since this had happened and it made her feel rather nervous, as well as . . . interested.

She was sorry when the music ended and the MC got up on the small stage as the band filed out.

'I'd better take you back to your seat. I think we're in for a few speeches. Phone number, address?' Edward crouched beside her, pulled out a pen and two business cards, giving her one with his contact number and using the other to scribble down her details before nodding and moving back to his own table.

Daniel smiled at her as she turned to chat to him. 'There is definite electricity between you two.'

She could feel herself blushing. 'Does it show that clearly?'

'Indeed it does.'

'I'm sorry.'

'Don't be. It's me who's out of step. Is he taking you out?'

She nodded.

'About time he started dating again. I think Renée will be pleased that you've accepted.'

Hang Renée, Beth thought, *I'm pleased.*

★   ★   ★

Towards the end of the evening, one of the waitresses skidded on something that had been spilled. Before she could stop herself, she'd fallen over and the tray of drinks had gone flying, sending its contents all over the three people nearest. One of them was Pete Newbury, who copped the main shower of drink.

There was a sudden hush as red wine dripped down his face and shirt front.

The waitress's face showed fear more than anything else and she hurriedly scrambled to her feet, glancing over her shoulder towards the maître d', who was making her way towards the group with an expression of frozen disgust on her face.

Pete stood up and looked down at himself, said

something to the waitress and burst out laughing.

Edward joined in the laughter.

When the maître d' joined them, Pete said something to her, and though she forced a smile, the look she threw at the waitress did not bode well for her future.

Pete took off his sodden dinner jacket and the waitress quickly took it from him. The maître d' gestured towards the rear doors. Pete nodded, grimacing at his shirt which was still dripping blood-red wine from the several glassfuls that had been spilled over him. He began to unbutton it, and as he reached Beth's table, stopped to slip the dripping garment off.

The maître d' took it from him, leaving him in a sleeveless white T-shirt that had plenty of splash marks on the front.

Edward rolled his eyes at Beth and followed his cousin out.

Conversation began again, staff hurried to mop the floor and change the tablecloth, and the band started to play a waltz.

★ ★ ★

'Are you all right?'

Beth realized Daniel was speaking to her and tried to pull herself together. 'Yes. Yes, of course.'

But she wasn't really. She felt as if the world had stopped spinning for a moment then speeded up. On Pete's right arm she'd seen a long scar, which ended near his wrist in a twist like a small sickle blade. It had faded to a thin white line now, but it was still very recognizable.

70

She'd seen that scar many times before — on her brother's arm.

Greg had always been a lively child and had fallen down the house steps once, cutting his arm badly on a rusty old bucket. She could remember blood pouring from the cut, her mother screaming, then the drive to the local hospital with Beth sitting in the back holding her wailing brother and trying to keep a clean tea towel wrapped round his arm.

There couldn't be two scars exactly like that one, in the same place on the person's right arm — just could not.

So the image of him as a child on the TV programme had been correct the first time.

Why had Pete's mother lied about it, then? And how had her brother Greg turned into Pete Newbury?

Beth felt slightly dizzy and was finding it hard to breathe properly. She couldn't take it in, couldn't believe it — except that she'd seen that scar, been near enough to touch it.

There was no doubt: *Pete Newbury was her brother.*

The noise of people enjoying themselves seemed to echo around her. All she wanted was a few moments' peace to come to terms with what she'd seen. 'Daniel, I feel — a bit woozy suddenly. Could we go out for some fresh air?'

'Of course.' He walked outside with her to the steps in front of the hotel. 'Something happened in there. Do you want to talk about it?'

She shook her head.

'Do you want me to take you home?'

'Would you mind? I'm sorry to spoil your evening, but I really can't — I'm not in the mood for dancing and . . . all that . . . now.' She waved one arm towards the room they'd just left.

'Of course I don't mind. I just wish there was something I could do to help.'

'You're taking me home and being understanding. That's an enormous help.'

She waited for him to collect her wrap and call a taxi. As they sat together in the back, she was grateful he didn't attempt to make conversation.

When they arrived at her block of flats, she fumbled in her bag for her key, her hand shaking.

Daniel eyed her with concern. 'Do you want me to come up? I don't think I should leave you alone. You don't look at all well.'

'I just had a bit of a shock, that's all.'

'You didn't move out of your chair, didn't say a word to anyone. And surely an accidental spilling of wine on someone else can't have made you react like that?'

She shook her head. 'I'm sorry. I can't talk about it. It's very — personal.'

'What number is your flat? I'm coming round tomorrow to check that you're all right.'

She'd told him before she realized what she was doing. 'There really is no need.'

'I took you out. Something happened while you were with me and I feel guilty about that. Humour me. We'll go out for lunch. I'll pick you up at twelve.'

He stood watching as she keyed in her security number and entered the block of flats.

She was glad when the lift whisked her out of

his sight. She'd ring him in the morning and cancel the lunch. What she really needed now was time to think.

The flat seemed horribly empty and she ached for someone to hold her and comfort her. For a moment, she almost wished she'd let Daniel come up with her.

Of course she got out the photo. Then she played the recording of the show and stopped it at the image of three-year-old Pete, holding her tattered, faded photo up against it. There was no doubt in her mind now that it was the same person. How could she have persuaded herself that it was a coincidence in the first place?

She watched Mrs Newbury's reaction to it very carefully, then played that segment twice more. The poor woman had looked terrified for a few seconds, then had pulled herself together. Rather clever of her to have had changes made that altered the photo of Pete as a child.

The photo of Beth's brother!

What had happened to Greg? How could he possibly have turned into Pete Newbury? Surely a woman like that, as middle-class as they came, with a gentle expression on her face, wouldn't have kidnapped a child?

You heard of children vanishing. You didn't often hear what happened to them. Or recognize one of them as an adult. Beth wasn't sure what to do about it.

Would Pete even want to know the truth about himself? He had a good life, was becoming more and more successful, might not want an old scandal revisited. And if he loved the woman

73

who'd brought him up, as his body language on the show seemed to suggest, he wouldn't want to do anything that might upset his mother, or worse still force her to answer a police investigation.

But Pete and his adoptive mother weren't the only people affected. What about Beth's mother, who had mourned her son for forty years? Was she to go to her grave grieving and thinking her son dead? No! The incident had blighted Linda Harding's life and thrown her into a nervous breakdown. It had also made Beth's own childhood very difficult. Childhood! She'd had to grow up quickly and young as she was, had been her mother's main support for the decade following the disappearance, because her father had moved on, got himself a new life.

It wouldn't be fair to leave Linda in ignorance that her son was still alive — not only alive, but a highly successful celebrity. Beth and her mother both needed closure, an explanation . . . a reconciliation.

But dear heaven, how was she to arrange this? How could she tell her mother who Greg had become without upsetting her all over again? How could she be sure Pete would want to meet his real mother?

★ ★ ★

Fran got into the front of the taxi with the driver to avoid getting smudges of wine from her husband's clothes on her oyster satin outfit. Pete lounged in the back, wearing a jacket the maître

74

d' had found for him over the slightly damp tee shirt.

'They'll never get the stains out of that shirt,' Fran fumed.

'If they don't, we'll buy another one.'

'Why should we have to? No, the hotel will have to pay. And there's the tux, too. That wasn't a cheapie, off-the-rack model. If the wine stains don't come out, if it doesn't look perfect when it's been cleaned, they can damned well replace that too.'

'Stop nagging, Fran. I'm tired. The poor waitress didn't do it on purpose. She looked terrified afterwards. I must get Edward to ring up on Monday and check that she hasn't got the sack.'

'She *should* get the sack.'

'Have a heart. The floor was greasy because Jack Garner had knocked food off his plate. He'd had too much to drink before the food arrived, he always does. He should have called for someone to mop the floor properly, not dabbed at it with his napkin.'

'The wait staff were all busy. There weren't really enough of them tonight. I don't know why you bother to go to Mettacom's annual bash, anyway.'

'Because it's a good evening out and I meet some useful people at their bashes. Don't nag, Fran. I'm tired.' And though she never seemed to notice such things, the taxi driver was listening avidly.

Fran threw him a dirty look over her shoulder then fell silent.

When they got home he had a shower, by which time Fran was in bed pretending to be asleep. He could always tell when she was pretending, because her breathing was too even and quiet. She snorted and snuffled like a puppy when she was really asleep. He used to find that appealing, now it just irritated him.

He went into the living room and got himself a glass of mineral water. He was thirsty but not in the mood for more alcohol. Moving out on to the balcony even though it was very chilly, he sat watching the city lights, wondering what his new segment would bring from viewers next week. He grinned and raised the glass in a silent toast to his own future. It was rather exciting to do these regressions. He wanted to do more than just chatting to celebrities and this was a good start.

Turning round, he raised another mocking glass to where Fran lay. He wanted more than her, too. But not quite yet, not till he had a good excuse for leaving her — and proper proof to satisfy a court about the lover she'd recently taken, the bitch.

He'd take legal advice about how best to divorce her. He didn't want to lose half of everything he possessed to a woman who'd contributed nothing to earning it and who poured out his money like water from a tap.

5

When Jo Harding went to pick up her son after work one evening, she saw that her friend Ghita had been crying. 'What's wrong?'

'Have you opened your mail yet?'

'No. I need a cup of coffee before I can face more bills.'

'Let's go to your place and look at the brown envelope.'

Next door, they left the children to play and Ghita put on the kettle while Jo tore the letter open. She read it quickly, screwing the single sheet of paper up in anger and hurling it across the room. Then she sighed and picked it up, smoothing it out again to re-read it.

Yes, it did say the small block of flats was being demolished and that the tenants had to vacate the premises by the end of the month. She looked at Ghita. 'Oh, hell!'

'I don't know what I'll do. I can't go back to my family. They disowned me when I had Kaleel.'

'I don't know what I'll do, either.'

'At least your mother will help you, Jo.'

'I'm not sure about that.'

'Of course she will. You said how happy she was when you phoned.'

'Yes, but she doesn't know about Mikey, does she?'

'Will that make a difference?'

'How do I know? I've not seen her for five years. And she never was the sort to drool over babies and small children, besides being the Queen of Neat and Tidy.'

'She'll be glad to meet her grandson, I know she will. And I'm sure she'll help you.'

They were both silent, then Jo said quietly, 'I don't want to be parted from you, Ghita. You're the best friend I've ever had, more like a sister. And our little boys love one another like brothers, too. Aw, don't cry. We'll think of something.' She put her arm round her friend and guided her to the scruffy old sofa, leaving the two toddlers playing together on the floor.

'I will think of something,' Jo repeated, patting Ghita's heaving shoulder and looking round. 'Mind you, if it wasn't for losing my home, I'd say it's not before time they demolished this dump. It's falling to pieces around us.'

'But at least we can afford the rent here.'

'And I have you to look after Mikey for me when I'm at work, to talk to when I'm sad. Why couldn't the damned owners have waited a few weeks to turf everyone out? I've had some big bills lately and I haven't got the money for a rent deposit on a new place, because you can bet the owners of this dump won't be in a hurry to pay us our deposits back.'

'I don't have the money either.' Ghita laid a hand on Jo's arm. 'Phone your mother. Tell her. She'll help you.'

'And what about you?'

'I'll think of something.'

'Maybe. And maybe I'd rather manage

without my mother's help. Besides, that doesn't keep you and me together. No, I'll have to think about it. One thing I've learned the hard way is not to rush into anything.' She glanced at the clock. 'Come back and have tea with me once you've bathed Kaleel. I've got some expired-date food from work.'

'You didn't steal it?'

Jo rolled her eyes. 'No, I didn't. I've not stolen anything since I got this job. I only stole when I was living on the streets, to survive. I don't do anything risky these days. I'd die if Social Services took Mikey from me.'

'Sorry. I shouldn't have asked that.'

Jo gave her a hug. 'You should if it worried you.'

* * *

Beth woke up feeling tired and headachey after another restless night. She couldn't face eating anything but lingered over a cup of coffee, trying to get her thoughts in order. She still wasn't certain about the right thing to do.

If she ignored the fact that Pete Newbury was her brother, it'd save everyone a lot of trouble.

But finding out that her son was alive would make a huge difference to her mother, who had mourned him for years.

No, Beth decided, she'd stick to her decision to bring things out into the open. The million dollar question was: how to start? Tell Pete first or her mother?

As she forced herself to finish a bowl of

muesli, she decided to approach Pete first and ask him to treat Linda gently.

She got through the urgent stuff at work, then closed her office door and told Sandy to hold all calls. Taking a deep breath, she went on the Internet, hunting for Pete Newbury's website, trying to find a phone number for him.

There wasn't one. There was only an email address, but she didn't intend to broadcast her personal details to whoever picked up his emails. A man so popular wouldn't be doing that for himself. She hadn't expected to get a direct line to him but she had hoped to get through to a personal assistant at least.

Baffled, she sat considering what to do, then realized she had the perfect person to find out from: Edward.

Only, she didn't want to tell him why she needed Pete's phone number, and it didn't seem fair to use him in that way. She really liked him. What would this do to their fragile new friendship?

Sandy knocked on the office door. 'Sorry, but Mr Bateman is here.'

'Oh, hell, I'd forgotten. Give me two minutes then show him in.'

She closed the website, tidied the papers on her desk and prepared to chat to one of their best clients, who had several apartment blocks for which Sherbright cleaned the public areas. Mal Bateman was a rather lonely older man who took her to lunch every couple of months and showed her photos of his grandchildren.

It always made her wish she had similar photos to show him.

Pete went round to see his mother, still feeling guilty about how he'd upset her on his show. She was entertaining a neighbour, but the woman didn't stay long, thank goodness.

When the friend had left, he looked at the dark circles under his mother's eyes in concern. 'Not sleeping properly? I thought you'd got over your insomnia. What's worrying you now? Whatever it is, I'm sure we can fix it.'

She shrugged. 'There's nothing worrying me, I'm just — not sleeping very well. It's been a full moon. That always disturbs me.'

'You're sure there's nothing worrying you?'

'Of course not. How can there be? Look at the lovely home you found for me after your father died. I still can't believe he made such poor investments as he got older. If it wasn't for you, I'd be sleeping on the street.'

'It wasn't Dad's fault. His memory was starting to fail. I'm glad he didn't live long enough to get full-blown Alzheimer's. Besides, I was happy to help, you know I was. I'm your son.'

Her eyes filled with tears and she nodded. 'I couldn't ask for a better son, either.'

He gave her a big hug. 'Mum, you're just an old softie.'

She dabbed at her eyes. 'So, how are the ratings on your show going?'

'They're rising. Did you see the last show?'

She nodded. 'With Cassadee.'

'Great viewing, wasn't it?'

She didn't answer for a few seconds, then said slowly, 'It showed people who were hurting. Do viewers really enjoy that? And Edward said the uncle committed suicide. Pete — are you sure you should go on with this segment?'

'Human emotion makes good television. Viewers love it. I can't wait to see the response we get for our opera singer.'

'But if it's going to upset people to that extent . . .'

'You leave me to worry about that, Mum.'

She let the subject drop and they chatted for a while. He knew something was still worrying her, though he couldn't think what. The trouble was, he'd never been able to make her tell him something if she didn't want to. She was a stubborn old bat, but he loved her dearly. A man couldn't ask for a more caring mother.

★ ★ ★

Early that Wednesday morning, after a disturbed night, Jo left Mikey with Ghita earlier than usual and took a bus to where her mother lived, still in the building where she'd once lived herself. How she'd hated that flat! Now she'd be deliriously happy if she could give Mikey a home half as good as this. The block of flats had been upgraded since she moved out and the whole district had gone upmarket, but nothing seemed to have changed drastically.

Could she do it? Could she ask her mother to let her come back here for a while? Would her mother agree to take her and Mikey in until they could find somewhere of their own?

Only one way to find out.

She walked slowly away and took out her mobile phone, dialling the familiar number. 'Mum? It's me.'

'Jo. How wonderful to hear from you. Are you well?'

'Very. Look — I reckon we should meet one day, catch up properly.'

'I can't think of anything I'd like more.'

'How about meeting at the little park where I used to play when I was a kid?'

'They've turned it into a shopping centre.'

'Oh. I never did go back there.'

'You could — come here, to the flat.'

'Um, not yet. Too many memories.'

'Don't hang up. Jo, *please* don't hang up. We'll find somewhere else to meet.'

Jo was startled to hear her strong, efficient mother getting so emotional. She remembered the days when her mother would go wooden-faced, giving short answers, hiding her feelings behind a barrier. Guilt flooded through her. This emotional fragility was all her fault. Could she cope with that sort of emotion? She'd have to. She'd lain awake racking her brain and had found no solution to her current problems, except asking her mother for help.

'How about the big park on Crayson Street, Mum? We could meet near the children's playground.'

'Fine. When.'

'Can you get there about six o'clock tonight? I have to work during the day.'

'Yes. Oh, Jo, you won't change your mind, will you?'

'No, Mum. I'll be there. I promise. And if anything crops up, I'll ring and fix a new meeting time. I'm a lot more reliable than I used to be. Give me your mobile number . . . Got it. I have to go now.'

She caught a bus back to work. The difference between where her mum lived and where she lived had hit her in the guts. No underground parking for her, even if she'd had a car. Just a pot-holed parking area full of old cars and overflowing rubbish bins. The narrow strip of garden hadn't been tended for years and wind-blown debris collected in the corners. She and Ghita picked it up and put it in the bins every now and then. No one else bothered.

Let's face it, her place was a slum. If she worked hard, if her mother helped just a little, Mikey wouldn't have to grow up in places like these. And maybe her mother wouldn't sound so desperate.

Jo shook her head at her own stupidity. When she ran away from home, she'd not really thought how deeply it'd upset her mother. She hadn't thought clearly about anything in those days, too busy rebelling against her parents and school, against the whole world in fact. And too full of raging hormones. Now that she was a mother herself, she understood a lot more about life and was learning to consider others. Well, she tried to. Didn't always succeed.

What if Mikey ran away when he was a teenager? How would she feel then? Upset big time, that's how. The mere thought of it hurt.

But could she cope with all the love she could hear in her mother's voice these days? She smiled wryly. Not to mention all that tidiness.

She didn't know. But whatever she did for herself and Mikey, she had to sort out something for Ghita as well. How her family could blame Ghita for getting raped, Jo would never understand. Her friend still worried that her father or brothers might come after her. She'd grown up in such a sheltered environment she was nervous of many facets of daily life, though she tried to hide it.

But if it wasn't for Ghita, Jo would be dead, and you didn't abandon someone who'd saved your life, someone you now loved dearly.

Jo would do anything to keep her son safe and look after her friend, but she'd try not to hurt her mother again, she promised herself.

★　★　★

Beth left the office early and was at the park by ten to six, terrified of being late and missing Jo. She found a bench near the children's playground and sat down, then changed her mind and began to walk up and down, so that she could see people coming from every direction.

Jo didn't arrive until five past six, by which time Beth was beginning to think her daughter had changed her mind.

Then a woman appeared in the distance, stopped at the far side of the playground, staring, before slowly making her way towards Beth. She too had fair hair, long and tied back. Her clothes were clean but worn, and surely she was taller?

She stopped in front of Beth, who ached to touch her but didn't dare. She was terrified if she did, Jo might pull back, walk away even. 'I've wondered so often what you looked like now,' she managed.

Jo grimaced. 'Older.'

'And not so — ' She hesitated, not wishing to offend.

'Not so out to shock people with what I wear. I've grown up a lot, Mum.'

'Shall we go and have a coffee? There's a café quite close. Um — my treat.'

'Yes, all right. That'd be nice.'

'It's this way.' Beth turned and began to walk. 'Goodness, you're taller than me now.'

'I take after Dad's side of the family there. How is he?'

'All right, I think. I've not heard from him for a while. Do you — keep in touch with him at all?'

'No. I don't suppose he misses me.'

'He does. He emails every now and then, mentions you, wonders how you are.'

'Does he really?'

'He has the same email address.'

Jo didn't say anything, so it was fortunate they arrived at the café. Beth led the way into a corner where they'd be fairly private. 'Would you like something to eat as well?'

'No. Thanks. Just a long flat white, please.'

The silence went on, then in desperation Beth blurted out the truth. 'I don't know what to say. I'm terrified of driving you away again.' Her hands were shaking and she put them into her lap to try and hide that.

'You didn't drive me away before. I ran. I was out of control in those days — out of touch with reality, full of raging hormones. Oh, Mum, don't cry!' Jo reached out and patted Beth's hand, then pulled back quickly.

'I promised myself I wouldn't cry, but I'm so *glad* to see you. You'll understand when you have children.' She made a huge effort, mopped her eyes and blew her nose. 'You — um, look well. Tell me about your life.'

Jo stared down at the table, drawing lines along the grain of the wood and back with one fingertip.

Beth kept silent, afraid of preventing a confidence by saying the wrong thing.

'I understand now how you must have felt when I ran away,' Jo said at last. 'You see — I've got a son.'

'A *son?* I'm a grandmother?' The room seemed to whirl round Beth and other people's voices echoed as if at the other end of a long tunnel.

'Are you all right? Mum? Say something.'

'I was — surprised. I never expected. Oh, how wonderful!' She reached out for her daughter's hand. 'Can I meet him? What's he called? How old is he?'

'Calm down. I'll tell you everything.' But she was smiling.

87

Beth put one hand to her forehead. 'Sorry. I feel a bit dizzy. I don't think I ate any lunch.'

Jo looked at her in concern. 'You're as white as a sheet and I'm sure you weren't this thin before.'

'I don't seem to get very hungry these days.'

Jo laughed suddenly. 'It's usually mothers who have to nag their daughters to eat. Looks like I'm the odd one out, as usual. Let's get a piece of cake each, eh? And if you promise to eat all yours up, I'll tell you about Mikey.'

'Mikey.'

'Short for Michael. I called him after Grandpop.'

Beth nodded. Mikey. She had a grandson called Mikey. 'You choose what to eat, but it's still my treat.'

Jo got up and went to the display of cakes, pointing to two and coming back just as their coffees arrived. The cakes were brought over soon after, huge pieces.

Beth stared at hers, feeling sick at the mere thought of eating.

'Geez, Mum, are you anorexic or something? You're looking at that lovely torte as if it's poisoned. Eat it, already!'

Beth picked up the fork and forced a mouthful down, then another, aware of her daughter watching her. Halfway through, she laid the fork on the plate and pushed it away. 'I can't eat any more.' When she looked at Jo's plate it was nearly empty. 'Do you want the rest of mine as well?'

'Well, it'll only go to waste and I've learned not to waste anything.'

'Are you eating properly? You're not short of money?'

'Yeah, Mum, I'm eating. I have a regular job, but it doesn't pay well, so I have to be careful. I can't afford luxury cakes like these, so I'm making the most of them now.' She reached into her shoulder bag and pulled out an envelope. 'Thought you might like a photo of Mikey. He's three, by the way.'

Beth opened the envelope and stared at a small, solemn little boy, who looked very like her brother had at that age. 'He looks well cared for, loved. Your grandmother always says you can tell by their expressions if children are loved.'

'I do love him to pieces and I do my best to look after him properly. Having him made me grow up fast.'

'And the father?'

'Couldn't get away quickly enough when he found I was having a baby. Good riddance to him. I registered Mikey as *father unknown*.' She looked up at the clock on the wall, then down at her watch.

Beth prayed she'd not leave yet.

Jo caught her glance and shook her head. 'I'm not rushing away, but I do have to keep an eye on the time. Look, I'm worried about you. Will you promise to eat properly from now on?'

'Yes.' She laughed. 'But not rich cream cakes. Will you tell me more about your life?'

'I work in the local supermarket. I'm full-time but I do night shifts stacking shelves sometimes, for extra money. My friend next door looks after Mikey. I couldn't manage without Ghita. She's like a sister to me now.'

'I'd love to meet her.'

'She has a son too. The boys are, like, best friends. Brothers couldn't be closer. The work's boring, but I'm a permanent employee and that's worth a lot these days.'

'Will you give me your address? Let me meet Mikey?'

'I'll give you my mobile number. Where I live is a dump.'

'Thank you.'

Jo looked at her warily. 'What for?'

'Getting back in touch.'

And then she was sobbing. Jo had to guide her out of the café and walk with her to her car.

'Geez, Mum, you're a mess.'

'I've . . . had a few other problems lately.'

'You're all right for money?'

'Money? Oh yes, I've plenty of that. There's something else that I need to sort out, nothing to do with you, but it's a bit of a worry. I'll tell you about it next time — there will be a next time, won't there?'

Jo hesitated and Beth thought her heart would stop, but when her daughter gave her a big hug, she began to think that if she was very careful, maybe Jo would stay found. 'Would you like to bring Mikey to tea, Jo?'

'I will one day. Not quite yet.'

'Your father will be pleased that I've seen you.' She saw Jo's expression harden. 'What have I said?'

'I don't want you to say anything about me to Dad yet.'

'But he'll want to know you're safe.'

'He ought to know already. You said he still has the same email address. I've emailed him three times, but he didn't reply, not once, though I put a trace on the messages and they'd been opened and read.'

'I can't believe that. Shane was as upset as I was when you left.'

'Well, he isn't bothered about me now. Promise you won't say anything about me to him until I tell you.'

'But . . . Oh, well, if you insist. I don't email him very often anyway. Though I think you're wrong.'

As she walked slowly home, Beth tried to understand why Shane would ignore Jo's emails. And she couldn't. She just couldn't. Then she wondered if his wife was intercepting them out of jealousy about his first wife and child. She'd always been very guarded about his first wife and child. But Beth didn't dare do anything that might drive Jo away again, so for the time being she'd keep quiet about seeing her daughter again, even to Shane.

★　★　★

That Wednesday evening the Pete Newbury Show attracted a record audience.

This time the celebrity in the *Who Am I?* segment was the famous opera singer. The reprise reminded viewers that Rosa had lost all her photos when her ex deliberately trashed her house after she split up with him. The opera

91

singer's deep grief at the loss of all her family mementoes was what had brought her to the show.

Pete had found his preliminary interview with her surprisingly moving. In fact, this segment continued to surprise him in many ways, both during the preparation and when it went live. He enjoyed doing it far more than the chats with the rich and famous.

Quite a few people had rung in offering old photos of the opera singer, some from when she was a child, a far bigger response than for Cassadee. Pete could provide Rosa with computer images of herself as a child, but real photos were so much better.

Who knew that better than him? He still wished he had proper photos of himself as a baby and toddler. Strange how that lack continued to irritate him. Why had no one who knew his mother come forward with photos, as they had for Cassadee? In fact, why hadn't his father and mother kept in touch with anyone from before the house fire? All their friends had been made later, after they moved into a new house in a new town.

When he saw Rosa walk on to his set, he was upset at how fragile she looked. He tried to set her at her ease, but it didn't work very well.

During the advert break he laid his hand on her arm. 'Are you all right?'

She tried to smile and failed.

'We've had several people ring in to say they've got photos of you as a child.'

She drew in a sharp breath. 'You have?'

'Yes. Old neighbours, distant relatives, all sorts of people. But if you'd rather not do the segment tonight, I've got some emergency tapes of interviews that we could put on instead.'

She clasped his hand for a moment. 'That's kind of you, Pete, but I won't spoil your show.'

'Sure?'

'Why are you being so understanding of my foolishness about photos?'

'Because my family lost all my early childhood photos in a house fire, so I know what it feels like.' He looked at the clock and added, 'Would you like to come out for a drink with me afterwards? I can never settle once the show's finished. Just a drink. I'm not propositioning you.'

'I'm the same after I've been performing on stage. All right, I'd like that. Just a quick drink.'

When they went on air again, she drew a deep breath and managed to answer his questions and comment on the computer images.

They'd selected two former neighbours, who were brought on to the set. She recognized one, apologized gracefully for not remembering the other.

'We have another surprise for you,' Pete said, 'but it'll have to wait for a later programme. It needs a bit of preparation. Keep watching, viewers, for a very moving conclusion to Rosa's story. Now, on next week's show, you'll meet someone else who needs your help. Here's a preview of why . . . '

★ ★ ★

93

Afterwards, while she was having her make-up removed, Rosa wondered whether Pete had meant it about going for a drink or had just said it to soothe her. But as she left, she found his PA outside ready to take her to a waiting room. He assured her that Pete wouldn't be long.

She was relieved. Even the few photos they'd found had raised memories that brought a lump to her throat and she definitely didn't want to go home yet, needed company to chase away the sad memories.

They went to a bar Pete knew, a quiet place with low lighting and gentle musak playing in the background.

She sipped her fruit juice. 'Those images on your show are amazing.'

'Yes. But only accurate for children older than six.'

'I saw the segment with your mother. It didn't look like you, she said. Did that upset you?'

'A bit. I'd like to know my baby self. And Mum said the revised image of me wasn't much good, either.'

She watched him stare into his drink, and waited in silence until he looked up and smiled.

'Tell me about your next concert. I don't know much about opera. I've always been more into popular music, really.'

'I'll send you two tickets for it. You and your wife might enjoy it.'

'That'd be great.'

She was surprised at how easily they chatted, but after an hour she'd relaxed so much she began to feel sleepy and couldn't prevent a yawn.

'Thank you for taking me out. It's been lovely. I wasn't ready for bed yet, but now I think I am.'

He patted her hand. 'And the photos upset you a bit tonight, didn't they?'

She nodded. 'Especially the one with my mother in it. She died when I was ten, so I never did have a lot of photos of her. I'd been having trouble picturing her face. Silly to let that upset me so much.'

'I always need to wind down after the show. And I'd really like to come and hear you sing. I'll look forward to it. I'm not sure whether Fran will be there. She's not into classical music.'

'I'll send two tickets anyway.'

As the taxi took her away from the bar, she sighed regretfully. What a kind man he was, not at all like she'd expected from seeing his show. Sometimes you could talk to strangers more easily than to friends and relatives.

His voice hadn't sounded warm when he spoke about his wife. Rosa had become an expert at picking that up. So many marriages broke up these days. How sad that was!

Even sadder to be like her, never married, when she longed for a real family, with children and pets, just like she'd had as a child.

6

Linda Harding answered the phone yet again at Bailey's Building Supplies, scribbling down the message and assuring the caller that Nat would get back to him.

It was a bright, sunny day and she had a sudden urge to stand outside for a few minutes. She always felt more cheerful when she could get some sunlight on her face.

She had barely reached the outer door of the prefab where the office was located before the phone rang again. Some days it hardly rang at all; other days it never stopped. In between calls she did the accounts, placed orders, got lunch for Nat, did whatever was needed.

The job was pleasant, busy enough that she didn't get bored, not too tiring for a woman of sixty-five. But if Nat didn't stop asking her out, she might have to look for another job. If she could find one at her age. She didn't want to retire, couldn't think what she'd do with herself if she had nowhere to go each day, no one to talk to.

She'd told him straight out she didn't date, was too old for that now, but he was like a steamroller when he wanted something. He said you were only as old as you felt. He clearly still felt young. She had days when she felt a hundred, others when she felt more bouncy. He was an attractive man, though, more because of his personality than his looks.

Talk of the devil. She'd recognize those footsteps anywhere.

He poked his head round the door. 'Any urgent messages?'

'Two. I've put them on your desk.'

'I like that outfit you're wearing, brings out the blue in your eyes.'

She'd given up answering remarks like that. 'Do you want me to order lunch for you?'

'Yes, please. Tell them to send steak pie and chips. Are you joining me today?'

'No. I have to go out.'

'Where?'

'Where I always go on Fridays.'

'I'll come to the shopping centre with you.'

She looked at him in exasperation. 'I'm going to the hairdresser's, Nat, not the supermarket.'

'Then come out for a drink with me after work.'

'No, thank you.'

He stopped smiling and gave her one of his piercing looks. 'I'll not stop asking until you do go out with me, Linda. You've not even given me a chance.'

'Because I don't want to date anyone.'

'You mean, you're afraid to date,' he corrected. 'Afraid to get too close to anyone.'

She didn't argue. Perhaps he was right. It didn't change how she felt, though.

★ ★ ★

Linda was walking into the nearby multi-storey car park after having her hair shampooed and trimmed when the mugger struck. Before she knew what was happening, she'd been knocked down and her handbag snatched. It happened so quickly she didn't even have time to scream before footsteps pounded away. She lay there for a moment, feeling dizzy with shock, then a young woman knelt beside her and helped her to sit up.

'Are you all right? I saw him. I can tell the police exactly what he looked like. Here, let me help you to your feet. That floor's dirty.' She pulled her mobile out and before Linda could stop her, had dialled the emergency number.

'The police will be here in five to ten minutes. Is there anyone you want me to call?'

Linda gave her Nat's mobile number and leaned against the wall, only half-hearing the conversation. Nothing had really happened, she tried to tell herself. She'd just been knocked down, not beaten up. But she couldn't stop shaking.

'He'll be here in two minutes. You really ought to sit down.'

'I'll be all right.' Already she was regretting sending for Nat. She should have given Beth's number. Only Beth was always so busy. Linda felt her temple gingerly. She'd gone down with a crash and must have hit it on the ground. Her hand came away with a smear of blood, but with her handbag gone she didn't have anything to wipe it with.

'It's more a graze than anything,' her companion said, pulling out some tissues and stuffing them into her hand.

There was a squeal of brakes and Nat's car

came up the ramp and pulled to a halt beside them. He left it to one side and jumped out, rushing across to her. 'Are you all right?'

'Just a bit shaken.' But she was glad when he put his arms round her and held her close for a moment before helping her across to his car.

The police arrived soon afterwards and took down the details of the attack, but it was the young witness who could tell them most, and though they asked Linda to go to the police station to make a proper statement, they took the young woman with them to make up a computer image of the attacker's face. There had, it seemed, been several muggings lately, all by men whose descriptions were very similar. But this was the first time anyone had seen the mugger's face.

When the police had driven off, Nat got in beside her. 'I think the police are right and we should take you for a check-up at the hospital.'

'No, I'll be fine. Honestly.'

'Shall I call your daughter, then?'

'No, she's busy. Look, Nat, I just want to go home. *Please.*' But her voice wobbled as she spoke.

'I'll take you home, then.'

'What about my car?'

'Donny can drive it out to your place. I'm taking you home.'

'You can't leave the business unattended.'

'Just watch me. No, don't argue, Linda. You're far more important than the few customers who're likely to phone on a Friday afternoon, and Jim will still be there to attend to anyone wanting supplies. It's usually amateurs wanting tiny amounts of this and that for DIY on Friday afternoons, anyway.'

She let her head fall back against the seat of his car, too shaky to argue.

'Where are your car keys?'

Then she realized. 'In my handbag.'

'Do you have a spare?'

'Yes, but it's at home. And my house key's in my bag too. I shan't be able to get in — and the mugger can.' She began to cry. It was all too much.

'We'll go to your home first and make sure it's all right. I'll break in, if I have to.' He pulled her towards him and let her sob against him for a moment or two.

He made her feel so safe that after a few minutes she stopped shaking. 'You must think me a weak fool,' she muttered into his shoulder.

'No, I don't. Anyone would be upset by that sort of thing.' He moved her gently to arm's length. 'Now, is it all right if I drive you home?'

'Yes. And Nat . . . thank you for coming.'

'I'll always be there for you, Linda.'

He didn't seem to need an answer, just drove off, weaving carefully in and out of the traffic.

Always be there, she thought. No one could promise that.

At her house, she remembered the back door key she'd hidden in the garden shed. 'It's in the — '

'Don't tell me.' He went into the shed and came out again a minute later holding the key. 'Not a safe place to leave it.'

'But I'd hidden it. How did you know where to look?'

'There are a few rather obvious places where people hide keys.' He looked at the back of her house. 'A child could break into this place. We have to do something about that, Linda.'

When they were inside, he insisted on making her a cup of sweet coffee, even though she never took sugar. She couldn't raise the energy to protest because it felt wonderful to be looked after and she was still a bit wobbly.

'Now,' he said, 'if you'll find those spare car keys I'll have them couriered to Donny and he can fetch your car. Then I'll have a look at your house locks. They're all old. You really should have updated your security. I could break in myself in two minutes flat — and without smashing a window.'

She shivered.

He came to put an arm round her shoulders. 'Don't worry. I'm not going anywhere till I'm sure you're safe.'

'You're a juggernaut,' she teased, trying to lighten the atmosphere.

'You've called me that a few times over the years. How long have you been working for me?'

'Five years, no, six.'

'Penny was already ill when you took her place. What a long time ago that seems now!'

'You must miss her.'

'I miss the old Penny, not the poor frail creature she became. I never believed in a 'merciful release' till she was in the final stages of that damned cancer.' He shook his head as if to

101

clear it of memories and smiled at her. 'How about another cup of coffee?'

'I'll make you one, but if I drink any more I'll not sleep tonight.'

'I'm a light sleeper, but I sleep soundly. I don't think anyone could break into my house without waking me. Should I call your daughter now?'

'No, she's got a date tonight. She goes out so rarely, I don't want to spoil it for her. She's too young to be on her own.'

'So are you.'

'I'm sixty-five.'

He grinned. 'A mere youngster.'

'You're only sixty.'

'It's a good age to be.' He made another cup of coffee for himself with his usual efficiency. 'You wouldn't have any biscuits, would you? I didn't manage to finish my lunch.'

'Home-made cake any good?'

'I'd kill for it.'

Everything seemed so blessedly normal, chatting to him, being complimented on her cake, that she relaxed still further.

'I'm staying here overnight,' he said after-wards. 'Or else you can come to my place. The thief's got your keys and I can't get anyone to come out and change all your locks till tomorrow morning.'

She opened her mouth to protest, but couldn't. The mere thought of being here on her own while someone else out there had her keys made her shiver.

'Thank you, Nat. I appreciate that. I've got a spare bedroom.'

'We can send out for some take-away.'

'Nonsense. I'll cook you a meal.'

He beamed at her. 'That'd be great. I really miss home cooking. I can't usually be bothered after a hard day's work.'

He seemed different from the busy, loud-voiced Nat she knew at work, calmer, gentler. And she loved cooking for people.

Somehow, the quiet meal and the pleasant conversation made the shock of the attack recede. And his solid, comforting presence was . . . just what she needed.

★　★　★

Edward rang Beth's doorbell exactly one minute before the appointed time on Friday and she told him on the intercom that she'd be straight down. She took a last look at herself in the mirror. The lilac skirt looked good and her new hairstyle really suited her. Renée was right.

But black was still the most serviceable colour to wear to work, whatever her friend said.

She opened the front door of the flats and accepted a kiss on her cheek. Only it didn't feel as cursory as the usual kissy-kissy ritual and she forgot to breathe for a few seconds. Edward paused with his head just a few centimetres away from her face, frowning at her as if puzzled.

The air between them seemed charged with undercurrents and for a moment she had an urge to pull his face towards hers and give him a proper kiss instead of this meaningless air kissing. That was so unlike her she couldn't move for a moment or two.

In the end, to her relief, he broke the impasse, straightening up and clearing his throat. 'I've — um, got a taxi waiting, and I'll bring you back in one because I like to have a glass or two of wine with a meal. Do you mind?'

'Not at all. I could have driven us, though, because I'm not a big drinker. Alcohol doesn't agree with me.'

'Another time, perhaps.'

They made small talk in the taxi, not hard to do with him, and by the time they arrived at the restaurant, she'd relaxed considerably. Indeed, he was one of the easiest people to talk to that she'd ever met.

The whole evening went well until the moment she asked if he'd tell her how to contact his cousin.

Edward stiffened and drew back. 'Why?'

'I can't tell you. It's . . . very private, personal.'

'It's that damned *Who Am I?* segment, isn't it?'

'In a way.'

His voice grew scornful. 'Have you lost all your childhood photos, too? Is that why you agreed to come out with me, to get to Pete so that you can go on the show?'

'No! I agreed to come out with you because — ' She could feel herself growing hot, fumbling for words. 'I thought we'd get on well.'

'I thought so too. But I'm not giving you Pete's phone number unless you tell me why.'

She shook her head. 'It'd not be right. I need to tell him first. It's about *his* childhood, you see.'

104

He snapped his fingers and the waiter who'd been hovering came forward. 'The bill, please. We're leaving.'

She sat motionless in sheer astonishment, then realized her mouth was open and stood up. She held her head high as she walked out, trying not to show how bitterly disappointed she was by Edward's reaction.

When the taxi arrived, she barred his way into it. 'I can go home on my own, if that's how you feel. It's stupid for you to come with me anyway. My place must be at least half an hour from yours.'

'I took you out and I'll damned well return you safely to your flat.'

He looked so fierce she slid into the vehicle without further protest. But they sat as far away from each other as they could.

At the flats, she didn't wait for him to open the car door, but got out and ran for the entrance, zapping the lock and trying to shut the door in his face.

He came after her and held it open. She stared up at his angry face.

'If you've something to write on, I'll give you Pete's office number,' he said in a tight, fierce voice.

'Thank you.' She fumbled in her handbag and found an old shopping receipt.

When he'd written the number he turned away, but she grabbed his arm. 'Just for the record, I did *not* accept your invitation for tonight in order to get Pete's phone number. I didn't even know I'd need it then. Something

105

cropped up after I'd agreed, something very important.'

He stared at her, his face expressionless, then nodded, stepped backwards and returned to the taxi.

She watched it pull away, then went up to her flat, feeling bitterly disappointed. Things never went right when she met a guy. Maybe it would be better to stick with male friends like Daniel and her girl friends. Less heartache that way.

Heartache? She tossed her head at the mere idea. She wasn't breaking her heart over Edward Newbury, a guy she'd met twice by chance and dated once. She was a capable businesswoman and she didn't *need* romance in her life.

She put the receipt with the phone number written on it on the kitchen surface, weighting it down with her phone index. She hoped this would be worth losing Edward's goodwill for. What if her brother didn't want to know them? How would her mother feel then? How would Beth feel?

Relationships were far too complicated and she wasn't good at them, as she'd well and truly proved with her daughter, and just proved again with Edward.

★ ★ ★

Jo got home from work to find that Ghita had prepared them a meal. They did this for each other sometimes. It was all very pleasant. The two little boys were watching the Wiggles on TV, jumping up and dancing sometimes, laughing

106

and singing tunelessly with the music.

They fed and bathed the boys first, moving from one flat to the other, then put them to bed together, which led to a lot of giggling.

After that Ghita served the meal, wonderful food, several plates of it. Nothing expensive but lovingly prepared and delicious.

'I can't eat any more,' Jo said at last. 'You could open a restaurant, you're such a good cook.'

'I'd like to do that, but where would I get the money? Or the courage?' She laughed softly at herself.

There was a knock on the door.

Ghita froze. 'No one ever comes here at night.'

'Shall I answer it?'

'No. Don't do anything. They'll go away.'

'They can see someone is at home and hear the TV.' Jo didn't wait, but went to open the door.

A man stood there, his black hair grizzled at the temples, his eyes dark and fierce.

There was a gasp from behind Jo. 'Father!'

'Can I come in?'

'Yes, of course.'

He took off his shoes and came inside.

Jo went to stand beside Ghita, feeling her friend trembling. She scowled at the visitor.

He not only came inside, but went to look in the bedroom, then investigated the small kitchen, before coming back to his daughter. 'No man in your life?'

She shook her head. 'No. There never was and hasn't been — since. This is my neighbour, Jo.

107

Our sons play together.'

He went back to stare into the bedroom at the two little boys lying peacefully among a pile of soft toys. 'Kaleel looks like your brother did as a child,' he muttered.

He stood there looking at the boys for so long, Jo was able to whisper, 'Do you want me to leave?'

'No. Please stay.'

Mr Haddad closed the door of the bedroom and studied Ghita. 'You look well.'

'I am well.'

'How do you live?'

'Social security, and I look after Jo's boy when she's at work to earn a little extra money. Will you take a cup of coffee?'

'Not this time.'

Jo's heart went out to her friend, who was looking white and shaken.

The father came across, hesitated, then placed one hand on Ghita's shoulder for a moment. 'It's not right that a man doesn't know his own grandson, however the child was created. Next time, I shall bring your mother. She weeps for you. And — we have decided to forgive you.'

Jo was furious and couldn't hold the anger back. 'Why do you have to forgive *her*? She didn't ask to be attacked and raped. Ghita is the most gentle person I've ever met. She'd never, ever encourage a man to behave like that.'

He looked angry for a moment then his expression grew thoughtful. 'You have a loyal friend here, daughter.'

'Jo is like a sister to me now,' Ghita said.

'Hmm. Give me your phone number so that your mother can phone you to arrange a time.'

He went without kissing his daughter or saying goodbye to Jo.

When the door was locked behind him, Ghita collapsed on the couch in tears.

'The brute!' Jo said angrily. 'Who does he think he is to blame you and forgive you?'

'He's my father. That's how it is with us. Fathers are gods in their own homes. But I don't care what he says as long as I can see my family again. I've missed my mother so much, and my older brother specially.' She sobbed some more, with her friend patting her on the back.

Eventually she managed to stop and smiled mistily at Jo. 'But you're my family too, now. Thank you for defending me.'

Jo nodded, but the encounter had annoyed her. Ghita had been so pathetically grateful, and yet her father had still checked for himself that there was no man living with her before he proceeded any further. On the other hand, it had obviously been difficult for him to come and see her, but he'd done it, going against his upbringing, from what Ghita had told her.

Jo's father hadn't even replied to her emails. Too busy with his new young wife and children, probably.

Her mother had wanted her, though, had replied instantly and had wept over her today. The tears had reassured her in a back-to-front way.

When Ghita had calmed down, Jo took her sleeping son home and lay in her narrow bed next to his, thinking about life, how strange it was, how hard to do the right thing.

What did she want from the future? She didn't know. She'd been too busy surviving to think far ahead. She wanted to look after Mikey, of course, and give him a decent life, but what were her dreams for herself? She couldn't live only for him.

She smiled in the darkness, allowing herself a dream or two. She'd like to live somewhere better than this place, that was sure, and have a more interesting job than working in the local supermarket. The other women there were very friendly, though, and that made a big difference to any job.

She had to tread carefully now and not stuff things up with her mother. She was going to try hard to find a new flat without asking for her mother's help. If she could move out of this place before she invited her mother round to see Mikey, she'd not feel so ashamed of where she lived.

Staring at the lighted numbers of her bedside clock-radio, she was surprised to find it was after midnight. Pushing her worries to one side, she started breathing deeply, trying to form pretty cloud images in her mind, an old trick of hers. If she didn't get some sleep she'd be dead on her feet at work.

She'd need to spend her lunch break flat hunting for herself and Ghita again. She'd tried several letting agencies now, with no success. It

110

reminded her of last time, how long she'd looked before she found their current flats.

Surely if she kept looking, wasn't too fussy, she'd find somewhere they could afford? Even if they had to share a flat at first.

7

Beth rang her mother at home early on Saturday morning, and to her astonishment, Nat picked up the call.

'Why are you — ?' No, she had no right to ask that. She compromised with, 'Is Mum all right?'

'She is now, but she had a bit of bother last night.' His voice went faint as he spoke to someone nearby, but Beth could make out the words. 'No, Linda, she needs to know.'

'What do I need to know?' she demanded.

'Your mother was mugged yesterday lunch-time in the public car park on her way back to the office. She wasn't hurt physically, but it was all a bit of a shock. He got her handbag and keys, so, I stayed in the spare bedroom last night. We're having all the locks changed today and some window locks installed.'

'I'll come straight round.'

'There's no need. I have everything in hand. Here she is.'

A moment later her mother came on. 'I'm fine, Beth, truly I am. I just got knocked over, not bashed. It was a bit of a shock, though, and it's a nuisance having to cancel the credit card. I'm going to have to get a new driving licence, too.'

'I want to come and see you, make sure you're all right. You can stay with me if you're nervous of being on your own.'

'I'll be just fine, especially after the locks are changed. No one's going to drive me out of my home.' Her voice softened. 'Anyway, Nat's been wonderful.'

It occurred to Beth suddenly that this incident might bring Linda and her employer together. She'd suspected for a while that Nat was fond of her mother, but her mother kept saying when pressed that she was too settled in her ways to change them for a man. Which was ridiculous when Linda looked ten years younger than her age and was in better health these days than she had been thirty years ago. 'Well, if you're sure you're all right . . .'

'Of course I am.'

'Phone if I can do anything.'

'Yes, darling. Oh, just a minute. How did your date go?'

'Fine.'

'Are you seeing him again?'

'I doubt it.'

'Oh, Beth, what went wrong this time? You keep pushing men away and you're too young to stay single.'

'Listen who's talking. You've been pushing Nat away for ages.'

There was dead silence, then, 'I have to go now. Bye.'

★ ★ ★

Linda slammed the phone down and glared at it.

'What did she say to upset you?'

She looked at Nat and blushed. It was one

113

thing to keep him at arm's length in the office, but here in her home, where the fringe of silver hair round his bald patch was sticking up at all angles and he was barefoot, with his shirt open down the front showing a body that didn't have a beer belly and was still pretty good for a man of his age, well, everything felt different. This was just too intimate.

She saw Nat look at her with eyes narrowed. 'It was nothing,' she insisted.

His wry expression said he didn't believe that.

'How about some breakfast?' she asked to forestall any more questions.

He grinned. 'You know I'm always ready for a good meal.'

'Yes, and you never seem to put on an extra inch, whatever you eat, which is so unfair. Bacon and eggs do you?'

'Bring them on. And how about a bowl of cereal and a few pieces of toast as well?'

He followed her into the kitchen, sitting at the breakfast bar, his presence so marked she got flustered and cut her finger when she was dealing with the bacon.

'Here. Let me.' He took the knife out of her hand. 'The mugging upset you more than you're admitting, Linda.'

And heaven help her, she blushed again. 'It's not that. Beth — um, reminded me of something.'

He looked at her shrewdly. 'You always get that expression on your face when you're telling fibs, even to someone on the phone.' He put one finger on her lips. 'Shh. If you don't want to tell me, that's all right, but don't lie to me, Linda. We've been friends too long for that, don't you think?'

She nodded, feeling her cheeks heating up even more, and went back to the cooking. How was she to stay calm with Nat there all day supervising the installation of the new locks? It was easier to keep her distance at the office, much easier, but here he was so large and male that he made her little house look too frilly and fussy, made her feel . . . soft and feminine.

It had been comforting to have him there during the night, and she was enjoying making breakfast for him, having someone to talk to.

Life was so complicated — or did people just make it complicated? Should she simply accept that he was here and enjoy his company? She did enjoy it, very much.

★ ★ ★

Edward went to play golf on the Sunday morning, but kept messing up even the simplest of shots.

'You're not on form today. Got woman trouble?' his regular partner asked with a grin.

'No.' He sliced the next shot into some bushes.

'She must be rather special to put *you* off your game.'

'I've got a lot on my mind.' Edward took a great deal of care with his next few shots, but his friend's words had hit home. After spending a few hours with her, he had hoped Beth might become special. Well, he'd been attracted the very first time he met her, who knew why? He certainly didn't understand it. But as she was the first woman who'd affected him like that for years, it seemed stupid not to . . . to follow up.

She'd assured him that the need for her to speak to Pete had cropped up *after* they'd agreed to go out for a meal. Why hadn't he believed her at the time? Why had he got so angry? He pictured her face, the direct way she looked at the world, and smiled involuntarily. She didn't seem like a liar.

Why would she need to see his cousin so urgently, though? She'd said it was personal, not business. What personal connection could she possibly have with Pete? His cousin had many faults, but Edward was pretty sure Pete hadn't messed around with other women since he got married. He'd seen him knocking back come-ons more than once, usually with a wry remark about being an old married man. The truth was, Pete was married to his career, was very ambitious and loved being a celebrity. He was scornful of celebrities who thrived on scandals.

For once, Edward was glad when the golf round ended. He excused himself from lunching with his friends, sat in his car tapping his fingers on the steering wheel, then gave in to temptation and drove round to Beth's. He owed her an apology and after that they'd see.

But she wasn't at home. Or if she was, she didn't answer the doorbell.

Had she gone out with another man? It was no business of his if she had, but still, he hoped she hadn't.

Beth went into work on the Sunday morning, because you could get a lot done when there was no one around and no phones were ringing. She tried to settle to checking the accounts but her thoughts kept coming back to what her daughter had said.

Had her ex really not replied to Jo's emails? It seemed out of character. Shane had been as upset as she was when their daughter ran away. Their shared anxiety had taken most of the animosity out of their relationship, though it was obvious his new wife had resented them being friendly again.

Perhaps the emails had gone astray. Yes, that must be it. Only . . . Jo had said she'd sent three emails and that they'd been marked as read. Next time she saw Jo, she'd suggest giving Shane another chance and would offer to act as intermediary. A personal approach was so much better than an email.

When Beth got home she found a message on her answering machine. She looked at the blinking light and wondered whether to bother listening to it now. She didn't want anything to spoil her calm, satisfied mood after several hours of productive work.

It was half-past two but felt later. She was going to clean the flat, make a proper meal, then have an early night and read in bed.

She walked past the phone then sighed and went back to listen to the message. If she didn't know what it was about, she'd only worry that it might be her mother or some crisis connected with work.

'Beth, it's me, Edward. I came round just before lunch, but you weren't in. I wanted to apologize for being so suspicious on Friday night. I really enjoyed our time together. I'm not going out today, so please ring me.'

She was surprised by that, she had to admit. From what Edward had said in his message, the coolness which had ended their evening together had upset him. Well, it had upset her, too. But if she rang him, he'd invite her out again, and who knew where that might lead? Did she want a relationship with anyone? Did she have enough spare energy to cope with that sort of thing? No, she didn't. She had enough on her plate with Jo and little Mikey at the moment, not to mention work.

An hour later, after cleaning her bathroom and kitchen in a furious burst of activity, she sat down and tried to relax. But she couldn't banish Edward from her mind or persuade herself that she didn't want to speak to him. Putting down her cup of herbal tea, she sighed and picked up the phone.

'Hello?'

He sounded so wary she almost put it down again then told herself not to be such a coward. 'Edward?'

His voice grew instantly warmer. 'Beth. I'm so glad you rang.'

'You — um, left a message.'

'I wanted to apologize for being so suspicious on Friday.'

'I don't blame you, and if it wasn't important, I'd not have dreamed of presuming on our friendship by asking you. But I couldn't find any other way to contact your cousin except by a fan email address, and this is too important for that.'

'You still can't tell me what it's about?'

She was tempted. Very. But no, this was for Pete's ears alone. 'I'm sorry. It's not my secret, you see.'

'All right. What have you been doing today? Something nice?'

'Working.'

'On a Sunday?'

'And cleaning my flat.'

'Busman's holiday.'

He still thought she was a cleaner, she realized, but as she opened her mouth to say she'd been working at the office, he spoke.

'When can I see you again, Beth?'

She hesitated. 'I don't know.'

'I really enjoyed our time together. Didn't you? Until I spoiled it, that is.'

Generous of him to take all the blame. And heaven help her, she couldn't tell him that she hadn't enjoyed herself, because she did want to see him again. 'So did I.'

'Let's go out on Thursday.'

'Look, I do want to see you again, but I've got a couple of crises with my family at the moment and I really need to sort those out before I do anything else. Can we wait a couple of weeks and then . . . we can do something together?'

Silence.

She hardly dared to breathe, worrying he'd

give up on her after such a lukewarm response. 'Is that all right with you, Edward?'

'You're not trying to let me down easily? If you don't want to go out with me, tell me straight out.'

'I'm telling you the absolute truth. Look, I can tell you about one of the things that's come up. It's my daughter. I've not seen her for five years, ever since she ran away as a teenager, except for a few emails to let me know she's alive. And now she's back in my life again. We met for the first time in years. And she has a son.'

His voice softened. 'That *is* a major change. Are you happy about it?'

'Yes, over the moon.' She laughed softly. 'You may not want to date a grandmother, though.'

He echoed her laughter, real amusement in his voice. 'I never have before, but there's always a first time. Two weeks?'

'Give or take. I'll ring you.'

'Promise.'

'I promise.'

As she put the phone down she smiled. She really liked Edward, had enjoyed his company very much. Well, they were both rather quiet, private people, she'd guess. He sounded tired of the hectic life of being Pete Newbury's manager.

Why she'd confided in him about Jo today, she couldn't work out, though. That wasn't at all like her. But he'd seemed to understand how important getting to know her daughter again was to her. And her grandson. She smiled. She had a grandson!

The following day, Beth went into the office

early to make sure the week got off to a good start. At half past nine she went out to reception.

'No calls till I tell you, Sandy. I've got something important to sort out.'

She found the piece of paper with Pete Newbury's office number on it and took a minute to steady herself before ringing the number.

A bright young voice answered her. 'Pete Newbury's office. How may I help you?'

'Could I speak to Pete, please?'

'Who's speaking?'

'My name's Beth Harding. Pete doesn't know me, but I have some rather important information about his — um, his childhood.'

'Could you give me more details?'

'I'm afraid not. It's personal.'

'Mr Newbury is a very busy man and he can't answer every query. That's why I'm here. I'd be very happy to help you if you'll tell me what it's about.'

'I can't. It's extremely personal and private. Believe me, he won't want anyone else to know this.'

There was silence at the other end then the bright young voice became sharper.

'How did you get this number, Ms Harding? It isn't publicly available.'

Beth didn't want to involve Edward. 'A mutual friend gave it to me.'

'I must ask you not to pass it on to anyone else. I'll give you the number for the PR firm that's handling our calls. Perhaps you'll be able to tell them what this is about. Do you have something to write with?'

'No. I mean, don't bother to do that. I can only tell Pete himself.'

'I'm sorry, but — '

'Look, it's Edward Newbury who gave me the number. He's a friend of mine and he knew I really needed to speak to Pete.'

There was another of those silences, then the young woman said, 'Here's Edward now. Perhaps you'd like to speak to him?'

Beth nearly put the phone down, feeling humiliated by the treatment she'd received, ultra-polite, but with a scornful edge. But this was too important to abandon. Her mother's life had been blighted for the past thirty-eight years. She needed closure — and so did Beth. She hadn't realized how much till now.

The blur of voices ended and Edward came on the phone. 'Edward Newbury here.'

'It's me, Beth. The person I spoke to wouldn't let me through to Pete.'

'She would need a good reason to do that. She's hired to be the dragon at the gates. Could you not have given her even a hint?'

'No. It's intensely personal. I promise you, Edward, that Pete wouldn't want it to be publicly known.'

He sighed. 'I'll speak to him and ring you back.'

'Thank you. I'm at the office today. I'll give you my direct number.'

She put the phone down and rested her head in her hands. She'd probably ruined her relationship with Edward completely now.

And that thought upset her. But not enough to stop her doing what was needed to help her mother. And herself.

* * *

Edward went through to Pete's office and found him skimming through a pile of requests from people wanting to appear in the *Who Am I?* segment. These were the better ones, weeded out from hundreds of letters before they got to him.

'Just look at this one, Ed!' Pete waved a letter at him.

'Can it wait a minute? I need to ask you something.' He quickly outlined what Beth wanted.

'You're sure she's not a wacko?'

'I'm certain. Um — I'm dating her. She's a sane and intelligent woman of about our age. You can spare her ten minutes, surely?'

Pete rolled his eyes. 'All right. But only for you. Are you sure she's not just using you to get to me? She must be a stunner for you to go to this much trouble for her. What does she do for a living?'

'I think she's very attractive in a quiet sort of way, but it's not just that. She's — a pleasure to be with. She works for Sherbright Cleaning Services. As far as I can make out, she works in the office and does some cleaning during the evenings when other employees are sick. Must need the extra money, I suppose.'

Pete made a scornful sound. 'I still say she sounds like a wacko.'

'She's not. But do it for me anyway. Ten minutes.'

'Oh, very well. Fix something up with Ilsa. Only ten minutes, mind. It's a madhouse this week.'

Edward went out into the reception area and arranged a time, then rang Beth again. 'Eleven-fifty on Tuesday is the only time I can get you in.'

'I'll be there,' she said curtly and rang off.

He sat frowning at the phone. Was Pete right? Was Beth just using him to get to his famous cousin? He was pretty sure she wasn't.

But how could you ever be completely sure about someone else? Especially when you'd not known them for long.

⋆　⋆　⋆

Jo went into work early that week so that she could take extra time off with her lunch break each day to go flat hunting. When she'd explained her problem to the personnel manager, he was happy to vary her working hours.

'Been meaning to say, Jo, we're very pleased with your work, and your reliability, especially given your circumstances. How would you like to train for a supervisor's job? It'd mean more money.'

She had a quick think, wondering yet again how such an inarticulate man had ever got a job managing people, but it didn't take her long to decide. 'I'd love to.' Apart from the extra money, there would be more interesting work.

'The child won't make it too difficult? You'd have to work all sorts of shifts.'

'I do that now. My neighbour babysits and she's brilliant.'

He nodded. 'Good luck with your flat hunting, then.'

That day she tried the last three agencies on her list and received the same knock-back from each of them. They could find her any number of luxury flats, but there was nothing available in her price range within easy reach of this district.

She got off the bus before her usual stop, calling in at shops near home, places she knew posted 'To let' and 'For sale' notices in the window. There was nothing new since her last visit the previous week.

Time was running short. What was she going to do? She didn't want to ask for her mother's help, even though she was pretty certain it'd be willingly given. She'd been so proud of standing on her own feet.

And there was Ghita to consider as well. Her friend would flounder if she didn't have help. Some people were just too gentle for this world.

Tonight Ghita's father was bringing her mother to see her. Jo went straight home, just as worried as her friend about the visit. Ghita had begged her to be present while her parents were there, which meant scrubbing up both herself and Mikey, and hoping he'd be on his best behaviour.

What they should really be doing was getting an early evening paper and checking all the 'To let' notices. Why did everything always happen at once?

8

On Tuesday morning Beth took a taxi across town to Pete Newbury's office, feeling sick with nerves. She had the childhood photos of her brother in her briefcase, but even now wasn't sure what to say to him. How did you tell someone that he wasn't who he thought? That his mother wasn't really his mother?

She arrived ten minutes early. She had to report to reception in the foyer and they rang Pete's office before she was allowed to use the lift, then told her to wear the identity tag they gave her all the time she was in the building.

The suite of offices was very luxurious, with carpets so thick they swallowed the sound of her footsteps completely. This added to her tension because it made everything feel unreal.

The receptionist looked up with a cool smile. Her name badge said Ilsa and her voice revealed that she was the one who'd answered the phone. 'Ms Harding? Please take a seat.'

A shadow passed across the frosted glass panel behind Ilsa and Edward appeared in a doorway. 'Come and wait in my office, Beth.'

'No need to disturb your work. I'm fine where I am.' She sat down.

'I'll see if Pete is free.' He tapped on the other door and vanished inside.

★   ★   ★

126

Pete was standing by the window, gazing down at the busy street. He didn't turn round for a minute.

'She's here.'

'Let her wait.'

'I'll have to wait too and I've a lot to get through today.'

With an aggrieved sigh, Pete swung round. 'I'm not speaking to her on my own. If she's a wacko, she can claim anything's happened today.'

'She says it's private, won't even give me a hint about it.'

'Since when have my business affairs been private from you?'

'This isn't business; it's personal, apparently.'

'You know about my personal life, too.'

'Not all of it.' Edward kept his temper with difficulty. Pete had been in a sour mood all morning, snapping at Gerry, at Ilsa, who simply snapped back, and at Edward, who walked away and refused to answer. A visit from a nondescript man whose reason for being there only Pete knew, had put him in an even worse mood.

This wasn't a good day for Beth's visit.

'I'll see her with you or not at all.' Pete folded his arms in one of his dramatic gestures.

'Perhaps you should see her another time. You seem upset about something.'

'I'm upset about a lot of things, including the way this woman's pestering me. *You* are the one who insisted I see her. So bring her in and let's get it over with. Now or never.'

Edward decided there was nothing he could

do to soften Pete's attitude. Beth would just have to tell him whatever it was and hope for the best.

He went to the door. 'Would you like to come in now, Beth?'

She did so, looking at him in surprise as he closed the door and stayed with them. 'I need to speak to Pete privately. I told you that.'

'Edward's my manager and my cousin,' Pete said. 'Nothing is private from him.'

'This is.'

He leaned forward. 'You have nine minutes left of your ten. You can spend them arguing about whether Edward should stay, or you can tell me what's got your knickers in such a twist.'

She stared at him in shock at this rudeness then stopped trying to cushion the blow. 'Very well. When my little brother was nearly three, he vanished and we never saw him again. I'm quite sure you're him.'

Both men gaped at her.

She reached for the briefcase and took out the folder she'd prepared. 'This is a photo of Greg a month before he vanished. This is an image of you, regressed on your TV show.' She laid them down on the desk, but Pete didn't bother to pick them up.

'And that's your proof?' He gave a scornful laugh. 'I think not. My mother said that image didn't look like me, and the people who wrote the computer program say the regression isn't accurate before about six years of age.'

'This time it was accurate and I also — '

He leaned back as if to distance himself from her. 'If you're going to ask me for money, you can forget about it. Now, get out or I'll call the security staff to escort you out.'

Edward stretched out one hand. 'Pete, there's no need to be like that.'

Beth moved right up to the edge of the desk. 'Stay out of it, please, Edward.' If anything, Pete's scorn had stiffened her backbone. 'There's one other thing that decided me. You have a scar on your arm. It's a very distinctive shape. Greg had just such a scar.' She pulled out her final photograph and slapped it down hard on the desk. 'Spare a few more of your precious seconds to take a really good look at it. You'll see I'm right.'

Edward and Pete both leaned forward. The three photos on the desk all seemed to show the same little boy. The scar showed very clearly on the third one, which was battered and cracked round the edges from much handling.

'The police used that one for identification purposes. It was in all the newspapers, if you want to check that it's genuine. I think they expected to find a body, but they didn't. My parents and I never saw Greg again, never knew whether he was alive or dead — until I saw you on television.

'My mother had a nervous breakdown at the time. I spent that first few months after the kidnapping being sent from one relative to another. When I went back home I had to look after my mother more than she looked after me, because my parents' marriage had broken up. I don't want or need money from you, Pete Newbury, *not one damned penny*. What I need is closure for my mother, who is also *your* mother.' She stepped back and folded her arms.

Pete gave her a sour look and picked up the third photo. 'You could have doctored this.'

'I wouldn't know how. But feel free to have it tested — as long as you give me your assurance that I'll get it back without further damage. I don't have many photos of my little brother.'

'Is your mother still alive?' Edward asked.

'Yes. She doesn't know about this yet. I wanted to speak to you first, see how you took it, and I'm glad I did.'

Pete looked at Edward, ignoring Beth. 'She can't be right . . . can she?'

'The evidence sounds convincing.'

'Well, I'm not believing anything till we've had some DNA tests done. And we'll check this photo too.'

Edward turned to look at her, upset by her white, hurt face. 'I'll look after the photo, Beth, I promise you. I don't think you're a liar, but Pete needs to be absolutely certain.'

She hesitated then gave him the briefest of nods before reaching into her briefcase again. 'This is a photo of me at nine, the age you were regressed to on the first TV programme.' She held it out to her brother.

Pete took hold of it as if it was poison-coated, looking at it with a scowl. 'This proves nothing.'

Edward moved forward to stare at it.

'There is a distinct likeness, though. We have the same hair colour. And this is my grandson, who is three. He's the image of what you were like at that age.' She pulled out the precious

130

photo Jo had given her.

Edward knew how much that meant to her, and she was right: there was a close resemblance.

Pete, however, was still in a bad mood. He gave it only a cursory glance and slid it back to her. 'So what if you can prove what you say? The last thing I need is another family hanging on to my coat tails. Even if I was once your brother, I've moved on. I don't want to change my life. And I definitely *don't* want to upset my mother.'

He stood up and moved round the huge desk, stopping at the door to say, 'Deal with her, Edward. Get rid of her. I don't believe what she says is true.'

He left the room without a word to Beth and they heard the outer office door slam.

'I'm sorry for his rudeness,' Edward said gently. 'Are you all right?'

She couldn't answer yet, was holding back tears only with difficulty.

'You're not all right. Come into my office. I'll find out about DNA tests and we'll have them done. I do think we ought to prove things beyond doubt, whatever we do after that.'

She let him guide her into his office but went to stand at the window with her back to the room. A few tears escaped her. She'd never expected Pete to be so rude and dismissive. He was nothing like the cheerful, friendly man he seemed to be on his TV show. If she'd known what he was really like, she might not have come here today.

Only, she had come now, so she'd just have to go through with it. But she wasn't letting him

131

near her mother in this frame of mind.

'Beth?'

She became aware that Edward was standing next to her, holding out a tissue. 'Thanks.'

'Give me a few minutes to find out about DNA testing.'

She stayed where she was while he made a few phone calls then heard him come across to her again. Not till he was standing next to her did she turn, and this time she had her emotions under control. Well, she'd stopped crying, at least, but shock and sorrow at his reception of her news were still churning round in her stomach, making her feel sick.

'We can go and get your side of the test done now, if you've the time.'

'I've plenty of time.'

'Look, Beth, I'm sorry he treated you like that. It was a shock to him. Pete's not normally so . . . rude.'

'I'm not lying, Edward.'

'No. I don't think you are. Once you've proved you're right, we'll figure something out. It won't be easy, though.'

She let him put an arm round her shoulders. 'I never expected it to be. What's his mother like?'

'I'm very fond of my Aunt Sue. She's gentle and kind, loves Pete too much, perhaps.'

'And his father?'

'He was a strong man who usually got what he wanted in business. He made a fair amount of money, then lost it again in bad investments later in his life. They were very happy together and I think Aunt Sue still misses him a lot. And your mother? You said she'd had a breakdown after your brother disappeared.'

'Yes. She was on anti-depressants for most of my childhood. She's picked herself up in the past couple of decades, has a job and a small house of her own. But she lives quietly, keeps herself to herself, finds it hard to get close to anyone. She really needs closure, Edward.'

'I don't really have to ask, but you will keep this to yourself, won't you? Whatever we find out.'

'Do you think I want to broadcast the news that I have a brother as rude as that? I don't need his money. I earn enough of my own, thank you very much.'

'I'm sure you do. But Pete's been in a bad mood all morning, which isn't like him, so something else must be upsetting him.'

As Edward gave her a quick hug, she turned in his arms and stared at him, putting up one hand to caress his cheek. 'I'm sorry you've been forced into the mediator role.'

'So am I. It's what Pete pays me for, but with you, it's different.'

'Is it?'

'You know it is. I want to see more of you. I don't want this coming between us.'

She had to ask, 'Do *you* think I'm lying?'

'No.' He bent to kiss her cheek. 'Right then. If you're ready, let's get this DNA test over with.'

'You'll be careful with the photo of my little brother?'

'I promise.'

He took her hand as they walked out and after

133

hesitating for a moment in surprise, she let him. She was feeling fragile under her bravado, and its warmth and strength comforted her greatly. She wasn't used to having support. It was . . . nice. More than nice. Wonderful.

★ ★ ★

The DNA test wasn't as simple as Beth had expected. She was questioned about when she'd last eaten or drunk, asked to rinse her mouth out with water, and had to provide two samples from the inside of her mouth.

Edward paid extra for a speedier test result, promising to bring Pete in to give a sample.

When they went outside he stopped. She thought he was going to reach out to her again, but after a moment's hesitation he dug his hands in his pockets.

She was disappointed.

'Shall I take you home, Beth?'

'No. I'd better go back to work.'

'No chance of another date now that I know what's upsetting you?'

She tried to be sensible, but it was difficult. 'Let's see how this comes out first, Edward. And if you're to get samples from Pete, you'd better stop him drinking alcohol or coffee with his lunch.'

'Hell, you're right.' He pulled out his mobile phone, waved goodbye as she got into a taxi and was soon talking urgently into it.

She smiled wryly. What had they all done before mobile phones? Even as she was thinking that, hers rang and she pulled it out.

Pete met Edward outside the clinic.

'You've not had any coffee or alcohol?' Edward asked.

'No. I told you on the phone, I was walking by the river, trying to get my head round all this. Though if you'd rung me half an hour later, I might have started on the wine. I'd just decided to call it a day and go home.'

'Were you going to tell Fran?'

'No. The less she knows the better.' He saw Edward stare at him, as if trying to work out what that meant.

'I thought things were improving between you.'

Pete turned away from the clinic and began to walk slowly along the street. 'Then you were being overly optimistic. I've been having her followed. The guy who came to the office this morning is a private investigator. She's still seeing that French fellow.' He waited for some response and when his cousin remained silent, said, 'I'm going to divorce her now I have proof she's been unfaithful. I've not been near another woman since we got married. *I* kept my vows.'

Edward said nothing, but clearly that surprised him.

Pete glared at his cousin. 'You don't believe me, do you? Well, it's the truth. If you think I've the time or energy to service all the little dears who offer themselves to me, then you can think again.'

'Sorry. Whatever you say.'

'It'll be bad enough getting divorced. What if the media gets hold of the news about my parents? You know what they can be like when they start digging for dirt. The last thing I need at the moment is another scandal.'

'Does it need to get out?'

Pete wished his cousin would sometimes lose that calm voice and show more emotion. 'It definitely won't get out from me, but I can't control what your lady friend does, can I? She could rake in a fortune if she went to the media.'

Pete got his wish as Edward stopped walking and spoke sharply. 'You're being unjust. Beth isn't like that.'

'How do you know?'

'I just do.'

'You've fallen for her, haven't you?'

Edward shrugged and began walking again. 'I'm certainly attracted, but it's early days.'

'You want to steer clear of entanglements with women. I can't believe how much I'm going to have to pay to get rid of Fran.'

'Is that how you think of it, Pete, getting rid of her?'

'What else? I'll pay a modest amount to get rid of Beth, too — unless you can sweet-talk her into keeping quiet about all this. If she's a cleaner, she won't be rolling in money. Fifty thousand pounds should fix her, seventy-five max.'

Edward stopped and grabbed his arm. 'Stop saying things like that. She does *not* want money. Her mother has been upset for over thirty years and needs closure. I reckon Beth does, too. The way she talks about the kidnapping shows that the hurt went deep.'

Pete stared at his cousin, not liking what he was hearing. 'Has it occurred to you that if we bring this out into the open, they might send Mum to prison for kidnapping?'

'Don't be stupid. If there's one thing I'm certain of, it's that Aunt Sue didn't kidnap anyone. She probably doesn't even know there's a problem.'

'If I was taken at the age of three, she'll know she didn't bear me, won't she? Why the hell didn't they tell me I was adopted?'

'You'll have to ask her.'

Pete stopped at the door but before he could say anything else, someone tried to get past him, so he stepped back.

To his annoyance, the woman stopped to look at him. 'Aren't you Pete Newbury?'

He summoned up the friendly guy who ran the show, something he could usually do at will. It had never been as hard as it was today. Grimly holding a smile that felt as if it was glued to his face, he chatted for a moment or two, then to his relief she left.

As they entered the building, he said in a low voice, 'You go to the reception and tell them I want to be kept out of sight and I'll sue if they tell anyone about the tests.'

'I've already told them that but they assured me everything is kept strictly confidential. A lot of their work is for the courts.'

'Let's get it over with, then.'

★ ★ ★

When Jo got home from work, she found Ghita a mass of nerves. Several little dishes of food were set out ready and the two small boys were dressed in clean clothes.

Jo hugged her friend and went next door to change, putting on her best clothes, a long skirt and a pretty top in toning colours. They weren't particularly in fashion or even new, having come from a charity shop, but the muted shades of green were flattering.

When she went back, they waited, trying to keep the boys entertained.

It was a relief when someone knocked on the door. She made a shooing motion to Ghita, who was shaking visibly as she went to open it.

Her father stood there, his face as stern as last time, and behind him stood a woman who looked so like Ghita it was a shock to Jo. This was what her friend would look like in a couple of decades.

'Please come in,' Ghita said.

They took off their shoes and would have left them outside, but Jo picked them up and put them just inside the door. 'It's safer that way.'

Ghita gestured towards Jo. 'This is my friend, Jo, who is now like a sister to me.'

But her mother's eyes were fixed on Kaleel, and after a quick nod of greeting to Jo, she took a step towards him, pushing aside her husband's hand when he would have restrained her. She bent to give the little boy a quick kiss, stroking his dark hair and smiling at him as she produced a small toy.

Ghita moved forward. 'This is your grandma.

Say thank you for the present.'

Jo could see Mikey waiting for his present, so pulled him to her and whispered, 'You can have a present when we go home.' He looked at her solemnly, then stayed close, as if aware of the strong emotions raging around them.

When her husband cleared his throat for the second time, Ghita's mother dragged her attention away from her grandchild and turned to her daughter. 'He looks very like your brother Nuriel did as a child.' She looked at Jo apologetically. 'Your son, too, is a fine boy.'

'Thank you, Mrs Haddad.'

The father folded his arms and stood there as if determined to stay apart from this, but Jo noticed his eyes kept going to his grandson.

'Won't you sit down, Father?' Ghita indicated the one armchair.

He did so, sitting stiffly upright, and his wife sat on the sagging sofa.

Food was offered and for once, the two little boys were so overawed they sat down on their towels without protest. Keeping quiet, they picked up their snacks tidily from small plates.

The visit lasted only half an hour, which upset Jo. To spend only thirty minutes with your daughter when you'd not seen her for more than three years seemed heartless.

When they'd gone, Ghita burst into tears and plumped down on the sofa, sobbing her heart out. Upset, Kaleel tried to get his mother's attention but though she hugged him close, it was a while before she managed to stop weeping.

'They didn't stay long,' Jo said.

'I knew they wouldn't. My mother held her grandson, though. I think she understands how I feel about him. However I got him, he is my son.'

Jo wasn't sure Ghita's parents understood much about their daughter's present life, but didn't say that. She helped eat up the food then stayed till the boys were both nearly asleep, before going back to her flat and putting her son to bed.

She sat in front of the television, but couldn't have said what was on. It took her a while to figure out what was upsetting her about the meeting: Mrs Haddad had cuddled her grandson but she hadn't touched her daughter.

Jo couldn't help comparing the visible love shown by her own mother, for all the awkwardness of their meeting, with the stiff visit that had just played out.

But was she ready to ask her mother for help, even so?

★ ★ ★

Beth was woken by the phone ringing at seven o'clock on Friday morning. She jerked upright in the bed, wondering . . . hoping . . .

'Mum? It's me.'

'Jo? Are you all right?'

'Yes. Sorry to ring at this hour, but I have to go to work. You used to wake up early.'

'I still do.'

'Look . . . are you busy this evening?'

'No.'

'How about I bring Mikey round to meet you after work?'

Beth closed her eyes and tried to swallow the huge lump in her throat that was stopping her from making any intelligible response.

'Mum?'

'Sorry. I was just . . . so happy. Yes. Yes, please do come round. What time do you finish work? Do you want me to pick you up?'

'No. Ghita will bring Mikey to meet me after work and there's a bus that will bring us to your place. You can drive us home afterwards, though, if you don't mind. It'll be safer.'

'I'll have some tea ready. What does he like?'

'He eats anything. So do I these days.'

It was a while before Beth realized she was still clutching the phone and it was buzzing loudly. She set it back in its cradle and went to make herself a cup of tea.

After nine o'clock she tried ringing Edward to find out if he'd got the results of the DNA tests, but the receptionist said Edward was out and she didn't know when he'd be back.

'Ask him to ring me, please.'

'I will if he comes back.'

How could she settle down to anything till she knew the results? Surely Pete would treat her and her mother differently when he realized she was telling the truth, that he was her brother.

She couldn't settle to anything. The waiting was killing her.

★ ★ ★

Linda was relieved to find the office at the building yard unoccupied on the Friday morning. It had been a fraught week. Once the locks had been fixed, Nat had gone home. And she'd missed him.

He hadn't mentioned his stay at her house, except for once asking if she'd had any more trouble. But she was more conscious of him than she'd ever been.

On her desk was a note. 'Out at a meeting all morning. You're lunching with me at Nonna Marianna's at one o'clock. I've already booked.'

She didn't want to go, was afraid of being too intimate with him. No, she was lying to herself. She did want to go, but she wasn't sure it was the right thing to do. Yet she knew if she pretended to be ill and went home early, Nat would come after her to check that she was all right.

Only she wasn't all right, hadn't felt all right since the mugging, not because of the attack, but because of Nat, comforting her, helping her, staying with her — and reminding her of feelings she'd not experienced for many years.

She locked her handbag inside the cupboard and tried to settle to work. There was always plenty to do. But she couldn't concentrate, kept watching the old-fashioned wall clock whose fingers were jerking round inexorably towards one o'clock.

At half past twelve, she heard his car and froze, even though she knew it was silly to be afraid of Nat. She couldn't move, could only wait for him to come into the office.

He stopped in the doorway and stared at her across the room. 'Oh, Linda. My dear, you look like someone waiting for the executioner. Am I that frightening?'

The warmth of his voice, the way his eyes crinkled at the corners when he smiled at her, made her fears seem suddenly foolish.

'No. It's not you, Nat. It's me.'

'Time you started living again, don't you think? I've waited long enough for you to come to life. I'm lonely, Linda. And so are you, I think.'

He moved over, took her hand and pulled her round the desk. He gave her a quick hug, not letting go of her hand as he took a step backwards again. 'Any messages that can't wait?'

'No.'

'Good. Let's go and have a long, leisurely lunch. We deserve it.'

He kept hold of her hand all the way to the car and she found she liked the warmth of his touch just as much as the familiar warmth of his smile.

It had been a long time since she'd wanted a man to touch her. Dare she get involved with Nat?

She smiled at that thought. Did she have a choice?

Although she knew Nat would leave her alone if she said she wasn't interested, she couldn't lie to him. She did fancy him — very much — scary though that was.

9

Beth spent most of the day at the office, catching up on paperwork, then left part way through the afternoon. She'd told Sandy about her daughter coming back into her life, and her friend had been happy to cover for her at work.

On the way home she called at a rather nice delicatessen that had opened recently to buy a few bits and pieces for tea, agonizing over what would please a three-year-old boy.

Next door was a toy shop and she lingered over the displays, wondering what to buy for Mikey. In the end the assistant helped her choose a book popular with children that age, one with brightly-coloured pictures of children playing various games. She could change it if her grandson already had a copy.

As the time for Jo's visit drew nearer, Beth couldn't concentrate on anything. The food was ready, the flat immaculate and she'd changed into casual clothes, not wanting to make Jo feel shabby. She'd noticed how well-worn her daughter's clothes were.

She began pacing up and down her living room, going to stare out of the window every few minutes, even though she knew it was too soon for them to arrive.

When she finally saw a young woman coming towards the flats pushing a child's buggy, she froze, suddenly terrified this might go wrong,

144

that she might lose her daughter all over again.

She didn't think she could bear that.

'Don't be stupid!' she said aloud. It seemed too impersonal to let Jo ring the doorbell and speak to her on the intercom, so she snatched her keys. Since the lift was being used, she ran down the three flights of stairs to the foyer to let them in, arriving slightly breathless.

Jo was standing a few yards away, studying the building, looking as tense as Beth felt.

The two women stared at one another for a few seconds then Beth walked towards the pair, her eyes drawn to the rosy-faced little boy. He'd been waving his arms around but suddenly grew shy and leaned back in his buggy, hiding behind a scruffy purple plush elephant.

'This is Mikey,' Jo said. 'Say hello to your grandma, darling. Remember I told you Kaleel has a grandma and so do you.'

He continued to hide his face.

Beth's voice came out thick with tears. 'He's beautiful.'

'Better not try to kiss him or anything till he stops hiding behind Huffilump. Mikey's a bit shy with strangers because he doesn't meet many.'

The air seemed so charged with emotion that Beth said the first thing that came into her head. 'I'm nervous. This is so important I don't want anything to spoil it.'

Jo patted her arm. 'That's all right. I'm nervous too.'

'Why are we standing outside like a pair of idiots? Come and be nervous inside.'

They went up in the lift in complete silence.

Mikey kept peeping at his mother for reassurance, and Huffilump was still very much in evidence.

When they got to the flat, Jo paused. 'The door's a different colour.'

'I've decorated inside as well, but your room's exactly as you left it. If there's anything you want, it'll probably still be there.'

Jo gaped at her. 'You didn't get rid of my things?'

'No. I couldn't. I kept hoping you'd come back.'

'Oh, Mum.' Her face crumpled and a tear ran down her cheek. 'I wanted to come back sometimes, but not till I'd achieved something. Dad would have been so . . . He'd have gloated about being right that I'd never amount to anything.'

'He was upset when you ran away. He'll want to know you're all right. I can't understand why he hasn't replied to your emails.'

'If I'd known he'd emigrated, I might have come to see you sooner, Mum. I couldn't face his scorn. He always made me feel such a loser.'

Beth didn't contradict her. Shane had been a bit like that, sharp with people who didn't meet his exacting standards. It had been one of the reasons they split up. One day she'd just had enough of his scorn.

'How can you be a loser with a beautiful child like this?'

Jo wiped away the tear with the back of one hand and gave a wobbly laugh. 'The only success of my life, Mikey.'

'Well, he's a gorgeous boy. I'd guess you've grown up, too. That's an achievement as well.'

Jo's face softened and she nodded. 'You're right. Mikey needs me, you see, so I have to be sensible. But I'm happy to look after him because I love him to pieces.'

She hesitated, then added, 'If I hadn't had Ghita to help out, I'd have been lost at first. She was in hospital at the same time as me and we got friendly because neither of us had any visitors. Afterwards I had nowhere to go, so she took me back to her flat and looked after me. I think I'd have died without her — or Social Services would have taken Mikey from me, which would have been nearly as bad. I was pretty depressed at the time, you see. Everything seemed — too much.'

'I'd have helped you.'

'I know that now. I didn't then.'

Beth swallowed that pain, didn't allow herself to protest, didn't dare. 'Ghita sounds a lovely person.'

'She is. You must come and meet her. Wait till you see her Kaleel and my Mikey playing together.'

The little boy started making noises and wriggling to get out of his buggy.

'All right if I let him run loose? Better check first if there's anything in reach that he can break.'

They had a quick look round and both women dived for dishes and an ornament that had belonged to Beth's grandmother.

'I've got some food, just stuff I picked up at the shops. I'm out of practice at cooking, with only me to care for and working irregular hours. You two will stay for a meal?'

Jo nodded. 'Yes. And you know what? It's not as hard as I'd expected.'

'What isn't?'

'Coming back here. Can I look at my old room?'

'Yes. Do you want me to keep an eye on Mikey and give you a few minutes on your own?'

'Thanks. That'd be great.'

'If there's anything you want, just take it.' Beth watched her leave, then turned to smile at the little boy, vowing to stay in his life from now on, whatever it took.

★ ★ ★

Jo walked down the short corridor to her bedroom, opened the door and stepped into her past, gasping and clapping one hand to her mouth as she stared round. Even though her mother had warned her, it was still a shock to see the room looking exactly the same as when she'd walked out of it five years ago.

Slowly, hardly daring to breathe, she moved across to the bed and stroked the familiar quilt, a little more faded but still pretty. When she slid open the wardrobe door, her old clothes were still hanging there. Most of them wouldn't fit now, unfortunately, because she'd grown a couple of inches and wasn't as stick-thin as before. No, some of the looser ones might fit. It'd be a big help because she was running short of decent clothes.

She moved the hangers to get a better look. Nearly all the clothes were dark. In those days, she'd thought it cool to dress in black, had bemoaned her naturally blonde hair, and worn chains, dark eye-shadow and black lipstick.

She'd frighten Mikey if she dressed like that now.

She looked at the floor of the wardrobe. Shoes. Now, those would be really useful if they still fitted her. She took out a pair of lace-ups she'd had to wear for school. How she'd hated them! Sitting down on the bed she tried them on and they fitted perfectly. She walked to and fro. These would be ideal for work, far better than the frayed trainers she couldn't afford to replace.

There was a school skirt, too. No one except her would know it was school uniform, as it was navy and of no particular style, but again, it would be perfect for work. She slipped it on and nodded. Great.

Sitting down on the bed, she tried to recapture how she'd felt all those years ago, what had driven her to run away. The room was comfortable. Her parents had provided everything a girl could need. Why had she felt they didn't love or understand her?

Seeing how upset her mother was, how terrified of frightening her away again, knowing how she'd feel if she lost Mikey, brought it all home to her.

Jo shook her head in bafflement at her younger self, felt like weeping for the stupidity of it all, but wouldn't let herself. OK, so she'd stuffed up big time, but she'd paid for her mistakes, paid dearly. And if that was what it took to get a son like Mikey to love, then she'd pay the price again without complaining.

As always, the thought of him lifted her spirits.

She went back into the living room, her shoes making no sound on the soft carpet, and stopped at the sight of her mother cuddling Mikey and reading a book to him, tears running down her cheeks. Oh, hell! Jo backed away. This was too private a moment to interrupt. She'd hurt her mother far more than she'd understood at the time. Perhaps she could make it up to her now.

She could try, anyway.

Opening the door of her old bedroom quietly, she banged it shut and walked along the short corridor once more. Her mother was still bent over Mikey, who had one chubby forefinger pointing at a picture in his new book.

'He loves being read to, doesn't he?'

'He always has. I often read to him.' Jo waved the pair of shoes. 'Can I take these? I hated them when I had to wear them for school, and they're still pretty ugly, but they're perfect for work. You bought me good quality shoes, didn't you?'

'Always.' She looked at Jo's feet, but didn't say anything about the ratty trainers.

Mikey wriggled down from his grandmother's lap and began to explore the room, touching things gently. His shoes were in a much better state than his mother's.

'He's not usually destructive,' Jo offered.

'It's good for children to explore. Don't you want any of your other things?'

'There's a skirt . . . and I can try some of the

150

clothes on after tea, but it's Mikey's teatime now, if you don't mind.'

'Come into the kitchen. It's almost ready.'

By seven thirty, Mikey was drooping, so they went into Jo's old bedroom, let him lie on the bed and went quickly through the things in the wardrobe.

'I can't take too much because I have to move soon.' Jo could have kicked herself. She hadn't intended to mention that yet.

'Oh? Where are you going?'

'I don't know. They're knocking the building down and we all have to get out. They've given us the minimum legal notice, the rats, even though they must have known for ages. I suppose they didn't want to lose any rent. But you know what the rental market's like. It's really hard to find somewhere cheap at the best of times, but just now, well, it's going to be very difficult. And I need to be close to Ghita and to my work.' She watched her mother start to fiddle with the plates.

'You could come here temporarily, then take your time to find a decent place.'

Jo tried to make a joke of it. 'Do you think we could stand one another full-time?'

'We could try. To be honest, I wouldn't want you living here permanently, but temporarily would be fine.'

'It'd drive you mad to have a three-year-old around. He'd break things, wake you up during the night, leave his toys everywhere, make so much noise and mess. You know what they're like at that age. And you've always been Mrs Tidy.'

151

Her mother's eyes were brimming with tears as she said huskily, 'He could break everything and I'd still want him. I've missed so much of his life.' She pressed one hand to her mouth. 'Sorry. I didn't mean to say anything like that.'

'And I didn't mean to come here and start asking for help on the very first visit.' Jo went to give her mother a quick hug. 'Hey, it's all right. We're both human. And it's really kind of you to offer to have me, but there's Ghita to think of.'

'Your friend? The one who helped you so much?'

'Yes. She can't manage very well on her own.' Jo tried to explain why Ghita's cultural background made her very self-effacing and nervous.

'So you're going to look for somewhere together?'

'Yes, though separate flats next to one another were ideal. I need her to look after Mikey while I'm at work and she needs me to help her cope with the world. It's a great partnership. We'll find somewhere soon, I'm sure.'

'Actually, I might be able to help you find a flat. I have some contacts in the rental industry.'

Jo looked at her in puzzlement.

'I'll tell you about my business success next time. Shane thought it a stupid idea and predicted I'd fail, but I didn't.'

As her mother drove them home, Jo felt as if the load on her shoulders had been lightened. So much for independence! She wished she hadn't waited so long to get in touch. She couldn't get the picture of her mother weeping over Mikey out of her mind, felt horribly guilty about causing her such pain.

It was heavenly to be driven home in comfort. 'Turn left. Second house on the right.' The place looked worse than ever, a huge old Victorian building that had been split into as many flats as could be crammed in, then neglected. 'Not very nice, is it?' Jo got out and paused by the driver's side. 'Next time you must come in and meet Ghita, but I'd better get her used to the idea first.'

'Am I so frightening?'

'Everything new is frightening to her. She tries to hide it, but I can always tell. It's better to give her some warning. Thanks for today. We enjoyed our visit. I'll — um, see you soon.'

'I'll look forward to it.'

★   ★   ★

Beth locked her car doors and sat watching till Jo had wheeled the sleeping child into the building, then drove slowly back home.

Mikey was such a lovely little boy. She couldn't help feeling resentful that she'd missed three whole years of her grandson's life.

Jo seemed a good mother, absolutely devoted. Who'd have thought that?

Beth's smile faded. She'd tried hard to be a good mother, too — and had failed. She still didn't really understand why Jo had done something as drastic as running away, and wasn't going to risk talking about that.

Parenting had to be one of the most difficult jobs on earth.

Pete watched his wife get ready to go out with 'the girls' and could stand it no longer. 'Tell Henri tonight that you'll be getting a divorce soon and he'll be able to marry you.'

'What?' Fran froze as what he'd said sank in, then plumped down on the bed. She opened her mouth as if to protest, caught Pete's eye and closed her mouth again. After a moment, when he didn't speak, she said, 'Henri was just a fling. I don't want to marry him. I want to stay married to you.'

'To my money, you mean. Well, sorry. That tap has been turned off. You'd better not try to use your credit cards from now on. They've been closed permanently.'

'Pete, don't! We'll discuss it, get counselling.'

'I don't want any bloody counselling. I want to be free of you, you disloyal bitch.'

There was a long, pregnant silence, then Fran stood up.

'I'd better change.' She put her handbag down and began to take off her clothes. When she was naked, she came across to him and tried to put her arms round his neck. But he stepped back, feeling disgusted that she was trying to use sex like this. He'd loved her once, but now he had a hard time remembering why.

'Don't!'

'But Pete, you know how well we go together.'

'Sex isn't love, Fran.'

'You don't know how to love!'

'Then it's a good thing our marriage is over. Put some clothes on, then we can talk.'

Sulkily, she slipped on a lacy dressing gown.

He led the way into the living room and steered clear of the big sofa on which they'd often made love. 'Right. Here's what I've worked out with my lawyer. If you move out, I'll pay for a flat and deal generously with you. If you try to stay here, I'll fight you for every single penny.'

She pulled her dressing gown more tightly around her. 'You have been busy.'

'So have you.' He watched her lips press tightly together and her hands clench into fists.

'I'll have to hire myself a lawyer before I agree to anything. Perhaps *you* had better move out for the time being. The man usually does.'

'I had this flat before we met. I like it. My lawyer says to stay put. After all, you've made sure there are no children involved, haven't you?'

She shrugged and turned away.

'I'll move my things into the guest suite, temporarily. I want you out within the week.'

He slept badly, tossing and turning, worrying about that damned DNA test, how much money Fran would rip him off for, how a divorce would affect his image.

Early on Monday morning, after a fraught day with Fran, during which they'd hardly said a word to one another, Pete went round to Edward's flat, desperate to talk about it all.

His cousin looked as if he hadn't slept well either, and greeted him with, 'What the hell are you doing here at this hour?'

'I told Fran last night that I was divorcing her. The flat isn't the most comfortable place at the moment.'

'What if she locks you out?'

'Then I really will break down the door.' Pete shrugged and went into the kitchen to get a cup of coffee. 'It's about time you got yourself a proper coffee machine.'

'Why should I? I drink tea in the mornings and water the rest of the day.'

'You don't know what you're missing.' It was an old joke between them but he hadn't the heart for it this morning. 'Have you got the results yet?'

'No. I'm going to collect them later.'

'I'll come with you.'

'Beth's meeting me there. I thought you didn't want anything more to do with her.'

'I don't. But I'm still coming.'

It was preying on his mind. He needed to know. Suddenly he understood the people on his show a bit better. They too needed to know.

Three hours later, as they were getting ready to leave, Pete asked suddenly, 'Do you think she really is my sister?'

'*She* is certain she is, and I consider it a strong possibility. There can't be two scars like that. And by the way, that photo hasn't been doctored.'

'I can't believe Mum would be involved in something like that.'

'I did some research into Beth's story. Her little brother vanished just as she said, and the scar on the arm was mentioned in all the media reports. There were other photos of it. I've checked them out.'

'What the hell are we going to do about her?'

Edward picked up his car keys. 'Nothing for the moment. We need the facts first, then we need to sit down calmly and discuss our strategy.'

There was no answer and he turned to see Pete staring out of the window, making no attempt to move.

'Pete? Are you coming?'

'What? Oh, yeah.'

When they parked near the laboratory, Pete blew out his breath in a whoosh of tension. 'You go in and get the results. I don't want to be seen there.'

'I'm waiting for Beth. And the results will be in an envelope. No one will know what we're collecting.'

'They might think it's a paternity suit. There's always someone who recognizes me these days.'

'And you love it.'

'Not today, I don't. Today I feel — strange. Who am I, if she's right?'

'The same person you were yesterday.'

Pete shook his head. 'I don't think so.'

Edward had never seen his cousin so subdued. 'Ah, here's Beth now.' He went to greet her. 'Pete's staying in the car. He's a bit upset. He and his wife decided to divorce yesterday.'

'That hurts.'

They produced some identification and collected the small package. Back at the car Edward gestured to his cousin to roll the window down. 'We should open this together. Shall we go back to my place?'

'I suppose so.' Pete made no attempt to greet

157

Beth and although Edward saw her open her mouth to say hello, she shut it tightly again when Pete didn't even look at her.

He gave her directions to follow them, got into the car and thrust the envelope into his cousin's hands. 'Here. Hold this.'

Pete took it gingerly, as if it was an unexploded bomb. Which in one sense it was.

★ ★ ★

At the flats, they waited for Beth to join them, then went up in silence.

'Nice location,' Beth said.

'It's convenient. I'd rather have a house and garden, though.'

Pete frowned at him. 'You never said.'

'You never asked. Anyone want a cup of tea?'

'Let's just get it damned well over!' Pete snapped.

'All right. Do you want to open it?'

He stared at the packet lying on the table. 'No. You do that.'

Edward looked questioningly at Beth and when she nodded, he opened it, skipping the preliminary explanations to find the information they both needed.

As the seconds ticked past, Pete asked, 'Well?'

'You're definitely related, with a high probability that you're brother and sister.'

His cousin leaned forward. 'Probability?'

'Didn't you read the information I gave you?'

'I had other things on my mind last night.'

'They can exclude you definitely from being

158

related, but they can't give a hundred per cent guarantee on a relationship, just offer probabilities. Yours are very high. Given the scar, this is proof you're related.' He held out the papers. 'Do you want to see them, Beth?'

She shook her head. 'I never had any doubts.'

There was silence, then Pete looked at Beth. 'How much will you take to forget about this? Fifty thousand pounds tempt you?'

She gave him a very level look. 'There's no amount of money that will buy my silence on this, because my — *our* mother needs to know you're alive, so that she can come fully alive again herself.'

'Oh, spare me the sob story. If that wasn't enough money, how much *do* you want? I mean, you're a cleaner, for heaven's sake. You must want a more comfortable life, mortgage paid, that sort of thing.'

She stood up. 'I don't want anything from you. Actually, I'm finding it hard to accept that I'm related to someone so horribly mercenary. If it's any comfort, I won't tell anyone apart from my mother because I'm not proud of being related to you. You'll have to ask Mum what she wants to do yourself.' Her tone became even more scornful. 'But it's a hundred per cent *probable* that you won't be able to bribe her, either.' She moved towards the door.

Edward went across to her, searching for words to excuse his cousin's rudeness, and finding none. 'I'm sorry for this. I'll be in touch.'

'Don't bother. A relationship couldn't possibly work out with a lowly *cleaner*.'

He watched her walk to the lift and wait there, foot tapping, back turned towards him.

He lingered for a moment even after the lift door had closed on her stony expression. He knew who had come out better from this encounter and it wasn't Pete. Reluctantly he went back inside.

'Has she gone?'

'Yes.'

'We need to have her followed, Edward. I'll call that detective. She must have some weak spot we can use to — '

'Beth's only weak spot is caring about her mother. And I'll not be part of having her followed or harassed.'

'It's your job to look after *my* interests, not hers.'

'Then I quit.' Edward went to get his car keys. 'Lock the door behind you when you leave. I need some fresh air.'

He was out before Pete had recovered from his surprise.

10

Beth walked back across town, going by the side streets because she didn't want to meet anyone she knew till she'd calmed down. At the office she held up one hand as Sandy opened her mouth. 'Give me five minutes and I'll be all right. If anyone calls during that time, I'm not here, not for anyone.'

She closed the door of her office and leaned against it, letting out her breath in a long, shuddering sigh. *That man* was her brother, the boy whose disappearance had ruined her mother's life? It was hard to believe.

He wasn't worth all the heartbreak!

If she told her mother he was alive, Linda would be desperate to see him, but how would he treat her? Only . . . could Beth keep quiet about this discovery? No, it wouldn't be fair. Her mother had the right to know.

Besides, Pete might send someone to bribe her to keep quiet, and that would be a dreadful way for Linda to find out her son was still alive.

It was going to be hard to sort this out tactfully. No, not hard, impossible. But there must be some way to minimize the damage.

When Beth's thoughts had stopped churning round in circles and she felt more herself, she followed her usual practice of giving herself an hour, during which time she'd try not to think about the pressing problem but would concentrate on something else. For some reason, a solution often came to her when she went back to review the main problem.

She took her little notebook out of her handbag and the first entry said: *Find Jo a flat.* Good. That would keep her busy.

She went out to Sandy. 'OK. I've joined the human race again. Any messages while I was out?'

'Several, but nothing urgent. Are you all right?'

'I had a bit of a shock today. It threw me for a while.'

'Jo again?'

'No. Something else entirely.'

'Anything I can do to help?'

Beth smiled at her friend. 'Not at the moment, but if there is, I won't hesitate to ask. Now, can you get Mal Bateman on the phone, please? I think he'll be the best person to help me find a flat for my daughter.'

'Jo came to see you, then?'

'Yes. And brought my grandson.'

Sandy let out a joyful cry. 'You didn't tell me you had a grandson.'

Beth gave her a quick summary of what had happened, cheering herself up as she did so. Not everything in her life was going pearshaped.

She went back into her office and when the phone rang, picked it up, expecting Mal to be on the line.

'Don't hang up!'

'Edward! How did you get through to me?'

'You gave me your direct phone number when we went out together.'

'Oh, yes. I'd forgotten. But I don't think we have anything more to say to one another.'

'Not even if I tell you I've resigned and no longer work for Pete?'

It was the last thing she'd expected him to say.

'Beth? Are you still there?'

'Yes. You surprised me.'

'I think I surprised Pete, too. But I meant it. I shan't be working for him again.'

She rubbed her aching forehead. 'At the moment you mean it, but the tie between you is too strong. He's your cousin and if he needs you, you'll go back to him.'

'Actually, he isn't really my cousin, is he? Besides, I've been intending to move on for a while now.'

'Even so, there's too much baggage between you and me now to — '

'Beth, give us a chance. *Please.*'

She hadn't expected him to plead with her and somehow couldn't hang up on him after that. 'What are you going to do now, Edward?'

'I haven't the faintest idea. I'm out of work and I've not felt so free for years. How about coming for a long holiday with me?'

'You're joking.' When the silence continued, she asked, 'Aren't you?'

'Half-joking. I'd love to get away.'

'I can't, not when I've just met my grandson for the first time and need to help my daughter find somewhere to live.'

'No, of course you can't. I'd forgotten about your daughter.' He laughed softly. 'I'm feeling too euphoric to think straight. Bear with me. Will you have dinner with me tonight?'

She hesitated, then decided she could do with a taste of euphoria. 'Tomorrow would be better, if that's all right with you. Tonight I have to tell my mother about Pete being Greg.'

'That'll be hard.'

'Yes. Hardest of all will be to tell her he doesn't want to see her.'

'I don't think Pete knows what he wants. He's not usually so . . . harsh. I know it's upset him that his wife's been unfaithful.'

'Well, now *he* has upset *me*. Great way to deal with a problem, don't you think?'

'He doesn't — '

She sighed. 'Let's not revisit that, Edward.'

'OK. I'll pick you up at seven tomorrow. Dress like Cinderella going to the ball. This is a big celebration.'

And he was gone.

Beth didn't move until Sandy poked her head into the office. 'I didn't get Mr Bateman for you because I saw you had a call on your private line. Shall I get him now?'

'Please. I'm not answering the phone again until I've spoken to him. If he's available.'

'He's usually available. I think it's mainly his son and grandson who run the business now.'

'Mal still keeps an eye on what's happening. Don't underestimate him.'

She waited, tapping her fingers impatiently, wondering if she should have refused the invitation to go out for dinner. No, she really wanted to see Edward again. And if he had resigned, surely they could manage to have a relationship without Pete spoiling it?

Oh, what did she know about relationships? She'd thought she had a reasonably happy marriage, but Shane had grown increasingly sharp and withdrawn. No discussions or counselling. He'd found someone else and left her to manage a very difficult teenager on her own.

The phone rang and she picked it up, glad of the distraction. 'Mal. Thanks for taking my call. Look, I wonder if you could give me some advice . . . ' She explained about Jo and Ghita, not hesitating to confide in Mal, who was about as close to a father figure as anyone in her life these days. He'd taken her under his wing when she was first starting up in business. Without his help, it'd have been much harder.

'I'm not sure I can help. Your daughter is right. That sort of accommodation is in very short supply. I'll ask around and get back to you tomorrow morning. I'm on the board of a couple of housing charities and I know they have long waiting lists. They may know of some temporary places, though. I presume the two young women would share a room, if necessary?'

'Yes, of course. They're pretty desperate.'

When she put the phone down, Beth frowned. If Mal couldn't help her, she didn't know where to turn. Could she cope with a crowded flat and small children? She didn't feel at all sure she could.

Leaning back, she allowed her thoughts to return to her mother. Somehow she had to work out a tactful way to tell her about Greg, who was now Pete.

Linda felt nervous as she packed up for the day at the office, dreading facing that car park again. When she was almost ready, Nat called, 'Wait for me and I'll walk you to your car.'

She went across and gave him a hug.

'What's that for?'

'Being so understanding.'

He held her at arm's length, hands on her shoulders, and looked at her very seriously for a moment. 'I'll always try to understand what you need.' Then he nodded and went back to being his normal brisk self as he finished closing the place up.

On the way to the car park he took her shopping bag from her with one hand and held her hand with the other. Did they look fools holding hands at their age? she wondered, then smiled. Had anyone else even noticed? Other people all seemed to be hurrying to get home, not strolling as she and Nat were.

At her car he stowed her shopping in the boot and stepped back. 'I'll follow you home. Can you give me some tea or shall we pick something up on the way?'

'I can always feed a guest.' But as she sat watching him walk away, hearing his cheerful whistle, she felt as if she was playing with fire. Worse, as if she wanted to play with it, which frightened her more than a little.

When she got home, she stared at her house. How small and shabby it was! She felt as if she hadn't really looked at it for a while. She'd been

166

cocooned here for years, scurrying home from work, rarely going out at night, living only a half-life.

Was she really ready to move on? She rather thought so and was pleased with herself for that.

As she slid out of her car, Nat drew up and got out of his vehicle with his usual energy. 'Penny for 'em.'

'I was thinking how shabby my place looks.'

'I can help you do it up, if you like. Or . . . '

'Or what?'

'You could move in with me.' He chuckled. 'Close your mouth, your shock's showing. My dear, we're too old to pussy-foot around and court one another for years.'

'Is that what we're doing? Courting?'

'I am. And I think you're starting to.'

She surprised herself, needing only a moment's thought to say, 'Yes, I believe I am.'

'Good. And actually, I don't want to live here among your memories. I moved after my wife died, chose a good house in an upmarket area, but it's too big for me. There's plenty of room for you, and for your daughter to visit, not to mention my sons. And no memories of others to intrude.'

'There are no memories here. My ex never lived in this house. But it is small.'

She was glad she'd pushed the front door open and could keep her back to him while she adjusted to the shock. She'd almost said yes to his suggestion!

He hefted the shopping on to the kitchen bench. 'What are we having for tea?'

'How about a stir fry? I've some chicken in the

freezer and plenty of vegetables and noodles.'

'Sounds great. And for afters?'

'Wait and see.'

'Can I help you?'

'Are you any good in the kitchen?'

'I like to think so.'

She'd forgotten how pleasant it was to cook together, then sit and chat over a meal while sharing a bottle of wine.

'Am I staying here tonight?' he asked, twirling the wine glass in his hand and staring at her very solemnly. 'I can sleep in the other bedroom if you want to wait a little to share a bed.' He reached out to caress her cheek. 'You're looking shocked again. You always tell me at work that I'm impatient. I'm just as bad in my private life, I'm afraid.'

'No, you're not going too fast. You can sleep with me, as long as you remember I'm not as young as I used to be.' She blushed as she added, 'My curves have all sagged a bit.'

He grinned and stroked his bald head. 'Nor am I a handsome young stud. I'm wearing pretty well physically, but I'm a bit bigger round the waist than I ought to be and my hair is long gone.'

'It's eyes that attract me, and warm smiles are far more important than hair.'

As they were finishing the clearing up, the phone rang. She leaned across to study the caller's number then picked it up, mouthing, 'It's Beth.'

'I'll wait for you in the sitting room.'

'Mum? Did I hear voices?'

168

'It's just Nat. He — um, came back for tea.'

'That's nice. I really like Nat.'

'Good. Because he and I are — what do they call it now? — an item.'

'That's *wonderful* news. I couldn't be happier for you, Mum. It's about time you found someone. Look, I don't want to interrupt your evening. Perhaps I should ring tomorrow.'

'Is something wrong, Beth? You sound tense.'

'You can always sense that, can't you? I think I'd better tell you this face to face. I can be over in quarter of an hour, traffic permitting, if you're sure I'm not spoiling your evening totally. It is rather important. Is that all right?'

'Yes.' Linda went into the sitting room. 'Beth has something to tell me, and from the tone of her voice, it's not good news.'

'I'm not going to offer to leave, because if it is bad news, you might need me, but I can go up to the bedroom when she comes, to give you some privacy.'

'No. Stay with me.' Her voice shook as she confessed, 'I don't cope very well with bad news. I had a nervous breakdown after my son vanished, and was on anti-depressants for years.'

'Well, whatever the news is, you won't be facing it on your own. You've got me to hold your hand from now on, literally and mentally.' He cocked his head on one side. 'What did Beth say about us?'

'She's pleased.'

'So am I.' He gave her a quick hug. When she moved away and began to clear the table, he helped her.

169

'I wonder what's happened? Perhaps she's heard from Jo again.'

★ ★ ★

When the four-wheel drive drew up outside, Linda went to open the front door before Beth had time to ring the doorbell. 'What's wrong?'

'Let me get inside first, Mum.'

'Sorry. I just hate to be kept in suspense.'

'I know.' She followed her mother into the sitting room, raising her eyebrows as she saw Nat standing by the fireplace.

He came across to kiss her cheek.

'I want Nat to be with me,' her mother announced.

'All right.' Beth took a deep breath and explained what had happened.

As her mother began to weep, Nat put his arm round Linda's shoulders, hugging her close and listening intently. When Beth had finished, she watched her mother lean against him, sobbing, watched how tenderly he held her.

It was such a relief not to be the one trying to offer comfort, because Beth was feeling more than a bit upset herself.

After a minute or two, Nat produced a big handkerchief and thrust it at Linda. 'Enough weeping, love.'

'I knew he wasn't dead. I just knew it. How soon can I see him, Beth?'

This was even harder. 'I'm sorry. There's no easy way to tell you — only he doesn't want to have anything to do with us, Mum. He was quite

170

rude about it, tried to bribe me to keep quiet.'

'Did he have any idea he'd been kidnapped?' Nat asked.

'No, none. I'm pretty sure of that. I don't think he even knew he was adopted.'

'Then he was probably in shock, not thinking clearly.'

'Well, that's no excuse for saying such horrible things. I don't intend to see him again, if I can help it. I'd not have told you at all, only he might contact you and try to bribe you.'

'You said he'd just agreed to get a divorce,' Nat pointed out. 'That's traumatic too. Poor fellow's had the angst piled on him this week.'

Beth snorted in disgust. '*Poor fellow!* I think not. Spoilt celebrity would be a better description.' She sneaked a glance at her mother, but Linda wasn't weeping now, just looking sad.

Her mother intercepted her glance. 'I'm all right, darling. I used to think I'd be hysterical with joy if I ever found Greg again, but I'm not. It's been so long. He'll be — what? — forty-one now. I'm a complete stranger, even if I am his birth mother, and you can never make up for the lost years. I saw him on TV with his mother and I can remember her quite clearly. She didn't look like the sort of woman who would kidnap a child.'

'Perhaps she didn't do the kidnapping,' Nat said. 'She may be a victim too.'

Beth waited and when neither said anything, she asked, 'So what do you want me to do about him?'

Linda drew herself up. 'Nothing. It's not your

problem now, Beth darling. I know you're trying to spare me, but I've been a lot better since I passed the menopause. I may weep, but I shan't collapse. Nor shall I rush into anything.'

'And she's got me this time,' Nat put in. 'I'll take good care of her, I promise.'

Linda smiled at him. 'And I'll take care of you, too, Nat.'

As they smiled at one another, Beth felt happiness replace the anxiety. It was wonderful to see her mother with someone as nice as Nat. 'I had to tell you, but don't let it spoil your life.'

★ ★ ★

For all her brave words, after her daughter left Linda began to weep again, finding comfort in Nat's strong arms. When she'd cried herself out, she blew her nose firmly. 'Sorry. I must look a mess.'

He moved his head back a little to study her. 'You don't look your best. But who cares? You're still my Linda.'

'And you're a lovely man.'

'I'm also a hungry one. What happened to that dessert you promised me?'

'I forgot about it completely. Ice cream all right?'

He beamed at her. 'I love ice cream. I saw you had some bananas. Let's make an ice cream sundae.'

By the time he'd rummaged through her cupboards and insisted on his ice cream and bananas being enhanced by a tin of raspberries,

172

some flakes of chocolate and some nuts, she had lost the urge to weep. She even managed to force most of her dessert down, because he was so very anxious to please her.

But the sadness was still there underneath, and always would be, she supposed.

How could her son not want to meet her? She wanted desperately to meet him. She didn't know how she'd manage to do that, but she would, somehow.

Nat touched her arm gently. 'Are you all right?'

Smiling, she laced her fingers in his. 'I'm fine, better than I'd expected to be, actually. Thanks for being with me.'

'Nowhere else I'd rather be.'

They went to watch television and soon she found herself in a corner of the couch, with Nat lying with his head on her lap, snoozing gently as the programme played on unwatched by either of them.

She wasn't going to tell anyone what she intended to do, she decided. Not Beth and not Nat, either. Both would try to stop her, she was sure. And she didn't intend to be prevented from seeing her son again, at least once.

★　★　★

When Pete arrived home, he found the locks had been changed and a suitcase was standing outside the door of the flat. He didn't give Fran the satisfaction of banging on the door and pleading to be let in. With a grim smile, he went back down to the foyer, took out his mobile and rang up a man he knew.

If she wanted a confrontation, he was very much in the mood for one.

Half an hour later two men came into the foyer, each carrying a bulging leather briefcase.

Pete said goodbye to the concierge, to whom he'd been chatting, and led the way up to his flat.

'I don't care how you manage it, but get me inside, then do whatever's necessary to mend the door again.'

'I have to ask: you're sure this is your dwelling, sir?'

'Oh, yes. My wife and I have agreed to divorce, but as we don't have children, there's no need for her to keep this flat. It was mine before we married and by hell, it'll be mine after we're divorced.' It had been the first thing he bought when he started making real money and he hadn't realized how much he loved the place till Fran insisted *she* was going to stay in it. Well, no way was the unfaithful bitch going to take his home from him.

The second man went to look at the door and smiled at Pete. 'No need to break anything down, sir. I am, if I may say so, quite an expert at picking locks. You should really have installed a much better one in a luxury place like this.'

'We have a concierge on duty downstairs all the time.'

'And there will be at least one back door, plus the entrance to the basement car park. This isn't enough protection, sir, not nearly enough.' He took out some tools and began to fiddle with the lock. After a short time, there were some clicking noises and it opened.

'After she leaves, can you come and fix me up with locks that can't be picked?'

'Yes, sir. But you'd better make sure you get a key for this new lock before we leave, hadn't you?'

Pete nodded. 'Would you mind waiting out here? I think there may be a bit of arguing before she agrees to do what I want.' He strolled into the TV room of his flat and smiled as Fran jumped to her feet with a cry of shock.

'How the hell did you get in?'

'Through the front door, how do you think?'

'But I had the lock changed.'

'Well, it's going to be changed again. This is *my* flat and you're not keeping it.'

'I like living here.'

'It was mine before we married.'

'I'll get a restraining order.'

He gave her a disgusted look. 'You're the one at fault here. What grounds could you possibly have for a restraining order? I'd hoped we could settle things amicably, but if you want to fight, I might remind you that I can afford to buy whatever help I need to defeat you.'

'I'll say you beat me up. I'll scratch myself to prove it. You won't win then.'

He moved back to the door and stood near it, arms folded. 'Go ahead. Do your worst.'

She picked up the phone and dialled the concierge. When someone answered, she let out a piercing scream and banged her arm on the

175

edge of the cupboard. 'Send someone to Flat 3!' She began to sob.

Pete had opened the door as soon as she started doing this and when she turned to look at him triumphantly, one hand curling up to scratch her own face, she found three men standing there, all staring at her quite calmly.

'He started to beat me,' she said faintly.

'He didn't touch you, Mrs Newbury,' one man said. 'I could see through the glass door that he was nowhere near you, even before he let us in.'

The phone in her hand squawked. 'Sorry, it was a joke.' She put it down. 'Pete, please! Don't do this. We can work it out.'

'We're way past that, Fran, as you just proved. How could I ever trust you again?' He turned to the two men. 'I think I'm going to need a chaperone till she leaves. Who knows what else she'll claim I've done? Would you be willing to stay with me twenty-four seven till she moves out, just in case?'

'We'll take shifts. It'll cost you, though.'

'I have plenty of money.' He chuckled at the sour expression on Fran's face as he added, 'More than she has.'

'Then we'd be happy to help you, sir.'

'Let me show you your bedroom.' Ignoring his wife, Pete went to open a door further down the corridor.

The nearest man shook his head. 'I think it'd be better if I slept in your room, sir, given what she's already tried to do.'

'Fine. Whatever you think best.'

Fran came to stand in the doorway of the

176

living room. 'You're a bastard, Pete Newbury, you know that?'

'I don't think so. You're the one who was unfaithful and I can prove it.'

'Everyone knows women throw themselves at you by the dozen.'

'But no one knows that I do anything with them.'

'I bet if I hire someone to look, they'll find you've been unfaithful.'

'They won't because I haven't. Now, I need to get some sleep. I've got long rehearsals tomorrow.'

'You men always stick together!' She glared at them and stormed off down the corridor.

'Good thing you had witnesses, sir,' the guard said. 'Nasty, that could have been.'

'Yes.' Pete went to have a quick shower. Not until he was safely under a stream of hot water did he let his emotions out. Men weren't supposed to cry — unless they were driven to desperation. He not only had to face the humiliation of having everyone know his wife had been unfaithful, but also the ridiculous claim that he'd been kidnapped as a child. And to top it all, Edward had resigned.

It was too much.

When he'd finished his shower, he towelled himself dry and went to sort out a makeshift bed for his guard before getting into his own. He felt relief at letting out his emotions. Now he'd settle in for a fight. No one was going to get the better of him. Not his wife, nor his damned inconvenient sister.

And they weren't going to upset his mother, either. She was looking a bit frail these days and still missed his father greatly, he knew. He ought to go and see her more often. He *would* see more of her from now on.

At least things were going well with the show. The new segment was drawing a bigger audience. People loved sob stories, that was clear.

He'd have to find a way to get Edward back, though, because he needed his cousin more than ever at the moment. He'd phone him first thing in the morning and grovel, if necessary.

11

The phone rang at seven o'clock in the morning, jerking Edward out of a sound sleep after a restless night. He peered at the clock and groaned, then fumbled for the phone.

'Feeling better today?' Pete asked.

'What the hell do you want at this hour?'

'Come and have breakfast with me. You can't have meant it about quitting, but clearly something is upsetting you, so we need to fix it. I apologize if it's my fault.'

'What I'm going to do right now is go back to sleep. Have a nice day.' Edward put the phone down and rolled over.

When it rang again, he ignored it. Five minutes later it started ringing once more. He sat up, unplugged it and quickly got changed for the gym.

The phone in the living room began ringing as he left his flat. Well, let it damned well ring.

He enjoyed a workout and started swimming a few laps to finish off the session. When he saw Pete come into the gym, he groaned, got a mouthful of water and spat it out but continued swimming. He wasn't jumping out to greet him like a tame dog.

When he'd finished his laps, he got out and Pete came across to join him.

'Breakfast now?'

'Which word don't you understand, *I* or *quit*?'

'I'll raise your salary.'

'It's not about money. You've always paid me generously — which was only right considering how hard you worked me. Look, Pete, I was thinking of quitting anyway. I want to live my own life, not yours. The way you treated Beth just brought the date forward. There was no need to be so cruel to her. You really upset her, and that upset me.'

Pete looked at him for a moment with eyes narrowed. 'Are you still involved with her?'

'I certainly am.'

'Bad timing, Edward. Bad choice of woman, too. She's only using you to get at me.'

'She isn't.' He smiled at the thought of that. Beth might be too blunt sometimes but she'd not lie about something important, he was quite sure of that.

'I'm going to pay her off, then we'll see who's right.'

'She doesn't want your money.'

Pete made a scoffing sound. 'She's a cleaner, for heaven's sake. Of course she wants money — clearly more than I offered her. You don't want to get tangled up with a greedy woman.'

Edward pressed the lift button, hoping it'd come before he punched his cousin. 'She damned well isn't greedy. Don't bother coming up. I don't want to talk to you till I'm feeling a little more charitable. I'll come into the office soon to collect my things.'

When Pete would have followed him into the lift, he shoved his cousin away forcibly, taking him by surprise, and shut the doors on him, glaring so fiercely that Pete stepped back.

Beth went home from her mother's house to a flat that seemed even emptier than usual. She fidgeted around, making cheese on toast and opening a can of soup because she couldn't be bothered to cook anything else. At least she was eating something, she told herself, and forced down an apple as well.

The evening seemed interminable and the only bright spot was an email from Jo, not a long one, but a promise to bring Mikey to see her next Saturday, if that was all right.

Beth typed a quick reply and went to switch on the television. But a promo about the next Pete Newbury Show upset her, and when they kept showing the stupid promo over and over, she switched off the television and tried to read instead. Unfortunately, the book wasn't good enough to grab her attention.

In the end she had a shower and went to bed, expecting a poor night's sleep.

To her surprise it was morning when she next opened her eyes. She stretched luxuriously. Nothing made you feel as good as a sound night's sleep.

Today would be better, she was sure. Tonight she was going out to dinner with Edward. *Wear something special*, he'd said. She only had the outfit she'd worn to the ball and it was too fancy for a visit to a restaurant, even a celebratory one.

She opened her wardrobe, but the selection of clothes revealed practical workwear, several pairs of jeans and tops, nothing glamorous. This was another time when she needed Renée's help.

Glancing at the clock she picked up the phone and rang her friend, explaining her dilemma.

'You're going out with a man more than once?' Renée teased. 'What's got into you?'

'He's interesting. I can talk to him.'

Renée's voice softened. 'I'm glad for you. You're usually so terse with people. And of course I'll help you. I'll pick you up at lunchtime. I know a great little boutique just five minutes from your office.'

Beth put the phone down, aligning its cradle carefully and staring at the surface for a moment or two. What had got into her to be buying more clothes that she'd only wear once or twice? Edward, that's what. He was frighteningly attractive, and yet so easy to chat to that she hadn't backed away, for once.

Did she dare risk spending more time with him? Hadn't she vowed not to get serious about a man ever again?

Serious! She wasn't serious about him, she just liked him.

She clapped one hand to her mouth as the realization sank in that she could very easily get serious about Edward Newbury.

What was she going to do about that? Stop it now or . . . dip her toe in the water again.

She looked down at her toes and smiled slowly, wriggling them inside her shoes.

★ ★ ★

Jo went to see a flat after work. 'Flat' was a misnomer, for a start. It was one room with a so-called kitchen in an alcove, and a shared bathroom that needed cleaning. A bedsitter wouldn't work with a small child. There needed to be at least two rooms or Mikey would never get to sleep in the evenings. When she turned to leave, the landlord blocked her way.

'Could do you a cheaper rent if you were the friendly type,' he said with a leer that made very clear what he meant by that.

'My girlfriend wouldn't approve,' she said.

His smile turned into a sneer. 'One of those, are you? Unnatural, that is. You need a real man to sort you out, you do.'

She pushed past him quickly, suddenly a little afraid, and when he grabbed her arm, she chopped at his throat with her free hand. She'd never actually tried any of the self-defence tactics she'd learned about in a class she'd once attended, had never needed to, because the first rule of self-defence was to avoid getting into dangerous situations. Though how you could do that when you were flat hunting was more than she could work out.

Hearing him coughing and choking behind her, she ran off down the street, groaning in relief when a bus came along almost immediately.

★   ★   ★

Ghita opened the door, expecting to see Jo, astonished when she found her father standing there again. 'Come in.'

This time he knew to leave his shoes inside the

183

flat. He still looked round suspiciously, but the sight of the two little boys playing with plastic cars on the rug seemed to reassure him.

Tears welled in her eyes. Would he always look at her so suspiciously? How could he think she'd ever do anything immoral?

Not till they were sitting with glasses of tea and a platter of untouched biscuits before them did he come to the point.

'Your mother and I think you should come and live at home again. She could help you with the boy until — ' He broke off with a frown.

'Until what?'

'Until we find you a husband. There are older men who'd be prepared to overlook what happened to you. It's just a matter of negotiating something.'

She stared at him in horror. She didn't want an arranged marriage and to her surprise, didn't want to live at home again, either. It'd mean waiting on her father and brothers hand and foot, keeping her opinions to herself, and she'd grown used to airing her thoughts and discussing her feelings openly.

Looking across at her rosy-faced son, she realized suddenly that she didn't want her Kaleel growing up with her father's attitude towards women. She hadn't appreciated how much she'd changed . . . until now.

'Well? What do you say?' he asked impatiently. 'This is no way to show your gratitude.'

She chose her words carefully, knowing they'd still upset him. 'I'm grateful you want to help me, but I've grown used to living on my own now. I don't think it would work to come back. And I definitely don't want an arranged marriage.'

His face grew red and angry, and for a moment she quailed before that anger, as she had done many times before, then pulled herself together.

'You will do as I say!' he thundered. 'You belong with your own kind, not with loose women like the one next door. To think of a daughter of mine acting as servant to one like that!'

The two little boys looked round fearfully at the sound of his raised voice.

'Jo isn't a loose woman and — '

He held up one hand. 'Enough. Your brothers and I will be round at the weekend to help you move back home.' He stood up. 'I shouldn't have to remind you that you owe a duty to your parents and family.'

She didn't protest as he slammed the door behind him, because she knew he wouldn't listen. And she didn't weep until she'd looked out of the window and seen him drive away.

When someone knocked on the door a few minutes later, her heart began to thump with fear, because she thought he'd come back for her.

The person knocked again and she couldn't move, didn't dare open the door.

'Ghita! Are you all right?'

She ran to the door and flung it open. 'Jo! Oh, Jo, I'm so glad you're back.' And couldn't stop weeping.

Beth went to check on how a new job was going. She made random inspections of every job that Sherbright contracted for, and the staff knew it. When a routine was well established, she put one cleaner in charge of the bigger jobs, paying that person a little extra.

The new office block was looking good and she complimented the cleaners on work well done. The woman in charge had a couple of suggestions for improving the way they tackled this job. Beth took them both on board and praised her employee for her initiative. She also made a mental note to keep an eye on the woman and promote her further if she continued to show initiative.

Some employees wanted only a part-time job, others were in transition, studying for better jobs, and one or two seemed to figure out that there might be long-term opportunities with Sherbright. Sandy had started off as a cleaner while studying at technical college, then had moved to the office. En route, she'd become a friend.

That morning Mal rang Beth.

'There's no accommodation free, not even for emergencies, and as usual we have a long waiting list.'

'Oh. Well, thanks anyway for trying.'

'I'm sorry I couldn't help you. What will your daughter and her friend do in the meantime?'

'They'll both have to come and live with me if they can't find anywhere.'

'That might not be wise.'

'It's better than them being homeless or living in a dangerous district.'

'You try to hide it by being brisk, but you're a kind woman, my dear.'

'And you're a kind man.'

He chuckled. 'My grandson doesn't think so. I gave him a telling-off yesterday for sloppy work. They can do what they want when I'm dead but until then we'll run this company *my* way, even if it does seem old-fashioned to the young money-grabbers of today.'

When she put the phone down, Beth was thoughtful. She didn't want to have two young women and two toddlers living in her flat, was sure they'd soon get on each other's nerves. She was too used to doing things her way, and she knew she was pernickety about cleanliness. That had been one of the points she and Jo had quarrelled about in the old days.

They'd have to set some firm ground rules. But surely with goodwill all round it'd work? For a time, at least.

* * *

At lunchtime Jo phoned her mother. 'Got a minute to talk? If not, I can ring later.'

'I'm meeting someone in half an hour but I'm free till then.'

'Right. We've got a major problem. Ghita's father came to see her last night and laid down the law. She's to go and live at home again and they'll forgive her — though what there is to

187

forgive about being raped, I'll never understand. And then they'll find her a husband, an older one who'll put up with Kaleel. You can imagine what sort of life she'd have — and poor little Kaleel, too.'

'I can indeed.'

Jo took a deep breath. 'I've looked everywhere, Mum, and there's nothing even half suitable. The flat I checked out yesterday had a sleazy landlord who offered reduced rent in return for my favours.'

'Ugh.'

'So . . . ' She'd practised saying it, but it was still hard to get the words out, 'can we come to live with you temporarily, just till we find somewhere?'

'Yes, darling. Of course you can.'

'Both of us? Me and Ghita?'

'Yes, both of you.'

Jo blinked furiously. 'Oh, Mum. How can we ever thank you?'

'By remembering when we quarrel — and I'm sure we will, however hard we try not to — that I still love you.'

'I love you too, Mum. Look, can you let Ghita move in tonight? Would you mind? I know it's short notice, but she's terrified her father and brothers will come earlier and take her away forcibly.'

'Why don't you both move in tonight?'

'Because there won't be time to pack up both flats.'

'I'll arrange that. Can you get the afternoon off work?'

'Yes. But how — '

'Trust me. I know a firm of commercial packers who're very efficient.'

When Jo switched off her mobile, she blew her nose hard, but it still didn't stop her eyes filling with more tears. What would she and Ghita have done if her mother had refused to help them? It didn't bear thinking of.

She hurried back to work to explain to her manager what was happening then, feeling much more light-hearted, she went home to tell Ghita the good news.

★ ★ ★

Beth had forgotten she'd agreed to go shopping with Renée until her friend turned up.

'Sorry. Something's cropped up.'

'Need any help?'

'No, but thanks for the offer. I'm organizing a team of professional packers to move my daughter and her friend in with me. They'll be in and out of her place tonight in three hours max.'

'What about the date with Edward? Have you put him off?'

'Oops! To tell you the truth, I'd forgotten him.'

'Do you want me to ring him for you?'

'No, I'll do it.' She made a quick note on her pad.

'I'll get out of your way, then.'

'Mmm. Thanks.'

Half an hour later the move was organized. Beth picked up the phone to call Edward.

'I'm sorry but I have to cancel for tonight.'

'Is something wrong?'

She explained quickly.

'Let me help.'

'I've hired a team of movers. You'd be in the way, I'm afraid. Can we put it off till next week?'

'I don't want to wait that long to see you. Tomorrow.'

'But — '

'Wednesday. I'll pick you up at seven.' He didn't wait for her to agree but broke the connection.

She stared at the phone, not sure she wanted this. She'd have enough on her plate with Jo and Ghita and two little boys.

And was he being masterful because he really liked her, or was he trying to bully her? She wouldn't put up with that.

She smiled and shook her head. No, he wasn't the bullying sort. For some reason he liked her. Well, she liked him too.

*　*　*

Ghita stood in the middle of the sitting room of her little home, bewildered by the rapid packing that was going on around her. Kaleel sat in his buggy watching, one thumb in his mouth. For once she didn't pull the thumb out.

'Do you want all the stuff in this cupboard?' a woman asked.

She nodded and watched in amazement as the contents of her pantry cupboard were rapidly transferred to boxes, labelled clearly.

It took less than two hours to pack all her

things and carry them down to a waiting truck. When she went to check on Jo, the flat next door was also empty.

Jo's mother came out of the bedroom and smiled at them. 'We're nearly finished. Your bigger pieces of furniture will be in safe storage, I promise you. I've got booster seats in my car for the boys. Let's get back to my place to wait for your things.'

The car was big and comfortable, easily taking the two children's buggies as well as a few bits and pieces. Ghita sat in the back with the boys, watching Jo's mother drive so confidently in and out of the traffic. She'd like to learn to drive, but had never been able to afford lessons. Her father would throw a fit if she even hinted at doing such a thing.

She let her head fall back and closed her eyes for a minute or two. No doubt her family would totally disown her now, and she was sorry for that, desperately sorry. But they couldn't expect women to remain the same once they'd moved to England. Things were different here. Frighteningly different sometimes. Wonderfully different at others.

For Kaleel's sake, she must become braver. She'd already started studying, but it was hard to learn these days when you couldn't afford a computer, and she couldn't use the ones at the library very often with two small children to take care of.

Her eyes went back to Mrs Harding. How kind of her to take them all in!

Ghita watched the street lights alternately

illuminate her son's face and leave it in darkness.

One day, she decided, she too would help others in repayment for all the help she'd received since that dreadful day when she'd been attacked. She felt sad that strangers had been more understanding than her own family.

12

In the morning, Ghita was woken by footsteps pattering down the short corridor that connected the bedrooms. She wondered for a minute what was happening, then memories of the previous day flooded back and she became aware that the children were up.

In the other narrow bed Jo raised her head and sighed. 'Morning already. And I'm on early shift.'

'I'll get your breakfast if you want to have a shower.'

'Did you sleep well?'

Ghita hesitated. 'No. I was worrying about whether I'd done the right thing.'

Jo raised herself on one elbow and stared at her friend in shock. 'Do you really want to go back to your father?'

'Definitely not. But I'm imposing on your mother.'

'We both are.' Jo swung her legs out of bed. 'If you want to use the bathroom, do it quickly.'

Ghita edged past the boxes in the bedroom and those lining one wall of the corridor. The boys were standing near the bathroom door, but she'd made sure all the doors that led off the corridor were shut last night, so the two of them would be trapped in the narrow space when they got up. She hadn't dared close their bedroom door because she wanted to hear if they woke in the night.

'We used the potty,' Kaleel volunteered.

'Clever boys!' She kissed them one after the other. 'I won't be a minute then I'll get you a drink.'

There was no way Mrs Harding could still be asleep, Ghita thought as she sat the two boys at the table. As if to prove her right, her hostess walked in at that very moment.

'I'm sorry if they woke you.'

'I'm an early morning person. I'm always up by this time.'

'Jo's in the bathroom, I'm afraid.'

'I have an en suite shower room off my bedroom, tiny but workable.'

'Oh, that's good!' She hadn't dared ask to look round the rest of the flat. It had seemed discourteous.

Mrs Harding studied her, head on one side. 'You're worrying about being here, aren't you?'

Ghita could feel herself blushing. 'I have no right to impose on you.'

'You've helped my daughter for years and looked after my grandson. That gives you the right, as far as I'm concerned, and if you want to consider yourself part of our family, I'd be very happy. You really are welcome, Ghita.'

Relief surged through her. 'Thank you. Now, if you'll tell me what you like to eat in the mornings, Mrs Harding, I'll get your breakfast each day.'

'Do call me Beth. And you don't need to wait on me.'

'I like to cook and I like to look after people.'

'Then we'll put you in charge of the kitchen. I

194

can't usually be bothered to cook. I work long hours and I never know when I'll get home. In the mornings, I just grab a cup of tea and a bowl of cereal.'

Ghita looked at her. Too thin by far. Dare she interfere? 'Jo likes a boiled egg or a scrambled egg on her toast. I could easily make that for you at the same time.'

She watched Mrs — no, Beth, hesitate then smile.

'Well, all right. That'll be sheer luxury. I'll have whatever you're doing for Jo each day. And tonight we'll sort out money and anything else we need to decide about running the house.'

The boys had been drinking their milk, but now Mikey interrupted them.

'You're my grandma,' he announced, staring hard, as if she were an alien creature.

Beth smiled at him. 'Yes, I am. That's nice, isn't it?'

'Yes.' He smiled at her shyly and waved one hand at the other child. 'Kaleel's my best friend.'

Ghita watched her hostess nod to Kaleel, who was much quieter and shyer than Mikey. Beth wasn't used to small children, she decided, and didn't seem used to living with other people, either.

She noticed that the sound of running water had stopped, and a couple of minutes later Jo rushed in, hair still wet from her shower. 'Mum, you're up. I hope we didn't disturb you. I'm on early shift today, I'm afraid.'

Ghita poured her friend a cup of coffee.

Jo groaned in pleasure as she sipped it. 'You

195

always make the best coffee, even with instant.'

Within five minutes breakfast was on the table.

'You *are* efficient,' Beth commented.

'I was trained in the household arts,' Ghita said. 'I wasn't expected to go out and work, only get married and look after my family.'

'Do you regret that you're not married?'

She stopped briefly to consider this, then shrugged. 'I'd like to marry, but a modern man, not the sort my father considers suitable.'

She made porridge for the two boys, gave them half a banana each then sat between them with the same breakfast. Jo didn't talk much in the early mornings, just ate quickly. Beth also said very little.

It was very different from Ghita's own family, but nice to be starting the day with adult company for a change.

Beth came into the kitchen again on her way out to work. 'Ghita, I've only got one spare front-door key. This is it and this one is for the outer door of the flats. There are some shops down the road, turn right out of the flats. Could you please have another two of each cut while you're out today, then you and Jo can get in and out as you wish? Here!' She thrust some money into her companion's hand. 'Get something nice for tea, anything, I'm not fussy. It's my treat tonight to celebrate you all moving in.'

'I shall have to look in your cupboards to see what you already have,' Ghita said anxiously. 'Also, to put away the food we brought. I hope you don't mind. And there are some of our boxes in your bedroom that I need to get things out of.'

196

'I have no secrets. Look anywhere you wish. Sort out whatever boxes you can and tonight we'll work together on fitting things in better.'

When Beth had gone, Ghita let a few tears of sheer relief fall, then bowed her head in prayer, saying thank you for all the kindness she had met from Jo and her mother.

She went to the window to stare out. She would see if there was a park nearby. The boys would like somewhere to run and play. And if she used only local supermarkets and shops, she should be safe in this area, because her family lived some distance away. She was still afraid they'd try to snatch her and her son off the street.

Turning back, she set to work to get the boys ready for the day and clear up the kitchen, then encourage them to tidy up all except a few toys. She frowned at her own bedroom. Jo, with whom she was now sharing, had said her mother was fanatical about cleanliness and tidiness. Well, so was Ghita. She began to pick up the various items Jo had scattered. She didn't mind doing that. She knew her friend well enough by now to understand that Jo tried hard to keep things clean, but simply didn't have a tidy bone in her body.

I'm the intermediary as well as the house-keeper and nanny, Ghita decided as she pushed the double buggy out of the front door. It'll be up to me to keep the peace. If I weren't here, Jo would soon irritate her mother.

She felt better to think she could make a positive contribution to her new life.

It was much more pleasant to walk along tree-lined streets, where older people nodded a greeting and smiled at the two little boys.

★ ★ ★

Linda had been doing her research carefully, using her computer at work and trying to find out how to contact Pete Newbury. She didn't say anything to Nat about what she was doing. In the end, however, she had to admit defeat. Her son didn't seem to have an office or any way of contacting him except via the television studio. She didn't want to accost him in the street for her first meeting. Why, he might call security to keep her away and walk on past!

In the end she decided to ask Beth how she'd found him, but her daughter's mobile was switched off. She nearly jumped out of her skin when Nat spoke from right next to her desk. She hadn't even heard him come into the office.

'What's bringing that frustrated expression to your face?'

She tried to think of something to say.

'I think I've already mentioned that you're the world's worst liar,' he said with a grin.

'I'm trying to find out how to contact my son,' she blurted out.

He took her hand. 'Oh, Linda, leave it be. You'll only get hurt. He doesn't want to see you.'

'But I want to see him. I *need* to. Only not in public.' She saw him open his mouth to protest and added firmly, 'I'm not going to give up, Nat. I've mourned Greg for years, imagined what he'd look like . . . ' She was annoyed when her voice shook and she couldn't continue for a moment or two. 'I'm his birth mother. I have a right to see him privately, at least once. If he doesn't want to see me after that, he'll have to tell me so face to face.'

'Promise me you'll not go to see him on your own, then, even if you leave me outside in the car.'

'I'm promising nothing, Nat, except to wait till after the show tonight. I think he'll be more open to a meeting once that's over.'

He looked at her thoughtfully. 'You know, there's more steel under your gentleness than people give you credit for. I've watched you sometimes dealing with our tougher customers and you don't let them get away with anything.'

'I used to be very weak but I've come a long way in the past few years, partly thanks to your help and support.'

'My pleasure, love.'

They were silent for a few minutes, then as they walked into the street, he changed the subject. 'It's wonderful not to be going home alone. Would you like to come and see my house tonight?'

'Yes, I'd love to.' She'd never seen his new house, though she knew the postal address, of course.

★   ★   ★

Nat's house was at the end of a cul-de-sac. It was pretty, with a gable at one end and a sprawl of garages at the other.

'Do you really need three garages?' Linda teased.

'That's how it was when I bought it. I added another room at the rear as well, a workshop.' He pressed the remote and the right-hand garage door, which was closest to the house, opened noiselessly. There was plenty of room inside, even for his big four-wheel drive.

He came to help her down, stealing a quick kiss before leading the way towards a door at the side. 'If you don't like this house, we'll find another.'

'Just like that?'

'You of all people know how comfortably off I am, Linda. What's money for if not to buy what you need to make you happy? Now, this is the mud room and through here is the kitchen.'

'Wow! It's a cook's dream.' She went to stroke the pink-tinged granite surfaces and run her fingers along the gleaming stainless steel of the six-burner cooker. 'It's a lot of house for one person.'

'Yes. It's a lot for two people as well, but my children sometimes come to stay when they're visiting London and we can invite your daughter round as well. I never thought my kids would both settle in the provinces.' He gestured to a photograph on the wall. 'I'll move that before you come to live here.'

'Why?'

'Well, you won't want number one wife staring down at you, surely?'

'I don't mind. I liked her the few times we met and I don't mind that you loved her very much.'

He framed Linda's face in his hands and gave her a gentle kiss on each cheek. 'You're a wonderful woman and I'm a very lucky man. She'd approve of me getting together with you. We always said if one of us went first, the other should look for someone else.'

He kissed her again, more urgently, and as he pulled away, they stared at one another breathlessly. Romantic love didn't just belong to the young, she thought in wonderment. She was lucky too, lucky to have met a man like Nat. 'Show me the rest of the house.'

When the tour had finished, he looked at her. 'Well?'

'It's lovely. I'd be very happy to live here.'

Nat beamed. 'When can you move in?'

'Give me a week or two. I'll need to sort out my things, decide what I want to bring, and that might mean you getting rid of some things here, too. I have a few pieces of furniture I'll definitely want to keep.'

'I want it to happen more quickly than that. I want everything about us to happen quickly. I'm thinking permanence here, Linda.'

She jumped in hurriedly before he could talk about marriage, because she wasn't rushing into that, wasn't even sure she believed in it any more. 'I think two weeks *is* quickly, for me at least. Don't push too hard, Nat. I still haven't told my daughter about us living together. And you might not like living with me, after all.'

'I've been spending my days with you for years. I think I know you pretty well by now, and you know me just as well. I don't grow horns

201

and a tail after I come home at night.'

'I'll phone her soon, then.'

* * *

Beth was so busy at work she didn't have time to think about herself for the first few hours. Only then did she realize she'd asked Ghita to buy stuff for a celebratory meal, completely forgetting that she had a date with Edward.

She rang home and no one picked up. She wondered if this was yet another example of Ghita treading carefully. When the answering system kicked in, she called, 'Ghita, please pick up the phone. It's me.'

To her relief the phone was answered. 'Is that you, Ghita?'

'Yes. I'm sorry. I didn't think I should answer your phone.'

'Oh, please do. And use it, too. It's much cheaper than mobiles.'

'You're very kind.'

'And very forgetful. When I told you to buy food for a celebration meal, I forgot that I had a date tonight. I've had to put Edward off once, so I don't want to do that again. Can we do our celebrating tomorrow instead? Would you mind?'

'It doesn't matter. You mustn't let your friend down.'

'How are things going?'

'Very well. The boys and I are going out to the park this afternoon, and I've unpacked some of our things.'

'That's great. I'll be home before seven, then.'

202

She only just managed that, because anything that could go wrong that day did, including one of their older vacuum cleaners breaking down and someone calling in sick.

As she rushed into the flat, she asked the others to let Edward in when he arrived and went to take a shower.

She hummed as she got ready, hearing the intercom ring and the front door go.

When she emerged, she found Edward playing 'little horses' with Mikey, while Kaleel waited shyly for his turn for a ride on Edward's knee. She stood in the doorway, amazed at how good he was with the children.

He looked up, winked, then put Mikey down. 'I think there's time for Kaleel to have a quick ride, don't you?'

'Of course.'

Mikey instantly threw a tantrum. 'Do it again! Do it again!'

'Ignore him,' Jo said. 'He thinks he's the only person in the universe.'

Kaleel began to look distressed as Mikey's crying continued.

'Stop that, you silly boy.' Jo picked her son up and talked softly to him as Edward gave the other little boy his ride.

'Have a good time, Mum!' she called as they left, winking at Beth.

'How are you coping?' Edward asked as they waited for the lift.

'Fine,' she began, then grimaced. 'Well, actually, I'm missing my peace and quiet already. The girls try hard to keep the kids quiet, but they're only three, for heaven's sake. Mikey's cries are particularly piercing, though.'

Again there was a taxi waiting for them. They got into the back and Edward continued the conversation, seeming genuinely interested in her situation. 'Ghita seems very good with the boys.'

'She's brilliant at looking after people, period. She ought to train as a childcare worker or a housekeeper, something on the caring side.'

'No reason why she can't.'

'She'd need childcare herself to do it. At the moment Jo couldn't manage without her.'

'It's hard for young women on their own, isn't it?'

Beth nodded. 'I employ a few who're single parents. I lean over backwards to help them.'

'You *employ*?'

She flushed. 'I own the cleaning business.'

He smiled. 'I'd wondered if it was something like that. Pete still thinks you're a cleaner.'

'I started off as one after my marriage broke up, just temporarily. I was desperate for some ready cash, you see, and Shane was being as awkward as he could about maintenance. I didn't want to ask my mother for help because she had enough on her plate, so I took the first job that paid quickly. I soon saw the opportunities in commercial cleaning, the way the people employing me were making the real money not the cleaners, so I continued cleaning to extend my experience while I took courses on setting up a small business. Then I took the plunge and started Sherbright Cleaning.'

She frowned, thinking over that time. 'I think I

was less attentive to Jo's needs than I should have been around then. I was working all hours of the day and night. Maybe that's partly why she ran away.'

'And maybe she'd have run away whatever you did.'

'Could be. We'll never know.' She hesitated then added quickly, 'I won't mention it again tonight, but has your cousin said anything more about my mother?'

'Not a word. I'm keeping away from him as much as I can, though. I didn't even record the TV show tonight. Pete's trying to persuade me to go back to work for him, but I won't do that.'

'I don't think my mother will let it rest till she's met him and spoken to him.'

'I can understand that. She must be desperate to see him. But he definitely doesn't want to see her.'

She decided it was time to change the subject. 'What's he done to replace you?'

'I doubt he's even thought about it, if I know Pete. He's brilliant at interviewing people, has on-screen charisma and the camera loves him, but he thinks things organize themselves.'

They arrived at the restaurant, which was so elegant in an understated way that it took her breath away. There were three celebrities she recognized, two other people whose faces looked familiar, and the food was exquisite. Since Edward was again using taxis, they were able to share a bottle of wine as they chatted.

'It's easy, isn't it?' he said suddenly.

'What is?'

'Us. Chatting. Spending time together. I can't remember when I've enjoyed an evening more. I hope we can do this again.'

'I hope my life settles down and lets me. I'm a bit worried about both Jo and my mother.'

'You're not responsible for everyone else in your family, you know.'

'It feels like it sometimes.'

'Take time for yourself, Beth. I'm going to. I've danced to Pete's bidding for far too long.'

Later, as they stood up to leave, he asked casually, 'Want to come back to my place?'

She hesitated. If she did, it would probably lead to intimacy. Did she want that yet?

She looked at him and was lost in his wry, patient smile. Yes, she did. He was right. She did need to take time for herself. And besides, he roused something in her that had been quiescent for years. She felt more alive with him, feminine, softer, happier. It wasn't a fiery feeling, more a question of like recognizing like.

Five years ago, she'd have dithered. But if she could carve out a niche in the business world, and a lucrative niche at that, she was more than ready for this . . . whatever it turned out to be. She looked him straight in the eye. 'I'd like that very much.'

'Good.' After they'd paid, she took his hand and they walked out, not needing to speak, simply enjoying being together.

Could a relationship possibly be so easy?

She felt the luxury wrap itself round her as they entered Edward's flat. 'You have a beautiful home.'

He closed the door and swung her into his arms. 'Never mind the flat, I've been dying to kiss you all night.'

Feeling as if she was in a dream, she raised her face to his and let the warmth of his lips, the closeness of his body fill her with happiness. Returning his kisses and caresses, she felt herself melting into the warmth of shared love-making as if she'd known him for years.

She'd expected embarrassment, awkwardness; she found pleasure, a man comfortable in his own skin who made the loving easy and joyful.

Much later, as they lay in bed nestled against one another, he asked, 'Are you staying the night?'

She sighed. 'I'd better not. It sets a bad example to Jo and Ghita.'

'I thought you'd say that. Pity. Next time, perhaps.' He planted a kiss on her nose then got out of bed, searching for his clothes, before finding a sweater.

'There's no need for you to come out again. It's too far. I can order a taxi door to door.'

He smiled. 'I'm old-fashioned. I like to pick my lady up and deliver her safely home again.'

Which made the warmth inside her burn up again, and it was a moment before she could speak coherently.

She'd been on her own for so long. She'd forgotten what it was like to have someone else care about her safety and happiness. Had she ever known this degree of caring?

Not with Shane, for all their early happiness together.

Edward could become . . . addictive.

Pete resented spending the money to keep two security men alternating at his flat, and he grew increasingly annoyed with Fran's greed. After all, she hadn't earned the money she was trying to take from him; he had. The divorce laws might be fair to couples who'd supported each other as they made their way in the world, but all Fran had done was be decorative and sexy after he'd achieved some success — and spend his money like water. That didn't make a relationship last, as he'd found out.

In fact, he grew increasingly irritable about this situation, knew it, but couldn't stop himself. People at the studio stared at him and began to treat him warily.

It took several days and a series of shouting matches for Fran to agree to his terms. It sounded to him as if her lawyer had more sense than she did.

In the end Pete wrote down exactly how much it cost for an hour of a lawyer's time, extending that to three months. This was money which would not be available for either of them after the divorce. 'I shan't change,' he said coldly. 'I'd rather spend my money defending what I've earned than hand it over meekly to you.'

She stared at him then, anger clouding her lovely eyes, making her lips go thinner, giving her face a predatory look.

'You're still beautiful enough to snare some other rich fool, after all,' he added.

'We shouldn't split up. We make a perfect celebrity couple.'

'I want more than good looks from a wife. I want children and a home.'

'*You do?*'

'I didn't know it till now, but you've made me think hard about my future. Do we waste our time and money on lawyers or do we come to an agreement? I'm not being ungenerous, after all.'

'I could get more if I hung on.'

'Doubtful. The lawyers would certainly get more, though — a lot more. And I'm not giving you anything except basic money to cover your daily living till we've come to an agreement. It could drag on for years. How will you manage without shopping and new clothes?'

In the end he felt it was that argument that was the clincher.

That evening she greeted him with, 'My lawyer wants me to accept your terms.'

'Good.'

'But I still think you're being mean and I'll never say a good word about you again,' she snapped.

'Better be careful what you say or I'll be suing you for slander.'

'I'm not moving out till I've found somewhere decent to live.'

The place she found to rent cost more than he wanted to spend, and he was sure Edward could have negotiated better terms for the lease. But without his cousin's help, Pete was finding details difficult and time-consuming to sort out. He just wanted to get her off his back.

Damn, but he missed Edward! Missed his cousin's company as well as his efficiency.

Pete made sure he was there to oversee the removal of Fran's possessions from the flat, making sure she took only what they'd agreed on. This led to some more sharp words, but eventually she clicked her way out, her legs as long and sleek as always in her high heels. Yet somehow he was unmoved by her beauty now.

The security men saw to the changing of the door locks then they too left.

Afterwards Pete walked round the place on his own, making a triumphant fist as he stood on the balcony. He made a cup of coffee, drank it slowly then hesitated, uncertain what to do with himself. Play some music? No, she'd taken the sound system. He must buy another. Read? He hadn't read a book in ages, must visit a bookshop and buy a few. Call friends? No, he wasn't in the mood for drinking or for sympathy.

He went out for a meal because he'd never learned to cook, choosing a small local café he'd not used before. Fran would have turned her nose up at this place, but the food was excellent and no one asked for his autograph.

He walked home and stayed in, surprised at how quiet the flat was without Fran. After drinking a couple of beers, he fell asleep in front of the television, waking with a start as music blared out suddenly.

He was in bed well before midnight, back in the master bedroom. For once he lay awake. He might have settled Fran's hash, but he still hadn't decided what to do about his mother. He needed answers, but didn't want to hurt her.

His meeting with his mother promised to be even more painful than his break-up with Fran.

13

The next morning Beth slept until eight o'clock, which was late for her. She wakened and stretched, feeling her body humming with physical well-being.

When she went into the kitchen she found Ghita clearing up the breakfast things while the boys watched a children's show on TV, jigging about to the music.

'Did you have a nice night out?' Ghita asked.

Beth couldn't stop herself blushing. 'Um — yes.'

Which made Ghita blush too. 'I didn't mean to pry.'

'You weren't. I'm not used to having a man friend, that's all. It's been a long time. Is Jo at work already?'

'Yes. Early shift all week. She'll be back about two.'

'Unless I get an emergency call, I'm clear for the day. Perhaps you and I could discuss food and money and that sort of thing, then run it past Jo? Or do you think we should wait for her?'

'She'll want to see what we've come up with, but she and I usually agree.' Ghita produced a neatly written list. 'I've checked your cupboards and we need to buy a few things if I'm to do the cooking. Sometimes I make dishes my mother taught me. Would that be all right?'

'That sounds great. I'll be happy with anything

212

that comes. I've been a bit remiss about eating properly lately.' She studied the list and whistled softly.

'Is something wrong?'

'No, this sounds fascinating. Real home cooking. How about I drive us to the supermarket and we buy what we need?'

Ghita hesitated. 'Jo and I don't have a lot of money. You won't want to eat our cheap food all the time. I was going to cook something different for you.'

'No need. I've been living off tinned soup, sandwiches and takeaways. Anything you cook will be better than that.' She laid one hand on Ghita's. 'Stop worrying. If you'll take over the housekeeping and cooking here, I'll pay you for doing it.'

'I couldn't accept money when you're letting me stay here for nothing! You won't even take rent.'

'I don't need the money. Use this time to save a bit. Or consider the housekeeping full payment for staying here. Don't undervalue yourself, Ghita. You have excellent skills, and if it weren't for Kaleel and Mikey, I could find you a housekeeper's job tomorrow.'

Her companion looked so astonished she waited to let it sink in, then casually mentioned how much a housekeeper might earn. 'Once Kaleel is of school age, there are places where he'd be allowed to live in with you.'

Ghita clapped one hand to her mouth, blinking her eyes furiously. 'I've been worrying about what sort of job I can get . . . later. Jo gives me money to look after Mikey, but she can't afford much.' Suddenly she was sobbing.

Beth had dealt with this before, young women working for her, shocked by the realization that they could earn enough money to cope decently. When Ghita had calmed down, Beth spoke briskly. 'Now, let's make a full shopping list. There are a few things I want as well.'

She drove them to the supermarket she usually patronized because it was closest, but as she slowed down outside it, Ghita started to say something then stopped.

'Is something wrong?'

'We can do better at Tesco's. This is the most expensive supermarket.'

'I go to it because it's close, but I'm happy to use another. Tesco's is a few streets away. With only one person it doesn't matter too much, with five of us to feed, I can see it's more important to keep costs down.'

She took charge of the double buggy the boys were sitting in and watched Ghita move round the supermarket like a professional shopper, making her purchases carefully, studying labels and unit prices. The two little boys seemed to understand that this wasn't a time to play up and sat quietly for the most part.

Only when they came to the checkout did Mikey ask, 'We've been good, Auntie Ghita. Can we have something?'

Ghita smiled at him. 'Yes. You've both been very good and I'm proud of you.'

They beamed at her.

She controlled them so easily, Beth thought in

amazement. Mikey was much better behaved for her than he was for Jo. What a treasure of an employee she'd make!

As they were coming out of the supermarket Ghita grew tense, looking round before she moved into the open and keeping an eye on the cars they passed.

'What's wrong?'

'I'm still a bit worried my father will come after me.'

'If he does, we'll take out a restraining order.'

'That won't stop him if he thinks the family honour has been blackened.'

'Does he know where you've gone?'

'No. And I'm hoping he won't find out. But you're Jo's mother and if he wants to find me, he'll check on her. He is . . . very set in the old ways, and I think my brothers will help him, so I try to be careful.'

Beth decided there and then to consult her lawyer. But she'd not say anything to Ghita about that.

★　★　★

When they got back there was a message from Linda asking Beth to call her.

'Hi, Mum. How are you?'

'I'm fine. Beth, dear . . . I've decided to move in with Nat, so, well, I thought I'd better let you know and give you my new phone number.'

'You're over twenty-one, you know. You don't have to get my permission.'

'You don't mind, though?'

215

'Why should I? I think it's great that you're not on your own and I told you before, I really like Nat.' She heard a sigh of relief.

'He has a house not far from you, Beth. It's a big place. This is the address . . . It'll take me a couple of weeks to sort through my stuff and decide what to keep, so I'm not moving in with him immediately.'

'If you're throwing anything out, you might think of Jo and Ghita. Their furniture is very old. We can always store it at my warehouse unit till they need it.'

'Good idea.'

There was silence and Beth quickly realized there was something else on her mother's mind. She waited, knowing Linda didn't like to be rushed.

'Beth, how did you contact Greg — I mean, Pete?'

'I got hold of his office address, which isn't public knowledge. But if Edward hadn't been there, I'd not have made it past his dragon of a PA, so I doubt it'd be much use to you.'

'Could you give the address to me anyway?'

'Edward's not there any more. He's resigned.'

'I still want to see your brother. Surely you understand that?'

'I don't want you walking into nastiness. How about I ask Edward's advice?'

There was a moment's silence, then, 'All right. But I don't want to wait too long.'

'Oh, Mum, is it worth it? Pete doesn't want to see us — and he wasn't nice about telling me that. You'll just get hurt.'

'I've been hurt already. Nothing can be worse than not knowing if your child is alive. I know you're trying to protect me, Beth, but I have a right to see him in person — at least once. It'll be up to him whether we meet again.'

As she put the phone down, Beth decided that if her mother did go to see him, she'd go with her, in case . . . Well, just in case.

★ ★ ★

The next day Pete drove out to visit his mother. He still couldn't quite believe he was adopted and it made him angry not to have known. Why hadn't his parents told him? That's what people did these days, surely? You were supposed to be open about such things.

Fate must have been watching over him, because his mind definitely wasn't on his driving as he made his way over to his mother's.

If he'd known he was adopted all his life, perhaps it'd not have been such a shock. A wave of pain ran through him. He was surprised at how much it had upset him. He couldn't get rid of the feeling that he didn't know who he was any more.

He felt guilty now about how rude he'd been to Beth Harding — he simply couldn't think of her as his sister, just could not, but there had been no need to be so cruel. He couldn't help wondering what his birth mother was like and how she had come to lose her son.

Another thing that upset him was if Sue Newbury wasn't his mother, Edward wasn't

217

really his cousin. He was still going to think of Edward as a relative. They'd grown up together, well, they had from about ten years old, after Edward's parents had been killed.

Once he grew older, Pete had thought it strange that his father hadn't associated with his brother before then. He'd never even met his cousin before Edward came to live with them. Had his parents kept their distance because of him and the adoption? *Surely they hadn't known that he'd been kidnapped?*

It made his head spin to think of the possible explanations. He had to find the truth.

After he'd spoken to his mother, the most important thing to do would be get Edward back as his manager and agent. He wasn't appointing anyone else because he didn't *want* anyone else. Edward could be trusted. Everyone knew that agents sometimes screwed their clients and Pete didn't intend that to happen. No way. He'd worked hard for his money and he enjoyed being well off.

Well, here he was.

As he drew up, he saw his mother working in the garden, hand watering some flowers that looked absolutely perfect. She was certainly good at creating beautiful gardens, he had to give her that.

She was also good at keeping secrets. Too damned good.

When she saw the convertible, she stood up with a smile and walked to open the gate. 'Pete, dear, what a pleasant surprise!'

He couldn't return her smile. 'I'm not sure

218

you're going to think that when you hear what I have to tell you. Shall we go inside?'

She turned so white, he wished he'd spoken more gently. He made her sit down while he got them each a cup of tea, then he took the chair facing hers. 'Drink that up then I'll tell you why I came.'

She made a pretence of drinking then set the half-full cup down, clasping her hands in her lap, but not before he'd seen them trembling. He felt bad about that, but not bad enough to stop.

'Don't keep me waiting any longer, darling. Something's very wrong, I can tell. What is it? You're not ill?'

'No. Nothing wrong with my health. There never is.' He fiddled with his cup, then put it down and took a deep breath. 'Why didn't you tell me I was adopted, Mum?'

She didn't move, not an inch, but tears welled in her eyes and rolled down her cheeks as if they had a separate life. He didn't touch her or try to comfort her — couldn't. He still felt cheated that his parents had kept such crucial information from him.

'Why didn't you tell me, Mum?'

'Your father thought it best.'

'And you? Did you have any opinion about it?'

She was silent for so long and was still chalky white, so he asked, 'Are you all right, Mum?'

She stretched one hand out towards him then let it drop when he didn't take it. 'I always did what Donald wanted. He was . . . very much in charge. You know that.'

'Tell me how you got me.'

She stared down at her lap. 'I couldn't have any more children, so we tried to adopt. They said it wouldn't be easy and the only possibility would be a child from overseas or a child with problems. Your father was much older than me, you see. But Donald was adamant: no mixed-race children, no problem children either.'

'But you found me in the end.'

'We adopted you privately. And — I think your father pulled some strings. I didn't ask, but I overheard him on the phone. I wanted a child so much, you see. I do know that he got the records changed — don't ask me how — and we took our own son's identity for you, even his name. *Don't look at me like that!*' She began to sob.

'How the hell did Dad manage that?'

'I didn't question anything. Donald told me he'd found an unmarried mother who couldn't manage on her own. He said she wanted to choose the adoptive parents who took her son, so she'd always feel she'd done the best thing for him.

'I met her. She was quiet, seemed very nice. She asked me questions, then she came back another day with her son. You. She said you'd been ill. You huddled on the couch beside her, looking so helpless and unhappy, I had to hold you in my arms. And you came to me, not her. It was as if you were meant to be *my* son.

'My main worry was that she might change her mind and try to get you back, though she never did. But because friends and family knew about our son dying, we had to move and change our whole lives. So we did. I'd have done anything to keep you, Pete, anything.'

He sat quietly, trying to take all this in. *She didn't know about the kidnapping.*

'We told everyone we were going to live in Australia, and we did for a while.'

'I remember that! Well, I remember the sun and going to the beach. But you told me later that we'd been living in France. How the hell many lies did you tell me?'

'Too many. I'm sorry.'

He stared down at his clenched fists and had to make a conscious effort to speak calmly. 'Go on.'

'From then on, you were our son in every way that mattered.'

'What about the baby who died, the one whose birth certificate I'm using? What happened to him?'

'He was premature, only lived for a few weeks. He was beautiful, but so small.'

He saw more tears roll down her cheeks, was choked with emotion himself. You read about this sort of thing, but you didn't expect to find yourself in the middle of such a horror story. His world had been turned upside down and on top of that, his parents had acted in a criminal way.

Whatever his father had told his mother, someone had actually snatched him from his real family and that thought made him feel hollow inside. Beth Harding said her brother had simply vanished one day and no trace of him had ever been found. So it was worse than a private adoption, much worse.

It was criminal.

He looked across at his mother as something else occurred to him. 'So the ReGress image was correct. That was what I really looked like when I was three.'

She nodded then said in a voice husky with tears, 'It was like a nightmare that evening, seeing you on the screen, knowing someone might recognize you. You shouldn't have done that to me, Pete! You should have asked me beforehand. I don't know how I kept calm, but I knew I must or I could lose everything that mattered to me.'

'You certainly kept your cool, even had me fooled.' He realized he was drumming his fingers on the arm of the couch and stopped. He'd known it'd be hard to talk to her about this, but not how much it would hurt.

'Someone must have recognized you that night. Who was it?'

'My birth sister.' He pushed his sweater sleeve up and brandished his arm at her. 'Not only did she recognize my face, but there was this as the clincher. You can't hide a scar as distinctive as this.'

She went very still, one hand at her throat where a pulse fluttered wildly, then she said, 'I didn't know your mother had another child.'

'There was a lot you didn't know.'

'What more could there be?' It was a whisper, a mere scrape of sound.

'There was no unmarried mother. Someone kidnapped me from my real parents and gave me to you. The woman you met must have been part of it. I wonder how much Dad paid for me.'

222

'No! *No!* I don't believe it. Donald wouldn't, he *couldn't* steal another woman's child!' She began to sob, so hysterical he had to move across and comfort her. She clung to him, weeping and sobbing, begging him not to hate her. He could only pat her back and try to make soothing noises, though he felt anything but calm.

He wished there was someone to comfort him.

As she began to quieten, she pulled away from him. 'I didn't know you'd been kidnapped, Pete, I swear to you, I didn't know.'

'I believe you. But Dad knew, didn't he?'

'He must have done.' She swallowed hard and more tears ran down her cheeks. 'That poor woman, your real mother! Is she still alive?'

'Apparently. I've only met my sister so far.'

'What's she like?'

'Thin, works as a cleaner — a cleaner of all things! How will that look? Oh, and she has the same colour hair as me. She's a bit older than I am, remembers me vanishing.'

'What does she say about her mother?'

He hesitated. 'She says her mother had a nervous breakdown after I was taken.'

'What about her father?'

'Her parents split up. She doesn't see much of him now. Don't look like that, Mum. It wasn't your fault they split up.'

'People do split up after they've lost a child. I've read about it. So I'm partly to blame.'

'People split up for other reasons, like me and Fran.'

She didn't seem to hear his last remark. 'How can I ever make it up to them both?'

223

He held her at arm's length and gave her a little shake to get her full attention. 'Mum, let's get one thing straight. There's going to be no attempt to make it up to them. If you admit to wrongdoing, the authorities might prosecute you, even jail you.'

'Prosecute?'

'Yes.'

She let out a whimper. 'But I didn't *know*.'

'We've only got your word for that. If they're mercenary, these two women may try to sue you for all you've got.'

'What I've got now wouldn't be nearly enough to make it worth their while,' she said bitterly. 'And money's the least of my worries. How can I ever forgive myself for taking another woman's child?'

'Mum, stop this. It happened a long time ago. You didn't know I'd been kidnapped and — '

She mopped away a tear. 'I did know the adoption wasn't being done in the usual way, though. I did know there was something underhand about it. But not that. I never thought of that, even in my darkest nightmares.'

'Promise me you'll do nothing without consulting me.'

She looked at him and it was the way she'd always looked at his father, submissive. As she nodded slowly, he let out his breath in relief, but he was finding it hard to stay calm and had to get out of the claustrophobic little house, so stood up.

'Don't leave yet, Pete.'

'I need time to think, Mum.'

'You must hate me.'

'Of course I don't! You're my mother in every way that matters.' He pulled her into his arms and gave her a hug, then a quick kiss on the cheek. 'I'll be in touch.'

She began to sob once more but he walked out, at the end of his endurance. He drove off as quickly as he could. For once, she didn't come to the doorway and wave to him, which was all part of the strangeness of the day.

He needed Edward now, he really, really needed to see him.

★ ★ ★

Without taking any conscious decision, Pete drove towards his cousin's flat, surprised when he found himself in the car park there because he didn't remember anything about the journey from his mother's. If his cousin wasn't in, Pete intended to camp out on the doorstep till he returned.

He rang the doorbell and the intercom buzzed. He groaned in relief. 'Edward, it's me.'

'I don't want to see you. Go away.'

And then he couldn't hold himself together any longer. He began to sob and plead with his cousin, as out of control as his mother had been.

'Oh, hell. What's wrong now? Come on up, Pete.'

Edward had to say that twice more before it sank in.

The front door clicked and opened with agonizing slowness. Pete stumbled through it, praying desperately as he hurried to the lifts that no one would see him in this state.

★   ★   ★

Edward felt only irritation when he heard Pete's voice on the intercom, then was shocked to the core as his cousin began sobbing. He'd never heard Pete lose it like this. He opened the door of his flat, heard the lift ping and saw Pete stumble down the hallway towards him, still sobbing.

Putting an arm round his cousin's shoulders, Edward guided him into the flat and sat him down on the sofa. He sat beside him till the sobbing died down.

'Here. Take this.' He thrust a wad of tissues into Pete's hand and moved further along the sofa, sitting sideways to watch, wondering what the hell had started this.

'Got a whisky?' Pete asked.

'At this hour? No. I can make you a coffee.'

'Just had a cup of tea at Mum's.' His breath hiccupped and he scrubbed his eyes again.

'You told her.'

'Yes. She didn't know I'd been kidnapped, I'd stake my life on that.'

'You don't have to persuade me. I can't imagine Aunt Sue doing that.'

'But she did know the adoption wasn't above board. Dad told her it was a private one, that a young unmarried mother wanted to be sure who was taking her son.' Pete tried to laugh and failed completely. He blew his nose hard before he continued. 'They had a son who died. Dad somehow managed to change the records and I became him. So I'm not really Pete, am I?'

Edward didn't know what to say or do.

'I've forgotten my real name. What did my damned sister say I was called?'

'Greg. Greg Harding.'

Pete stared at him. 'I've never liked the name Greg. Perhaps I remembered something subliminally.'

The silence was laden with so much pain that neither spoke for a moment or two. What must it be like, Edward wondered, to suddenly find out your whole life had been a lie, that your parents were not related to you, that you had a birth mother still mourning your loss, and a sister?

'You're not even my cousin. That hurts too.' Pete looked at the crumpled tissues and let out a sigh that was nearer a groan. 'I think I need to wash my face.'

'No hurry.'

'I've never thought myself weak, but I lost it today, Edward.'

'Anyone would in the circumstances.'

There was silence, then, 'What the hell am I going to do?'

'Do nothing till you're sure what you want.'

'I want it never to have happened! That's not possible, though, is it?' He stood up. 'I'd better wash my face. I'm ready for that coffee now.'

Edward watched him go before heading for the kitchen.

When footsteps crossed the sitting area of the big main room, he turned, expecting to see his cousin looking better. Instead Pete was glaring at him.

'You're sleeping with her now, aren't you?'

'What?'

'That woman. Beth. My sister. You're sleeping with her. You've got her phone number on the pad next to the bed — and two people slept there last night.'

'If that's any of your business, yes, I am.'

'She's using you — and you're dumb enough to let her.'

'She's not like that.'

Pete spun round and marched towards the door. 'Be sure to tell her what an idiot I've been today. Why don't you take her over to meet Mum while you're at it? Call yourself a friend! You're a damned *traitor*! We brought you up when you had no one. It's *us* you should be loyal to, not them.' He slammed the door after him.

'Can't I care about both of you?' Edward murmured. He didn't chase after Pete. He didn't think anyone could talk sense into him at the moment.

But he was utterly certain Beth wasn't using him.

He wished she weren't Pete's birth sister, though. This was going to complicate things horribly. And Pete was right. His aunt and uncle had taken him in after his parents died, had brought him up with love, as if he too were their son. He did owe them loyalty.

But that didn't mean he was going to give up the woman he loved. He blinked in shock at this thought. How could he fall in love with someone so quickly? Then he smiled. How could he not when it was Beth? It seemed as natural to be with her as it was to breathe.

★ ★ ★

By the following teatime Pete was going stir crazy in his flat. He couldn't remember the last time he'd spent Saturday evening on his own. Fran had always had something lined up for them to do. She'd been a good social organizer, he had to give her that.

Not that he wanted her back, not bloody likely.

He picked up the newspaper and flicked through one of the pullout sections. Entertainment. He checked the TV pages to see whether *In Focus* had been mentioned and it hadn't. He'd have to see if he could stir up some more publicity.

Idly, he flicked a few more pages and found the theatre section. One advert jumped out at him: a concert with Rosa Caralina. He smiled at the memory of having a drink with her. He'd really enjoyed her company. Then he remembered that she'd sent him a couple of tickets for that particular concert. What had he done with them?

He went into his home office, which wasn't much used, and hunted through the jumble on his desk. He usually threw bits and pieces here, letting Fran sort them out every day or two. But there was no sign of the tickets.

Remembering that Rosa had sent them to the

studio, he went back into the bedroom and searched the pockets of his jackets.

'Aha!' He pulled out two crumpled tickets and waggled them triumphantly, then studied the details. The concert started at eight o'clock. When he turned over, he saw 'Drinks in the green room afterwards, Rosa', scrawled on one.

'Why not?' he said aloud. There was plenty of time to grab something to eat and get to the concert.

Should he see if Edward fancied coming too? No, his cousin would probably be with her.

Feeling a lot better, Pete went for a shower, dithering over what to wear, something Fran usually sorted out for him. She'd definitely had her uses. In the end he went for a dark grey suit and pale pink shirt, no tie. It looked all right to him.

Stuffing the tickets into his pocket he called for a taxi and went into the City. There were dozens of eating places near the theatre. He chose a Chinese restaurant which had dim lighting. He wasn't in the mood for being recognized.

Replete, he walked to the concert hall, delighted to be given an excellent seat. He'd never really gone mad for opera and classical stuff, but he didn't want something with loud, thumping rhythms tonight. He wanted something that would soothe and relax him.

14

After Beth had taken Ghita and the shopping back to the flat, she went into the office to check that everything was going well for the weekend. Sandy was just getting ready to leave.

'No problems?'

'None at all. You didn't need to come in.'

'Oh, you know me. I'm a control freak.'

'You're not. You're just a super-efficient manager. Got anything planned for tonight?'

'I'm having dinner with Jo and Ghita, a special welcome dinner, postponed from earlier in the week.'

'Not seeing Edward again?'

'I don't know. I hope so. But not tonight.' She could feel herself blushing and was relieved when Sandy didn't comment on that.

'Why don't you give him a ring and invite him along too?'

But she didn't need to ring him. Midway through the afternoon one of the security staff at the office phoned her.

'There's a man to see you, Ms Harding. Name's Edward Newbury.'

'Send him up.' She went to meet him at the door of the suite, which she kept locked when she worked outside normal business hours.

Edward smiled and pulled her into his arms for a kiss. Only as he drew back did he say, 'Hello there.'

'How did you find me?'

'I remembered your company's name. It wasn't hard after that.' He looked round. 'This place is rather like you, no frills and yet — attractive.'

'You don't need frills when you run a cleaning service. Mostly clients don't even come here. I go out to see prospective clients and I look over their premises at the same time. Come into my office. I'll make you a cup of tea.'

'I'd love that.'

Edward watched Beth walk across to the kettle. She was smiling, looking relaxed and at home here. 'Where would you like to go tonight?'

'I can't go anywhere, I'm afraid. I'm having a celebration meal with Jo and Ghita, to make them feel welcome. Ghita's cooking something special.'

He was disappointed. 'Tomorrow, then?'

'Tomorrow would be fine.'

'Let's go out for the day, drive into the country, have a leisurely lunch at a pub.'

'Sounds great.'

He sipped his drink. 'What time are you due home today?'

'Not for a couple of hours.'

'If you've nothing pressing to do, we could go for a walk . . . or visit a museum . . . or anything else you fancy.'

'I'd enjoy a walk. How about we go along the Embankment? There's always something to see there.'

'Great.' He could feel himself grinning foolishly. She did that to him, made him feel happy, partly because he didn't have to guess her moods or pander to them. He'd never met a woman who was so up front about everything. 'How's it going with your house guests?'

'Crowded. Noisy. They're lovely children, but I'd forgotten how omnipresent toddlers are: toys, mess, tantrums. Ghita is brilliant with them, thank goodness.'

He decided to be just as up front with her. 'How am I to court you with so much going on in your life?'

She froze, staring at him as if she couldn't believe what she'd heard.

He was a bit surprised himself. 'I shocked you, didn't I? I didn't intend to blurt it out like that, but I'm so tired of spin doctoring and being tactful to people I don't like, not to mention keeping Pete on an even keel. And I do want to court you.'

She put out one hand to steady herself on the table, as if she felt disoriented.

He wasn't going to back pedal. 'It's an old-fashioned word, but I've got old-fashioned feelings for you.'

She flushed and one of her hands went up protectively to her throat. 'You're going too fast, Edward.'

'Am I? It didn't seem too fast last night. We're good together, and sex isn't what I'm talking about.' He grinned. 'Though it doesn't hurt that we suit in bed too. The thing is, I didn't want you to leave after we'd made love. I wanted us to sleep together, wake up together, have breakfast and laugh together. I've not felt like this about anyone for years.'

'Oh.'

He felt a little angry. 'Is that all you can say? *'Oh!'* Don't you feel anything for me?'

'I am . . . attracted. Only, I'd shut down that side of me, put all my energy into my business. I'm a bit surprised by what's happening between us, if you must know. I don't usually hop into bed with near strangers.'

She spread her arms in a helpless gesture that made him want to hold her close and tell her it was all right, he'd never hurt her or let her down. But he didn't want to frighten her off. 'How about I slow down a little, then?'

She nodded, giving him a shy half-smile. 'Yes. Do you mind?'

'I'll do whatever it takes to make you happy.'

Her eyes were suddenly very bright. 'What a lovely thing to say.'

'So . . . about this walk? Courtship, stage one, eh? Just like our grandparents.'

'I'll enjoy walking out with you. And please don't stop — courting me, I mean.'

'Care to seal that agreement with a kiss?'

She stepped forward and cupped his cheeks in her hands, kissing him sweetly and firmly on the mouth. He liked her doing that, didn't want to have to make all the running. Love should be a two-way thing.

He took her hand as they left the building and they alternately chatted and enjoyed the walk. But it was over all too soon.

'I'll take you home by taxi.'

She laughed at him. 'The Tube is cheaper and there's a station nearby.'

'I'll come with you, then.' As they sat on the rattling train, he said, 'It's certainly cheaper.'

'And more eco-friendly.'

'I'd better get used to it then. I'm out of work now.'

'Short of money?'

'No. I've got some put by. I'm always careful with my money. I don't need to rush into anything now, which is a good thing, because I'm not sure what I'm going to do with my life. They say it happens in your forties, don't they? Reorientation of life and career.'

'Yes. It happened to me.' She stood up, balancing easily in the swaying vehicle. 'My stop.'

They lingered for a moment or two outside her flat. He took hold of both her hands and pulled her to him for a quick kiss, then stepped back and watched her go inside. He didn't want to say goodbye, didn't move away till she was out of sight.

With a sigh he began walking, asking himself why he liked her so much, why he'd fallen in love with her so quickly.

She was attractive, but not beautiful or glamorous as Pete's ex had been. Edward grimaced. A woman devoted to looking glamorous would take a lot of living with. He liked the fact that when he kissed Beth, it was her soft skin and lips he touched, not a layer of coloured grease.

He'd teased Fran once about make-up being only 'coloured grease', when she'd kept them waiting to set off on a trip to a small country town where Pete was making an appearance.

She'd nearly hit the roof at such sacrilege, and to listen to her, you'd think people came to see her, not Pete.

In some ways, Beth seemed old-fashioned. Or was she normal and he'd been associating with folk who lived an unreal life in the fast lane?

He passed a florist's shop and grinned. What was more old-fashioned than sending flowers to the woman you cared about? He went in and ordered a small bunch of roses. She'd not want a lavish bunch, he was sure. But he ordered red ones. That would send the right message.

★ ★ ★

Beth went into a flat that no longer seemed hers. The corridor was still full of boxes, but they'd been rearranged into smaller piles. The smells coming from the kitchen made her mouth water. The two little boys were clearly being bathed by Jo because shrieks and giggles kept erupting from the bathroom. She paused for a moment in the hall, taking it all in, then shouted, 'I'm back!' and went into the main living area.

Ghita peered out of the kitchen which led off it. She had flour on one cheek and was flushed, but looked happy. 'You have a wonderful kitchen, Beth! It's a pleasure to cook here.'

'Do you think so? It came like that. I'm not much of a cook, I'm afraid, but I'm glad you're enjoying the facilities.'

She put her things away in her bedroom then walked along to the bathroom, where Jo was kneeling beside the bath, sailing a little plastic boat across the water and up Kaleel's chest to tickle him under his chin with it, then doing the same to her son.

Mikey waved at Beth, sending drops of water scattering. 'Granma! Granma! We're having a bath.'

She went to kiss him and then kissed Kaleel and Jo for good measure. It must be her day for kissing people.

'You don't usually go for touchy feely stuff, Mum.'

Beth frowned. 'I didn't think you liked being kissed.'

The awkwardness was back briefly, then Jo grinned. 'I didn't like anything then. But I do like you kissing me now, so don't stop.' She bent over the boys suddenly, blinking her eyes.

'I won't.' Beth could feel herself tearing up too, so went to get changed before any of the moisture in her eyes overflowed. Jeans, she decided, and a colourful top Renée had once persuaded her to buy, which she'd hardly ever worn.

Someone rang the doorbell and she went to answer it, her breath catching in her throat as a florist gave her a bunch of red roses. When she'd shut the door, she looked at the message. *Courting, Stage 2. Love, Edward.*

When was the last time someone had given her flowers?

Jo came down the corridor with the boys. 'Flowers?'

Beth could feel herself flushing. 'Yes.'

'They're lovely. From Edward?'

Beth nodded.

'That's a good sign. Ghita, look what Edward's sent my mother?'

Both young women admired the flowers, looking a little wistful, then Ghita announced she was ready to serve the meal as soon as Beth had put the flowers in water.

The boys stayed up for the first course, a range of finger foods served on a low table. They'd clearly eaten like this before because they both waited to start till Ghita had bowed her head and said a blessing. Then she turned to Beth. 'You're our guest of honour, so you must choose first.'

Beth had to ask what a couple of the dishes were, but made sure to take something from each platter.

Then Ghita helped her son and Jo helped Mikey, after which the boys sat quietly on two towels with their dishes in front of them, eating steadily with their fingers.

'We've done this before,' Jo said. 'They love it, and when they've had enough to eat from the first course, we put them to bed and enjoy the rest of the food in peace.'

'I have some wine or fruit juice.'

'Ghita doesn't drink alcohol, but I wouldn't say no to a red wine.'

The little boys went happily to bed and could be heard giggling for a short time, then silence reigned.

Three more savoury dishes were served, fork food this time, slightly more spicy and utterly delicious. Beth again revised her view of what jobs Ghita could do. If this was a sample of the

238

food she could produce, she was very good.

'She's a brilliant cook, isn't she, Mum?' Jo whispered as Ghita went to get the desserts. 'And she loves cooking.'

'I'm going to put on weight.'

'You need to. Why have you let yourself get so thin? You look run down. Do you have to work so hard? You're not short of money now, if you can run a luxury flat like this one on your own.'

Beth was so surprised she couldn't think of an answer, then shrugged. 'I was busy and I never felt hungry somehow. When you live alone, eating seems more of a necessity than a pleasure.'

'You're not alone now. Are you going to see Edward again? If he's sent flowers, he must be seriously interested.'

'I — um, saw him this afternoon. We went for a walk.'

'You're blushing. Mum!' Jo beamed across the table at her. 'Are you two an item?'

'Maybe. It's a bit early, but yes, I think we might be.'

'Good. That's Gran settled and you too. Maybe it's catching and I'll find someone. What do you think, Ghita? Do we want husbands?'

Her friend shuddered visibly. 'My father has someone in mind, but he and I don't share the same taste in men. He thinks of money and position in the community, I think kindness. I'm only going to get married if I like and respect the man.'

'What about love?' Beth asked.

Ghita looked thoughtful. 'That too, but love alone isn't enough for me. I'd want a kind man,

239

who could love Kaleel as well as me, and who'd let me do more with my life than act as his servant.'

They settled down to an earnest discussion of the qualities that appealed to them in men, and went on to say what they didn't like. It was as if they were three friends chilling out together, Beth thought in wonderment. She caught her daughter's eye and Jo winked.

'That was fun,' Beth said as the evening wound down. 'I've enjoyed your company. Now, let me do the clearing up.'

Ghita stood up quickly, shaking her head. 'That's my job now.'

Beth didn't want anyone to wait on her hand and foot. It wasn't her style. 'Not all day, every day. We'll all share the clearing up in the evenings. With a dishwasher it won't take long. Anything that doesn't fit into the machine tonight can wait and go in the next load tomorrow.'

'I don't know how to work a dishwasher,' Ghita confessed.

'I'll give you lessons tomorrow.' Beth yawned suddenly. 'Come on. I'm tired. Let's make a start.'

She felt happy as she lay in bed, optimistic enough to hope that Pete wouldn't hurt her mother too badly and Edward would continue to be so attentive.

Could life be so good? Could this state of affairs continue?

★ ★ ★

As the concert ended Pete applauded loudly with the rest of the audience. He hadn't realized quite how wonderful Rosa's voice was, because it sounded so much richer in this building than it did on a recording. He went to find one of the theatre staff and showed her the ticket Rosa had written on. With a smile, the woman led him behind the stage and showed him into a room full of people holding drinks.

He wasn't in the mood for chatting, but knew two or three of the men so had to exchange greetings with them. He prowled on, taking a glass of wine when it was offered to him and sipping it, not really interested in drinking tonight. Strange, that. He usually enjoyed several drinks in the evening, too much according to medical research, but hey, something would kill you so why not make it a sin you enjoyed?

Only he was too upset to enjoy a drink tonight, it seemed.

'Pete. You came?'

Rosa was there, smiling at him, looking tired, wearing a simple white dress with a trail of lace down one side. She had a gold chain round her neck and her dark hair curled loosely on her shoulders. Compared to Fran she looked a bit out of date, but he rather liked that quietly feminine look, he decided.

'I enjoyed the concert very much, Rosa. Your voice is beautiful.'

'Thank you. Mario is great to sing with. Our voices match well.' She looked round. 'Is your wife not here?'

'Ex-wife. We split up recently. We're getting a divorce.'

'I'm sorry. That must be hard.'

And damned if tears didn't come into his eyes, not because he cared about Fran — he certainly didn't — but because everything had been upsetting this week.

Rosa reached out to grasp his hand and he held on to her tightly. 'Can we get out of here? I'm in no state for socializing, but I'd enjoy a quiet drink with you.'

'I'll have to speak to a few people on the way out, Pete, but yes, I'm tired too.'

A tactful way to cover him being tearful and emotional, he thought. Tired. She seemed sorry for him. He didn't want her sympathy, just some gentle, undemanding company.

When they got to the now-empty foyer, he asked, 'Where would you like to go?'

'Why don't you come back to my house for a nightcap? You don't seem in the mood for public places.'

'No, I'm not. But I'm not in the mood for my own company, either.'

She stopped walking to stare at him. 'We need to get one thing straight. I'm not inviting you round to sleep with me. I don't hop in and out of bed with people.'

'I'll behave myself.'

Outside they picked up a taxi and he leaned back with a sigh. 'Thank you for your company. It's comforting. You're very easy to be with.'

'If we can't help one another, we're not much as human beings, are we? Anyway, you were kind to me after I appeared on your show, and the photos people sent in afterwards have been a great joy to me.'

The taxi ride was longer than he'd expected and they drew up in front of an older semi-detached house, one of a row of old-fashioned dwellings, not a block of flats. 'I'd not expected you to live in a place like this.'

'It was my parents' house. I grew up here.'

'I've got a flat overlooking the river.'

'I like having a garden.'

He followed her inside. She switched on lights, revealing old-fashioned furniture, a worn rug, books everywhere, not just in the many bookcases, but on the low table and even stacked on the floor by an armchair. Some of the books looked very battered and there were scratch marks on a table. He remembered suddenly that her ex had trashed the place.

'You read a lot.'

She smiled. 'It's my favourite pastime. I can take books with me wherever I go. They've kept me company in countless hotel rooms. I like gardening too when I'm at home.'

'So does my mother.'

'It's very satisfying to grow plants and vegetables. Would you like a drink of wine or brandy or something?'

'No, thanks. I'm not in the mood for alcohol.' He laughed bitterly. 'It must be the first time in years.'

'Something's upset you. Not the divorce, I think.'

'Yes, something has. And you're right, it's not the divorce.'

'If you'd like to talk about it, I promise I'll keep your secret. But if you don't want to talk, we can listen to music or simply chat.'

'Don't you watch TV?'

'Not often. Mainly the news. I'm away so much, I can't keep up with the various series, though I do quite enjoy archaeology programmes.'

To his surprise, he found the old-fashioned armchair with its frayed armrests far more comfortable than the low, ultra-modern furniture in his flat.

'I usually have hot milk with honey in it. Can I get you one too, Pete?'

He smiled at the thought. 'That's a children's bedtime drink.'

'It helps me sleep. I sometimes have trouble after a performance.'

'I'm not surprised. You were brilliant tonight, must have given a lot of yourself. I can't get over the way your voice soared across the theatre.'

'Thank you. I love singing. Now, I won't be long.'

She went out and he felt himself relaxing in the quiet room. No accent lights here to show off an expensive art piece, just two frilly table lamps glowing softly pink in the corners.

He opened his eyes as Rosa came back. 'This is a very relaxing house.'

'I like it. I moved into a flat once and it never felt like a home to me without a garden. When my parents went into a retirement village, I came back here.' She put a mug down on the low table between them and took the armchair on the opposite side, sipping her drink.

He picked up his mug. It was made of thin, translucent china, with flowers painted on it and a gold rim. Steam rose gently and there was a sweet smell. He couldn't remember the last time he'd had anything with honey in it. It had far too many calories for Fran even to allow it into the house. The sweet warmth slipped down very easily. 'I must have this more often,' he said, setting the mug down carefully. 'It's delicious.'

The next thing he knew, Rosa was shaking him gently.

'You fell asleep. I hate to disturb you, but it's getting late.'

He blinked, disorientated for a moment, then focused on her. 'Sorry. I'll call a taxi.'

'You can sleep in the spare bedroom, if you like.'

'Are you sure?'

'Of course. My friends often stay over.'

'I'd like that.' Not to wake up to an empty flat would be wonderful at the moment.

Smiling, Rosa switched off the sitting room lights and led the way upstairs, showing him to a small bedroom whose single bed was covered by a virginal white cover. She opened the wardrobe. 'This is an old dressing gown of my brother's. And his pyjamas should fit you too. There's only one bathroom. You can't miss it.'

He took her hand and raised it to his lips. 'Thank you. I'm really grateful to you.'

'I've done very little.'

'You've given me some peace in a very troubled time and that's worth a lot to me. I'll tell you about the other thing tomorrow, if I may.'

'Of course. Sleep well.'

She was gone and he wished she'd stayed. Which was silly. They weren't lovers, just friends. He wondered briefly what sort of a lover she'd make. Not as skilled as Fran, he was sure, but undoubtedly more loving.

He snuggled down in the narrow bed, murmuring in pleasure at its soft feel. He didn't know why it helped not to be on his own tonight, but it did.

★   ★   ★

On the Sunday Edward took Beth for a drive in the country, stopping for lunch at a pub. They talked easily and the time flew.

He grinned at her as he dropped her off at her flat. 'See. Taking it nice and easy. But still courting you.'

'Oh, Edward — ' She broke off, not knowing what to say.

He kissed her cheek. 'No need for words. We enjoyed one another's company, and we're going to continue doing that.'

She was sorry he hadn't tried to persuade her to go back to his flat. She was sorry he'd come into her life at such a complicated time.

No, she wasn't. She was glad she'd met him, whatever the circumstances.

15

Beth got up on Monday feeling hopeful that things had taken a turn for the better, even though so much was still to be resolved. She didn't feel like breakfast and didn't want to disturb the others, so left a note for Ghita and was at work by just after five. Someone had to be there to make sure the early shifts went off smoothly and it was easier to sort things out from the office than from home.

When a woman rang in sick she called in a standby cleaner. It was a house rule that you rang in if you couldn't make it, one of the few things for which she had dismissed people who offended more than once. When a second person rang in, none of the other standbys answered their phones. In the end she raced along to the office block in question and filled in herself. She worked quickly and efficiently, noting that parts of the floor had been skimped last time.

As they all trooped outside at eight o'clock, she caught up with the group supervisor. 'Who's been doing the sixth floor, Rachel?'

'That student, what's he called? Tom.'

'He's been skimping. Do you want to have a word with him or shall I?'

Rachel flushed. 'I can't seem to get through to him about our standards. I've already spoken to him twice, and he's apologetic, promises to do better next time, and he does for a while. Then things start to slip again.'

'I'll come in tomorrow and speak to him myself.' She patted Rachel's shoulder, knowing that even though her companion had three small children at home, she was an extremely conscientious and reliable worker. 'If warnings don't work in future, let me know. It doesn't mean you're failing. I'm the next step up the chain of command, so it's normal and right for you to turn to me.'

She smiled. 'The rest of the place looks good and those changes you made seem to be working well.'

Rachel's expression brightened. 'Thanks. It is more efficient, I think.'

'I've been wondering if you'd like to go on a people management course?'

'I'd love to, but I can't afford to lose my pay.'

'You won't lose anything. It's paid training. I'll get Sandy to ring you and discuss arrangements.'

Rachel flushed in pleasure. 'Thank you. I'd love to do that. I've not been on a course since I left school.'

Beth walked to her car, knowing she'd have to sack Tom. He'd had two warnings about sloppy work and if that hadn't done it, experience told her nothing would. She remembered him clearly. Good-looking, full of himself, but she'd been doubtful about him from the start, only he'd applied at a time when they'd taken on a new contract and were short of cleaners. He'd said he was a student, but she'd seen him around during the day a few times so he couldn't be studying full-time.

She left a message on his phone as soon as she got back to the office then sat back, feeling tired.

Sandy came in, looked at her and said tartly, 'Don't tell me. No one else was available, so you had to do the work yourself.'

Beth shrugged. 'You know how it is.'

'You look exhausted. Did you eat any breakfast before you started?'

She had to think for a moment. 'I forgot. Besides, I had a huge meal yesterday. Edward took me for a drive in the country and we stopped at a pub.'

'You mean you had a huge lunch. What did you have for tea?'

'What is this, the Inquisition? I had some supper. Ghita made it.'

'I'm your friend as well as your employee, so I'll continue to question you when you look like that. I care about you so I'm going out to buy you a sandwich and I'm standing over you till I've seen you eat it.'

'I'll go and buy myself one. I could do with some fresh air.'

But before she even got to the door, a new client phoned and she had to change her plans.

'You need another member of staff,' Sandy said. 'A personal assistant. You can afford it.'

'Perhaps. I'll think about it.'

'I'll draw up some job specs. Now, promise you'll get something to eat on the way there.'

'Yeah, yeah.'

She meant to, she really did, but she was thinking about Jo and Ghita and it slipped her mind.

Edward woke feeling happy after a thoroughly relaxing day out with Beth on the Sunday. It wasn't until he'd finished breakfast that he began to wonder what to do with himself. How wonderful to have the whole day stretching before him! Normally he'd have been at the office by nine, discussing the coming week's show with Pete, sewing up any loose ends, answering a dozen phone calls.

It was no use calling Beth. She'd be working hard.

When the phone rang he checked the caller ID before he picked it up. He didn't intend to be dragged back to the office. 'Hi, Aunt Sue. How are you?'

There was silence, then, 'I'm a bit upset, dear. Pete came to see me on Saturday.'

'Yes.'

'You knew about it?'

'He told me.'

'I didn't know he'd been kidnapped, Edward, I *swear* I didn't. Have you seen Pete? I tried to contact him yesterday, but he's not answering my calls.'

Her voice was so shaky, he said at once, 'Do you still make the best scones in the universe? Good, then I'll come out to see you mid-morning. We'll talk about this quietly. I'll be there in about an hour.'

Annoyed, he rang Pete at the office.

His cousin greeted him with, 'Ready to come back to work?'

'Nope. I want to know what you said to your mother on Saturday. She's very upset and says you're not answering her calls.'

Pete's voice turned sulky. 'I was out all day. The last thing I wanted when I got back was to have my mother weeping all over me.'

'Then you shouldn't have treated her so harshly. You know what she's been like since your father died. What *exactly* did you say?'

'I asked her why they didn't tell me I was adopted, and as usual she said it was Dad's idea. Then I told her what had really happened, that I have a sister and a birth mother hounding me and — '

'They're hardly *hounding* you.'

'It feels like it. That sister of mine has a steely look in her eye. If my birth mother is at all like her, I don't want to know either of them.'

'What you mean is, you don't want anyone to upset your happy little bubble. Well, get over that, Pete, because your real family aren't going to go away.'

The phone was slammed down on him.

Edward went to the gym to do twenty minutes' swimming, then drove out to his aunt's.

★   ★   ★

No sooner had Pete put the phone down, than it rang again. 'Oh, hi Gerry.'

'Is Edward coming in this morning for the show briefing? He's not been in touch today.'

'Oh, er, he resigned last week. I'm sure it's only temporary. We can manage without him for

251

a week or so, surely? You can take his place.'

'I don't have his notes, don't know the details of what's been planned.'

'I'll look for them in his office and get back to you. You will, of course, be paid at a higher rate while he's off.'

'But you do think he'll be coming back? I can't manage for long without him, Pete. I've never made all the arrangements myself. I've been mainly in charge of the research for the *Who Am I?* segment.'

'Look, I know Edward. He's my cousin as well as my manager and he won't let me down. I just need to give him a few days to get his head together. I have every confidence in you in the meantime, Gerry.'

Pete glanced at the clock, eager to end this conversation. He was having lunch with Rosa and was looking forward to it. He'd enjoyed being with her at the weekend. Strange that, with no sex involved. He wasn't feeling the lack as much as he'd expected, either. Well, no wonder. He had too much on his mind.

★   ★   ★

Edward drew up outside his aunt's house. He'd have expected to find her in the garden on a day like this but there was no sign of her. He went to rap on the door and when she didn't answer, he pushed it open.

She was in the kitchen, sitting weeping over a batch of burnt scones, and she looked dreadful. She didn't even notice him coming in.

'Aunt Sue?'

She jumped visibly. 'Oh, Edward. I'm sorry. I can't seem to do anything right today.'

'The scones don't matter.' He'd only suggested them to give her something to take her mind off the situation. 'Come and sit in the living room. We can talk there.'

He guided her to the couch and sat beside her, worried by her pallor. From the look of her, she'd been doing a lot of weeping. 'Pete shouldn't have told you about the kidnapping,' he said gently.

'Yes, he should. That's the only thing I'm certain of in this mess.' She blew her nose and let him take her hand again. 'I didn't know they'd *stolen* him. I met a young woman they said was his mother. He was very confused for a while after we first got him, but the psychologist who helped us said it was because of being taken away from all he knew.' She stopped to stare pleadingly at him. 'You do believe what I'm telling you, don't you?'

'Of course I do.'

'Edward, what am I going to *do*? I keep thinking about that poor woman.'

'I don't think you should do anything at the moment. There could be legal implications. Leave that to Pete and me.'

She shook her head. 'I can't. I must see her, make her understand that I'd never, ever have done such a dreadful thing.' She began weeping again.

It was soon clear that he couldn't keep her out of this, nor should he. He too was upset by the thought of what Beth's mother must have gone through. And Beth. She'd had a difficult childhood after her brother disappeared, from the sound of it.

'Pete says the sister wants money off us.'

'He's wrong. She doesn't. She's not like that.'

'How can you be so sure?'

He'd been hoping to avoid this, but wasn't going to add any more lies to the pile already festering. 'Because I'm seeing her. I'm in love with her, actually. She doesn't need money nor is she asking for it. Pete thought he could buy her off, but he can't. What she does want is closure for her mother.'

Sue looked startled. 'You're going out with this woman?'

'I certainly am. Her name's Beth. You'll like her, I'm sure.'

'I doubt she'll want to see me. If this comes out, how can I ever show my face again?' She began weeping, a soft, despairing sound.

He put his arms round her. 'Shh, now. Shh. I can't see any reason for it to come out. I told you Beth isn't after money and would hate the notoriety she'd face if it did come out, I'm sure. Let me feel my way, try to settle this quietly.'

He stayed for lunch but had to leave around two if he was to do as he'd promised and try to reconcile the various parties. Beth would understand that his aunt hadn't known what had happened, he was sure. But would her mother? He had no idea what Linda Harding was like.

★ ★ ★

254

The day had started badly and was rapidly getting worse, Pete thought resentfully. Rosa rang just before noon to cancel their lunch date and wasn't free to see him for several days.

Instead of working on the first interview for his coming show, he kept trying to figure out what to do about his sister. Surely, if he raised the stakes financially, she and her mother would leave him in peace? He didn't *want* another family. Most of all, he didn't want this to get out. The media would have a ball with all the lurid details. He shuddered at the mere thought of that. And what if the police prosecuted his mother? It'd destroy her.

He told Ilsa he wasn't taking any calls, but she came into his office an hour later. 'Look, Pete, if I don't let Gerry speak to you, he's threatening to resign. We can't manage without him.'

'Oh, very well. Put him on.'

Gerry rang three times that afternoon for clarification of some point or other in connection with this week's show.

In the end Pete lost patience. 'How the hell am I supposed to know every sodding detail? You'll have to get hold of Edward and ask him.'

'I've tried. He's not answering his phone.'

'Use your initiative. Send someone round to his flat. Go yourself.'

'But — '

Pete slammed the phone down.

It rang almost immediately and Gerry said, 'Don't put that phone down on me again, Pete, or I'm out of here. I need an assistant and if I don't get one, I'm resigning forthwith. There's far too much work for one person, especially when that person is still feeling his way.'

'You can manage for *one week*, surely?'

'No, I damned well can't.'

'Well, hire a temp then. Yes, pay what you think fit. Just sort it.' Pete kept himself from blowing up again, put the phone down and rested his head on his hands. He was finding out how much they'd all depended on Edward, who was an amazingly well-organized person.

There must be some way to get his cousin back.

★　★　★

Edward slowed down as he reached his former office building. He didn't want to go inside again but was worried about his aunt and wanted to talk to Pete about her. She was in a very agitated state and at her age that could be dangerous.

He walked inside and went up to the suite of offices, feeling the building close round him like a tight grey shroud.

The receptionist didn't even look up as the door opened. 'Go straight in, Gerry.'

'I'm not Gerry.'

Ilsa stared at him. 'Edward! Thank goodness you're here. Everything's falling to pieces without you.'

This greeting from the dragon-lady amazed him, but he wasn't going to be blackmailed into working for Pete again. 'Is he in?'

'Yes.'

He walked across to Pete's office, not

bothering to knock on the door. He never had before so why start now?

Pete was leaning back in his chair with his eyes closed, a frown creasing his forehead. He looked up and groaned in relief at the sight of his cousin. 'Thank goodness you're back! Look, can you just — '

'I'm not back in that sense.'

'What do you mean? You're here, aren't you? Are you really going to let the show fall to pieces?'

'It won't do that.'

'It's already shaking on its foundations. Gerry's useless. He can't cope.'

'He's not useless. You're asking him to do a job he's not done before. He's only been with us for a couple of months. What do you expect from him, miracles?'

'*You* managed all right.'

'I'm older and far more experienced. Besides, we built up your career gradually. I had time to learn on the job. Gerry's intelligent and hard-working. Give him a chance.'

Pete's voice became coaxing. 'You'll manage this show, though, won't you, Edward? You'll come back, just for this one week?'

And then it'd be just for another week. 'No.'

To his astonishment Pete looked ready to burst into tears at his blunt refusal. He'd never seen his cousin look so . . . human. Gone was the easy charm, the relaxed smile, and even Pete's clothes looked less smart. He should never have worn that garish shirt for a day at the office. Probably Fran had monitored what he wore

257

before. They'd need to get someone else to supervise his wardrobe for the show and —

Edward stopped himself mentally. Not his business now. But maybe he had left Pete too abruptly. All he knew was, he couldn't face coming back to the constant demands that sucked him dry of energy. 'Look, Gerry can ring me and I'll give him a few pointers, but I'm not, repeat not, coming back to work for you. Ever. Give him my personal mobile number.'

Pete's expression became vicious. 'I've checked your contract. You need to work out your notice. We agreed on a month's notice either side.'

'So sue me. And I'll bring up in court the fact that you've never allowed me to take a holiday in peace, or a weekend even. I'll claim I'm having a breakdown.'

Pete folded his arms. 'Why did you come here if you're going to be such a shit?'

'Because I went to see Aunt Sue this morning.'

'So?'

'I've never seen her so upset. She's too old for such stress and you know her health isn't the best. I'm worried about her. Really worried.'

'She deserves to be upset after what she did to me. And she's not the only one who's upset, if you remember my visit to you on Saturday. I've not lost it like that since I was a small child. I'm not sure I even cried then.'

They both fell silent, contemplating this. Yes, Edward thought, Pete hadn't cried as a child or got into quarrels and fights. He'd been sunny and charming with everyone, the centre of attention, the beloved son of the house.

'I don't want to see Mum again till I've got myself together,' Pete said sulkily.

'You can't bury your head in the sand. In fact, your attitude to this whole crisis isn't leading anywhere useful. But first and foremost, you have to see your mother. She needs you desperately.'

'Well, she can't have me. She and Dad got me into this. She'll have to wait till I find some way to sort it out.'

'You could do that quite easily by agreeing to see your birth mother and making peace with her. If she's anything like her daughter, she'll be — '

'*I'm not seeing that damned woman!*'

'If you don't see her and you don't see Aunt Sue, how exactly are you going to fix things?'

'I don't know. I haven't had time to think, dammit.'

'So what do I tell your mother?'

'Tell her I'm furious about all this. And tell my birth mother the same thing. I'm definitely not going to see *her*, and she can like it or lump it.' His voice softened. 'You go and talk to her for me, Edward. You're good at negotiating agreements. Get her daughter on side. Find out how much they want to keep quiet and I'll pay it in a blink.'

Edward turned on his heel, stopping at the door to say curtly, 'I'll say it one final time. The Hardings do not want money, Pete, they want closure. And for your birth mother, that means seeing you.'

He walked out, so angry he didn't stop when

Ilsa called his name.

He didn't stop until he was several hundred yards away.

★ ★ ★

In the reception area, Ilsa and Gerry exchanged shocked glances. Gerry had arrived shortly after Edward and they'd heard most of the conversation because the door hadn't been shut and both men's voices had risen higher and higher.

'We'd better keep that information to ourselves,' she said.

He nodded.

Pete yelled from his office, 'Get Gerry round here.'

'He's here already.'

Pete came to the door. 'How long have you been here?'

'I just arrived. I — um, passed Edward on the way. He looked furious.'

'I'm the one who should be looking furious, the way he's dumped me in the shit.' He looked up at the clock. 'We'd better get down to the studio and run through the show. Get us a taxi, Ilsa.'

'It's only a short walk,' Gerry protested. 'We'd get there more quickly on foot.'

'And on foot we'll be an open target for anyone who wants to stop us. I'm not in the mood for chatting up gushing women today, so just do as you're told and get the bloody taxi.'

Pete heard Gerry breathing deeply and Ilsa had that tight expression on her face that she got

260

when he'd been too brusque. His head was thumping and he turned to find the painkillers he kept in his desk.

He tossed two tablets down quickly. He'd smooth things over with Gerry later. At the moment all he wanted to do was sort out the damned show and then hide for the rest of the day.

★ ★ ★

Three hours later, there was still so much to do that Pete lost it again and roared at everyone. He watched their expressions go wooden and knew he'd blown it, but didn't have the energy to mend things.

He turned to Gerry, who was still frowning. 'Get your bloody finger out. You're supposed to be in charge. Do something. Sort this mess out. I've got a blinding headache and I'm going home.'

When he got there, he took some more painkillers and began pacing up and down the flat, wondering what the hell to do with himself that evening. He was sure he and Fran had had several engagements booked, they always did, but he couldn't find the social diary. She'd probably taken it with her on purpose.

Well, if he was supposed to see anyone tonight, he'd say he was ill. He'd get a meal sent up from the café across the road and he'd chill out, watch TV or a movie.

He opened a bottle of wine with the meal and about an hour later realized he'd drunk the lot.

When he stood up, he felt pleasantly distant from all his troubles, so walked across to pour himself a generous whisky as a nightcap. He'd feel better after a good night's sleep.

Some time later he staggered along to the bedroom, flung himself on the bed fully-clothed and let all the pain and hassles fade away.

16

Sue woke feeling so strange she knew something was seriously wrong. She couldn't move properly but managed to press the alarm button beside her bed before she lost consciousness.

The warden on duty that night came to investigate and dialled the emergency number as soon as she realized what had happened.

Joyce stood watching as Mrs Newbury was rushed to hospital, feeling upset as she always did when a resident was taken ill. Pulling herself together she rang the next of kin listed in the retirement village records. But Mrs Newbury's son didn't answer.

She tried several times over the next hour, then rang the hospital. They told her Mrs Newbury was holding her own and asked if the next of kin had been contacted.

Joyce went back to Sue's house to try to find someone else to ring. She hated going into their homes without permission, but this was an emergency. A quick check of the phone book revealed an Edward Newbury, so she rang him.

★ ★ ★

Edward was jerked out of sleep by the phone ringing. If it was Pete, he'd unplug the damned thing, but first he'd give his cousin an earful.

'What do you want now?' He jerked fully

awake as a woman's voice answered him.

'Sorry if I woke you. I'm Joyce, the warden from Sunny Meadows Retirement Village. Um — are you related to Sue Newbury?'

'Yes. I'm her nephew. Is she all right?'

'I'm afraid she's just been taken to hospital. Thank goodness she managed to press the emergency button! It looks like a stroke to me, but of course that's for the doctors to decide.'

'How is she?'

'Barely conscious and confused.'

Edward took down the details and rang Pete. There was no answer, so he rang the concierge at the luxury gated community and explained what had happened.

'I can see the flat from here, sir, and the lights are on. I'll just go up and knock.'

'Take your master key. He's a sound sleeper, especially if he's had a drink or two. This is my mobile number. Call me if he's not there. I'll be with his mother.'

As he was walking into the hospital, his mobile rang.

'Concierge here. I'm sorry, Mr Newbury. Your cousin's had new locks fitted and I don't have a key to them. He's not answering the door.'

Edward bit back a curse. This wasn't the concierge's fault. 'Look, keep an eye open in case he's out and returns, but don't stop phoning the flat. He's a heavy sleeper. If you get through to him, tell him where I am.'

Edward walked into an emergency department that looked like hell on earth at this hour of the night, with small groups of people in anguished huddles and a young child crying with penetrating shrillness. A man with blood streaming from his forehead was helped in by a friend just then, and it took Edward a few minutes to get anyone's attention as they attended to the accident victim.

The receptionist sent him up to the stroke unit. There, a ward clerk showed him into a small waiting room. 'Your aunt is having a CT scan at the moment to help determine what sort of stroke it is, which will affect treatment.'

'Is she conscious?'

'Yes, but she's a bit bewildered by it all. These things can happen so suddenly. Has she been under treatment for high blood pressure or anything like that?'

'No. But she had a bad shock yesterday. Could that have caused it?'

'I can't say, sir. The doctor will be able to tell you more when they've done the scan.'

Edward would have paced up and down, but the waiting area was too small, so all he could do was sit — and try in vain to contact Pete.

When the doctor came, she said it was a stroke, but luckily not too major.

'My aunt will recover, then?'

'Nothing is ever certain with strokes, but she stands a good chance.' She smiled. 'You can go and sit with her, if you like. I'm sure it'll comfort her to see you when she rouses.'

He found a nurse straightening the covers and adjusting the position of the call button. His aunt had always been slender, but now she hardly made a bump in the covers and she was nearly as pale as the sheets beneath her. Her eyes were closed but she opened them when Edward spoke to the nurse. He turned to her at once.

'You've had a little stroke, Aunt Sue. Don't worry. It's not a serious one. I'll stay with you till you feel a bit more yourself.'

She managed a tired smile and he was sure her eyes were saying thank you, then her eyelids fluttered and she seemed to sleep again.

He looked round the ward in distaste. They'd partitioned off the huge, old-fashioned room into smaller sections of six beds, in an attempt to give the patients more privacy, but the stroke unit wasn't a restful place. Several people in his aunt's section were lying still. From other parts of the unit, however, sounds carried all too clearly, echoing from the high ceiling. Somewhere a woman was weeping, another was calling out incoherently and from a room at the side a man's voice rambled on and on, the words blurred and incomprehensible.

Edward went back to the ward clerk. 'My aunt has private medical cover. Isn't there somewhere quieter she can be transferred?'

'If we transfer her, she won't be in the specialist stroke unit, sir, with staff experienced in caring for and diagnosing her problem. It really is for the best, at least till we're sure she's stabilized.'

'Are there no side rooms, then?'

'They're occupied by people who are worse than her, sir.'

He went back to sit by Sue's bed, nodding to a woman sitting by a bed further down the row.

He'd read somewhere that the first twenty-four hours were critical, so he wasn't going anywhere yet.

Every now and then he tried phoning Pete. It wasn't until four o'clock that his cousin picked up the call and it didn't take Edward long to realize that Pete was still drunk.

'Your mother's in hospital.'

Silence. Then, 'What happened?'

'She had a stroke. I'm with her now. You might like to join us, if you're sober enough. I've been ringing you for several hours.'

Pete ignored his comment. 'I'll have a quick shower first.'

'Clearing your head? You've got to stop hitting the booze so hard, Pete. Your face is starting to get puffy. That's not good for your image.'

'Will you get off my back!' The phone was slammed down hard.

* * *

Early on Tuesday morning Beth picked up the phone, hoping the call hadn't woken the children. Her heart lifted when she heard Edward's voice. Then he explained about his aunt.

'Oh, dear! I'm so sorry.'

'I'm staying with her. At the moment I'm waiting for Pete to arrive. I hope I didn't wake you. You said you always got up early.'

'I'm in the kitchen enjoying a peaceful cup of coffee. The others haven't surfaced yet.'

'We'll have to play it by ear as to whether I can

267

still take you out tonight, as we'd planned. I hope you don't mind.'

'Of course I don't. Your aunt must come first. Is Pete with her?'

'Yes.'

'I'll be thinking about you.'

★ ★ ★

Ghita walked to the supermarket, strapping the boys into their double buggy and enjoying the afternoon sunshine. Soon they'd be too old to push around then things would be more difficult. They were a lively pair and Mikey in particular was always into mischief.

As she was coming out of the supermarket, a car screeched to a halt and she jerked back in shock as her father jumped out of it and strode across to her.

He grabbed her arm. 'Why didn't you let me know you'd moved? Where are you living now? If you're with a man — '

She tried to pull away and the security officer outside the supermarket moved forward a little. 'Let me go!' she muttered. 'People are staring.'

He looked round, then did as she'd asked, but his expression was dark with anger. 'Give me your address at once.'

She knew he'd make a scene if she didn't do as he asked, and for a moment wondered whether to give him a false address, but she knew she couldn't hide for ever unless she left London completely. Then what would Jo do? And how would Mikey and Kaleel cope without one another?

268

She raised her chin and for the first time stared right back at him. 'Jo and I are living with her mother temporarily, while we search for somewhere to live. They're pulling down the flats we used to live in.'

'Those hovels! I was ashamed to think of my daughter living there. And why did you go to Mrs Harding when you could have come home?'

She felt her knees tremble, but she had to do it, had to tell him that she wouldn't obey him. 'I told you it wouldn't be right to live at home again. I'm a mother myself now and I need to make a home for my son.'

'You can't possibly give him a home like ours. And what sort of home is it with only women?'

'My home may not be as comfortable as yours, but I can give him love and happiness. I'm not bringing him to a place where he'd be scorned — and where I would, too.'

'How dare you speak to me like that?'

He raised his hand, as he'd raised it so many times before, and she cowered back.

To her shuddering relief, the security officer stepped between them. 'Excuse me, sir. I hope you weren't going to hit this young lady.'

'She's my daughter. I'll do as I like with her.'

The officer grew grim-faced. 'It's against the law to assault people, sir, whoever they are. If you hit her, I'll call the police.'

Breath whooshed into her father's mouth and he seemed to grow bigger, his face dark red. Oh, she knew that look, knew it all too well.

Kaleel began to cry and it was the fear in his voice that gave her the courage to say, 'Please leave us alone, Father. You won't change my mind.'

'Perhaps you should move away now, sir?' the officer said, and though his voice was perfectly polite, there was steel beneath the quiet tone.

Ghita's father swung round and strode back to the car.

She watched it drive away then reaction set in and she began to tremble.

'Come over here and sit down a minute, love.'

Before she knew it, she was inside a small office, sitting on a hard metal chair, and the two boys had somehow been released from their safety straps and followed her in. They clung to her, one on either side, terrified. Even Mikey was weeping. The man who'd saved them stood in the doorway, his eyes kind.

'I've asked my friend to get you a cup of tea. Nothing like it for shock.'

'Thank you. I'm sorry about the disturbance. My father ... hasn't grown used to British ways.'

'There are a lot like that and some of them aren't from overseas. I think bullies are bullies, whatever their background.'

She blinked at him in shock. 'You do?'

He nodded. 'My old man was Irish. He used to beat us up till my brother got big enough to thump him back, and by the time Sean had left home, I was big enough to protect myself and our mother.' He looked at her, worry creasing his forehead. 'Will you be all right going home?'

'I don't know. My father will probably follow me to find out where I live.'

'Look ... I've got a van. I come off duty in a

270

few minutes. I could take you home. If you and the boys ride in the back, no one will see you.'

She looked at him, amazed that a stranger could make such an offer. She was going to say no, but he had such a kind, open face, she trusted him instinctively. 'Would you really do that?'

He grinned. 'Sir Kevin O'Galahad, that's me.'

She smiled involuntarily. 'You do feel like a knight coming to my rescue.'

'That's agreed, then. Now, drink your tea and I'll just finish my shift.' He paused in the doorway. 'I'm Kevin Daly, by the way. If you want me to bring the manager to vouch for me being respectable, I will.'

'No need. I trust you.'

'Well, I've never hit a woman and I never shall, nor do I go around frightening little lads.'

'Your wife is a lucky woman.'

His face grew sad. 'Mary died last year. Cancer, it was. And I was the lucky one to have even a few years with her. She was a lovely woman.'

'I'm sorry.'

'Ah well, life goes on, don't it?'

Fifteen minutes later Kevin came back and took them out through the staff entrance, fastening her and the little boys carefully into his elderly but immaculately clean van. She gave him her address and they drove off.

As they passed the front of the supermarket she saw through the back window that her father had parked his car to watch for her, and she shivered.

'My father was waiting for us.'

'Well, he didn't see you.'

When they arrived at the flats, Kevin insisted on helping her and the boys in with the shopping.

Jo had just come home off an early shift and when Ghita explained what had happened, she grew angry. 'You're going to have to get a restraining order.'

'They don't work,' Kevin said. 'My sister tried that with her ex.'

'My father will keep on till he finds me. He won't care about restraining orders.'

'We'll think of something,' Kevin said. He coloured slightly. 'If you'll let me help you, that is?'

'Why should you?' Jo asked.

'I don't like bullies. And I'm fond of kids.'

Jo studied him through narrowed eyes and looked questioningly at her friend.

Ghita blushed and it was left to Kaleel to solve the dilemma. He fetched one of his books in and dumped it in Kevin's lap.

'Read it.'

Kevin picked up the book and beckoned to Mikey, then looked at the two women. 'I think the lads have just voted for me but I'll leave if you want me to.'

'I still don't understand why you want to help me,' Ghita said.

He shrugged. 'Loneliness, if you must know. I've nothing much to do after work now I'm on my own. Mary always said you should help others, so that's what I try to do. Besides,' he looked at the boys, 'I love children. Trouble is, you have to be careful of going near them these days if you're not related. If you want me to get a police clearance, I will.'

Jo shook her head, smiling now. 'I think you've just talked yourself into a friendship, Kevin.'

He smiled back at her, but his eyes immediately returned to Ghita.

Beth came home just as Kevin was leaving.

'Hello, Mrs Harding! How've you been keeping?'

'Kevin!' She looked at his uniform. 'I see you got yourself one of those security jobs. You all right?'

'Yes.' He looked at the girls. 'Small world, isn't it? I used to do odd shifts for Mrs Harding when Mary was ill.'

Ghita explained how she'd met Kevin and Beth assured both girls that he was indeed trustworthy.

'I think he fancies Ghita,' Jo said after he'd left.

She went bright red. 'I've only just met him.'

'And he's already talked himself into seeing you again. He's coming round to take you shopping tomorrow.'

'If you don't want to see him, you have only to say so.' Beth looked at her questioningly.

Ghita hesitated then avoided their eyes as she said, 'The boys like him. It's not good for them only to be with women.'

'Well, invite him round to tea in return for the shopping.' Jo winked at her mother.

★　★　★

273

Linda looked at Nat mutinously. 'I know I'm going to get hurt, but I can't let it go. He's my son.' She watched him rub his right temple, a habit he had when he was worried about something. She knew he cared about her, but she had to do this for herself. Had to.

'How are you going to see him if he keeps avoiding you, love?'

'Beth's given me the address of his office.'

'And you'll just push your way in?'

'If I have to.'

'You'll let me come with you?'

'As long as you promise not to try to stop me.'

He mimed crossing his heart. 'I doubt anyone could. But I want to be there for you. When are you going?'

'Thursday. It wouldn't be fair to do it just before a show. This way, if he's upset, he'll have time to get over it before the next show.'

'And you? Will you get over it within a day or two?'

'I don't suppose so. But I shan't have a nervous breakdown this time. I'm much stronger than I used to be.' She went across the office and put her arms round him. 'Dear Nat. Thank you for caring about me.'

He hugged her back and his voice came out muffled as he said, 'I don't want to lose you.'

'Why should you? This has nothing to do with you and me.'

'Who knows? I don't trust family crises. People can be cruel to one another, or they can act out of character.' He pulled away from her as the phone rang. 'No peace for the wicked.' He

274

picked it up. 'Nat Bailey here. What? I don't believe it! I'll be there in five minutes.' He slammed the phone down. 'Damned fools. What do they think they're doing? That lorry cost me a fortune.'

As she watched him go, she murmured, 'No peace for the good, either.' What a lovely man he was!

But she had trouble concentrating on her work that afternoon, kept thinking about her son.

17

Early on Wednesday evening Pete went to the make-up department. He'd seen his mother that morning and she'd looked a lot better, thank goodness. He'd met Edward at the hospital and they'd had another row afterwards about how he'd told Mum about his birth mother. Well, how was he to know she wasn't well? She always said she was all right when he asked, didn't she?

The older of the two make-up women had been in the job for a long time and was one of the best in the business, so spoke her mind to everyone without fear or favour.

Today Di scowled at him in the mirror. 'Did you have to dress young Gerry down in front of everyone the other day, Pete? The lad's doing his best. No one can do more than that.'

'Mind your own damned business, Di.'

Lips tight she carried on with his make-up. When she'd finished, he thought he didn't look as good as usual, but there wasn't time to have it redone. He looked at her suspiciously and she smirked.

Had she deliberately made him up wrongly? He peered into the mirror. No one would believe him if he complained because if she had, it was very subtly done. Or maybe it was because his face looked puffier. Could Edward be right about the drinking doing that?

He was still worrying about his appearance

when the show began.

For the first time ever, things didn't run smoothly, and it was going out live. Furious at this, Pete pinned on a smile and at one stage confessed to his viewers that he'd lost a valuable member of staff that week, which was why things weren't running as smoothly as usual. 'The young guy who's taken over is doing his best and I'm sure he'll have things under better control next week. A big hand for Gerry!'

The studio audience applauded wildly.

Gerry's smile was unconvincing.

The regression segment went well, though, thanks to the computer gurus, who continued to produce their wonderful images at the drop of a hat. It was a continuation night, with two follow-up stories. One was particularly touching. An elderly man, who'd been separated from his family and taken to Australia when he was a child, was back in England desperately searching for any surviving relatives. Thanks to ReGress he'd been able to get an image of himself at the age when he'd been sent to Australia by the authorities, and had made an appeal when he first appeared on the show. A major newspaper had taken up the story, publishing the image and asking if anyone remembered that child.

The man's brother and sister had recognized him and this continuation segment showed the reunion. A real tear-jerker, which the viewers loved. Most people in the studio audience were dabbing unashamedly at their eyes and even Pete felt moved by the three siblings' joy. He listened to tales of the English pair's desperate search for their lost brother, whom they'd believed to be in Canada, marvelling at how keen people were to find their families.

They mentioned how upset their widowed mother had been when her son had been taken away from her while she was recovering from a serious illness. But the authorities in those days had been more autocratic and had decided the boy would do better with a fresh start. She'd never managed to find out what had happened to him and had died grieving over that.

For the first time, Pete wondered what his birth mother had gone through when he'd vanished. He simply hadn't connected with the emotional side of the affair before, had only seen it as an annoying disruption at an important stage in his career.

He was thoughtful as he walked out of the studio. He still didn't want to rock the boat, nor did he want to see his birth mother — definitely not! — but he was beginning to realize how unhappy she must have been.

Perhaps Edward could find some way of letting her down gently.

No, dammit, Edward wasn't there any more.

Well, he'd think of something to do himself. But not tonight. He was exhausted.

★ ★ ★

As Pete left the studio, Gerry scowled at him. Not only had he not said thank you for all the extra effort and hours Gerry had put in since Edward's departure, he'd blamed Gerry on the

278

show itself for the problems, though most of these stemmed from last-minute changes Pete had ordered. Not content with that, as he left the studio he'd made yet another dig at his acting manager's ability to organize things, one that had been overheard by several of the other guys.

Gerry wrapped everything up, remembering to thank people for what they'd done, which Edward said was important. He tried to brush it off when some of them commiserated with him on the way he'd been treated, hoped he hadn't shown how upset he was.

Afterwards he went across to the bar opposite, which was used by quite a lot of television staff and the inevitable journalists on the hunt for a juicy story. He found a quiet corner and sat sipping a beer, feeling gutted.

People who didn't know the situation were now going to think he was incompetent. Edward had always managed to control his cousin and hide how volatile Pete could be, but no one else could keep him in order. Maybe Gerry should resign. But if he did, people might think he'd been sacked.

What the hell was he to do? He knew he wasn't in a position to manage next week's show.

'You look a bit down in the mouth.'

He glanced up. 'Maggie. Hi. Haven't seen you for a while.'

'Been doing a stint in the EU, Paris and Brussels mainly.'

'Lucky you.'

'I saw the show tonight. Bit harsh of Pete to blame you publicly.'

'Yeah. Tell me about it.'

'I heard Edward Newbury had quit and you'd taken over. They say Pete's upset quite a few people this past week. I didn't know he was such a prima donna.'

Gerry shook his head sadly. 'The stories I could tell! Though I won't. It was mainly his fault things went wrong tonight, not mine. He's always wanting to chop and change the show at the last minute. If Edward had been there, *he* might have reined him in. I tried but Pete wouldn't listen to me. He's been even more of a pain to deal with ever since — ' He realized he'd nearly revealed what he'd overheard in the office and cut himself off short, gesturing to the seat next to him. 'Buy you a drink?'

'Yeah, that'd be good. My friends don't seem to have fronted up tonight.'

'I'm avoiding the crowd from the studio.'

The drink arrived and she sipped it, smiling. 'It's nice to catch up with old friends. I'm sorry you're upset.'

She laid her hand over his and gave it a quick squeeze. He took hold of it, enjoying the comfort of a sympathetic listener.

'What were you going to say about Pete? Ever since what?'

Gerry tapped one finger to his nose. 'Confidential stuff.'

'Oh, sorry.'

After a while, she suggested going out for a curry and he agreed. By the time they came out of the restaurant, his head was spinning from drinking too much too quickly, but he reckoned he was going to score with her.

When he woke up in the morning he had little recollection of coming home, though from the looks of the place, he'd shared his bed with Maggie. It wasn't the first time. They'd been casual friends for a while.

In the kitchen he found a note. 'It was good. See you soon. M.'

Smiling, he got some coffee, took a couple of painkillers for his hangover, then frowned. Damned if he could remember the last part of the evening. He didn't usually get bladdered. But he'd been so upset about the way Pete had treated him.

Reluctantly he went to work. Someone had to pick up the pieces. But if Pete snapped at him once more, he was out of there. OK, so it had been a big opportunity to get this job, and while Edward was teaching him the ropes, it had been an excellent learning experience.

But no one, not even the oh-so-great Pete Newbury, was going to treat him like a doormat.

* * *

Edward invited Beth round to his place on the Wednesday night. He made her a simple meal and they ate it at his breakfast bar.

'Would you mind if we watched the show?' he asked afterwards. 'I don't want to bore you, but I'm a bit worried about how it's going.'

They sat close together on the sofa, but he forgot about her as the show started, muttering occasionally, or shaking his head and making irritated noises.

'It doesn't seem to be flowing as smoothly as usual,' she commented.

'No. I'm sorry I'm such poor company.'

'Doesn't matter.' She sneaked a quick look at his grim expression and didn't comment on anything else about the show. If he wanted to talk, she was here.

When *In Focus* ended, Edward looked round for the remote, couldn't find it so got up to switch off the television. He stood staring down at the blank screen, hands thrust deep in his trouser pockets. 'I shouldn't have walked out on him like that. I should have hired a replacement first. Gerry's a good kid, but he's not had enough experience and he's too young to stand up to Pete.'

When Edward sat down beside her, she took hold of his hand, waiting. Minutes passed, then he gave her a wry smile. 'I think we're experiencing the Chinese curse.'

She smiled her understanding and chorused with him, '*May you live in interesting times!*'

They both laughed.

'Well, I've certainly not been bored lately,' she said ruefully.

'Neither have I. It's distracting me from my main purpose, though.' He raised her hand to his lips and her heart did a little skip. But he didn't take her in his arms, as she'd hoped.

'I'll have to go and see Pete. I can't let the series flop.'

'Won't he find someone else to co-ordinate things next week?'

Edward let out a scornful snort. 'Pete? He's

good at talking, not so good at doing, and he's the world's worst organizer. Fran had her uses, believe me, keeping him in order socially. And I've always been there to keep an eye on him at work.'

'Now you're feeling guilty for leaving him.'

'Sort of. Though I'd been thinking about it for a while.' He began to play with her bracelet in an absent-minded way. 'It's as if he hasn't grown up in some ways. I believe he always means well, I really do, but he uses his charm to get things and win people round. He's never had to struggle to achieve things as others have.'

He looked at her very directly. 'Do you think you could ask your mother to hold back on contacting him until I've sorted out the show?'

She shook her head. 'Even if I asked, it'd do no good. Edward, she's waited for thirty-eight years to find out what happened to him. It's a credit to how strong she is these days that she didn't rush round to see him straight away, but she knew it wouldn't be fair to do it just before the show. She's absolutely desperate to see him.'

'I'm sure she is. And look — I don't want that Pete thing to come between you and me.'

'It's going to make things awkward.' She took her hand away and stood up, moving across to the big picture window. 'Perhaps you and I had better stop seeing one another till it's been sorted out. It's not just Mum, I've got Jo and Ghita to deal with as well.'

'And I've got my Aunt Sue to look after. She'll need to go into some sort of care for a time, till they've done some physio and rehabilitated her.'

'How is she? I realized she must be on the mend for you to invite me round.'

'Yes. It'll take a while for her to recover, though. She's still upset about Pete, which isn't good. She didn't know he'd been kidnapped, Beth. I swear she didn't.'

'I believe you. But he was. Perhaps someone was selling children and — '

'I think my uncle might have bought a child, but I doubt he'd have got involved in a kidnapping. My aunt says she met the supposed mother, who was giving up her child because she wanted a better life for him.'

'What a mess it is now!' Beth said quietly, staring out at the lights of the nearby houses and apartment blocks. She watched the red lights of cars braking in the street and the more distant lights that twinkled on a nearby hill. She didn't know what to do next. Did he want her to stay tonight?

He came to join her, enfolding her in an embrace, so that she leaned back against his chest.

'Do you really want us to stop seeing one another, Beth?'

'Definitely not.'

'Nor do I. I meant it when I said I was courting you.'

It made her glow with pleasure. 'I like it when you say that.'

'Good. Somehow we'll work our way through this mess. Trust me. And I'll try my hardest to prevent your mother getting hurt any more.'

Beth hesitated. 'I'd better tell you. At the

284

weekend I gave Mum the address of Pete's office. She promised to do nothing till the show was over for the week.' She could feel him stiffen.

'I wish you hadn't done that, not yet anyway.'

'She was sobbing, Edward. You should have heard the pain in her voice. She threatened to go and confront him at the studio next week if I didn't. Surely it's better to settle this privately, not make a public scandal of it?'

'Yes, you're right there. But I'm thinking of her, too. Her timing's really bad. Pete's been in a foul mood lately.'

'I couldn't have guessed there would be trouble with the show, or I'd have asked her to wait a little longer. But I have to confess, I don't think she would have done. I've never seen her like this, so quietly determined.'

'When is she going to confront him?'

'Tomorrow, I suppose. She's not a confronting sort, though, so I'm sure she won't make a big fuss.'

'He might.'

★ ★ ★

On the Thursday Linda took a deep breath and pushed open the door of Pete Newbury's office, which had only PN Enterprises on the window outside.

The receptionist looked up. 'Can I help you?' Her voice was chill, her body language saying she wanted only to get rid of an annoying intruder.

'I need to see Pete Newbury.'

'I'm afraid he's busy. If you'll tell me what it's

about, perhaps I can help you? And could I ask how you found this address?'

'That's irrelevant. It's a personal matter and you can't help me. I'm not leaving till I see him.'

'In that case, I'll have to call the police to have you removed.'

Voices had been coming from behind one of the closed doors, two men arguing by the sounds of it. Linda decided to risk it and darted across the room before the receptionist had realized what she was doing. Flinging open the door, she saw Pete Newbury, face red with anger.

Both men turned to look at her.

'Who the hell are you?' Pete said. 'Get rid of her, Ilsa.'

As the younger woman tried to pull her away, Linda clung to the door and yelled, 'Does the word 'kidnapping' mean anything to you.'

The other man came towards them, and for a moment she thought he was going to help push her out. Instead, his voice was gentle.

'I'm Edward Newbury. I know your daughter.' He held up one hand to stop the receptionist moving to intercept her. 'Please leave this to me, Ilsa.'

For a moment it seemed as if the younger woman was going to ignore his quiet request, then Pete flapped one hand in a back-off gesture and she returned to her desk.

Linda took a couple of steps forward, her eyes devouring the man her son had become. This was nothing like seeing him on the television. He was bigger than she'd expected, starting to put on weight around the middle. He reminded her

286

so much of her own father it hurt. 'You're taller than your father was and you look more like your grandfather than him.'

He took a step back as if trying to keep his distance, but his voice was shaky. 'What do you want?'

She stopped moving and told herself to be calm. 'To see you. Is that such a surprise? You are my son, after all. I've dreamed about this moment so many times and I — ' Then the room began to spin round her and she cried out in fear as she felt herself falling.

* * *

Pete saw the woman's eyes roll up and realized she was going to faint. Automatically he stepped forward to catch her. She wasn't very heavy, but was more sturdily built than his mother — his *real* mother, he reminded himself.

He looked at Edward for help but his cousin shook his head slightly and slipped out of the room.

As the door closed behind him, Pete looked down and saw she was starting to come round again. He scooped her up into his arms and carried her across to a sofa by the wall. Uncertain what to do next, he hovered for a moment then went back to his desk and pressed the button for Ilsa.

She usually answered his calls within seconds, but this time there was no sign of her. He guessed Edward was preventing her from coming in, and he was about to go out to fetch her when

Mrs Harding groaned. She moved incautiously, nearly rolling off the sofa, so he had to rush back to make sure she didn't hurt herself.

Her eyes opened and she blinked at him, looking disoriented. Then she let out her breath in a soft 'Ohh' sound, as if it had all come back to her.

'I'm sorry. I don't usually faint.'

When she tried to sit up, he stopped her. 'Lie still a minute. We don't want you keeling over again.'

She smiled knowingly. 'Your grandfather used to speak gruffly like that when he was being kind. I'll be all right now. Could I have a drink of water, please?'

'Sure.' He helped her to sit up then went across to the water cooler and brought her back a paper cup of water, watching as she held it in a hand that trembled and sipped it slowly.

'Thank you.'

'How much money will it take to persuade you to leave me alone?'

She looked at him in shock. 'Beth said you'd offered us money and I thought she was exaggerating. I don't need *money* and I'm not intending to make trouble for you, I promise. I just want to see you, get to know you. You're my *son*.'

'Well, I don't feel like it.'

She swallowed hard, staring down for a moment. When she looked up, she asked in that same quiet voice, 'Have you had a happy life?'

'Very. You couldn't get better parents than I had.'

'It's a comfort to me to know that, at least.'

Hell, her voice was wobbling and her eyes were bright with tears. He didn't like upsetting people and wished Edward were here to help him get rid of her gently. He looked resentfully towards the door then back at her. 'You've chosen a bad time, I'm afraid. I'm very busy today and — '

'Can you not spare me even an hour?'

'Won't that make things worse?'

'For you, perhaps. Not for me. It'll give me a few memories at least.'

If she was speaking the truth, she really didn't want money, which was good. But that didn't mean he wanted to spend time with her, stirring up things best forgotten. He realized he was looming over her and pulled up a chair, straddling it and leaning forward against its back. He surprised himself by saying, 'It'd have been better if you'd never found me.'

'No, it wouldn't. Believe me, it's far better for me to know you're not dead and have had a good life.'

Her eyes made him feel uncomfortable. They were both penetrating and yet understanding. She was nothing like he'd expected. At one stage since his discovery of the kidnapping he'd wondered if she or her husband had sold their own son. He'd bet his life this woman hadn't. He was reserving judgement on his birth father.

'I've been lucky,' he admitted. 'Things have fallen nicely into place.'

'I'm glad for you.'

He moved his shoulders helplessly. 'I don't

want things to change.'

'Things always change, Greg — I mean, Pete. Even grief passes. Did you realize that your sister had nearly as bad a time of it as I did after you disappeared? I was too distraught to care for her and she was passed round our relatives like an unwanted parcel. After I got back from hospital, *she* was the one supporting me for a few years, young as she was.'

It was out before he could stop himself. 'What about my father?'

'He moved out after a year or so, remarried, has other children now. You'll have to ask him yourself how he feels about you.'

'If he doesn't thrust himself upon me, I'm certainly not going to contact him.'

She stared at him incredulously. 'Is that what I've done? *Thrust myself upon you?*'

He flushed slightly. 'It feels like that, the way my sister came to see me uninvited, then you barged your way in here. I've said I don't want to . . . to go back. Why can't you both leave me alone?'

Her heart twisted with anguish — and with recognition. He'd been spoiled, had had things too easy, was weak, just like his father. *I've spent half my life mourning for him and he regards that as an intrusion! He wasn't worth all that pain.*

She stood up, not feeling like weeping now, letting her anger carry her out with dignity intact. 'If that's what you want, so be it. Don't worry. I won't *thrust myself upon you* again.'

She walked out without looking to left or

right. Even so, to her shame, she kept listening for footsteps running after her, a voice calling her back.

But the corridor stayed quiet behind her and her son, the child she'd mourned the loss of every day of her life, simply let her walk away. Someone closed the office door with a sharp click before she'd taken even half a dozen steps.

Nat got up from a seat further along the corridor. He didn't say a word, just folded her in his arms and said, 'I'm taking you home, love.'

She leaned against his shoulder for a moment or two then straightened up and walked out with him. She was relieved that he didn't ask her what had happened, because she'd have burst into tears if she'd tried to speak.

It's over, she thought. *All those years of grieving and wondering. It's over, just like that.*

★ ★ ★

Edward watched Linda Harding walk out. Her face was white and set, her head held high. It was obvious how badly she'd been hurt.

When Ilsa went to close the outer door, he nearly pushed past her, but Pete came and beckoned him into the office.

'What happened? What the hell did you say to her?'

Pete shook his head very slightly and sat down at his desk as if his legs wouldn't hold him upright. 'Get me a whisky, would you?'

'No. That's not the answer and you'll become an alcoholic if you keep turning to the bottle every time there's trouble.'

'Then I'll damned well get one myself.' He lurched across the room and poured himself two fingers of whisky, spilling some. Picking up the glass he tossed the amber liquid down like water, then poured some more before taking the glass back to his desk.

'What did you do to her?' Edward repeated.

Pete stared down into his drink, shaking the glass slightly to make the whisky swirl round. 'It was horrible. I didn't handle it well, I admit. You should have stayed with us. You deal with these ticklish situations far better than I do.'

Ticklish situation. Is that all it was to him? Edward had seen Beth's grief about her brother first-hand, and was sure her mother would have been even more harrowed by the kidnapping. Suddenly his anger boiled over and he went across to the desk, grabbing Pete by his expensive shirt and jerking him to his feet. '*What did you do to that poor woman?*'

'Told her I didn't want to see her, what else?'

'There's more to it than that. A woman wouldn't walk out with that look on her face unless someone had hurt her very badly.'

Suddenly Pete swept the tumbler of whisky off the desk and everything else with it. 'Do you think I don't know that?'

'So what exactly did you say?'

'I offered her money. Then I said . . . I said she'd thrust herself upon me.'

'I always knew you were a selfish sod, but I never realized quite how selfish till now. I don't know why I'm even wasting my time with you.'

He turned on his heel.

'Come back! I need you.'

'Well, too bad. I need some fresh air. There's something rotten in here and it stinks to high heaven.' Edward strode out.

★ ★ ★

As Thursday passed and his head cleared, Gerry kept getting flashbacks to the time he'd spent with Maggie. They got on well and always had a lot to say to one another, but it seemed to him that he'd done most of the talking last night. She was too damned sympathetic — it was what made her a good journalist — and he'd needed to unburden himself about the show.

What exactly had he told her? A chill feeling settled in his belly as more memories fluttered into his mind. He couldn't have! Surely not? By the end of the day he was pretty certain he'd let the cat out of the bag about Pete's real mother.

But even if he had told her, Maggie was a friend. She'd keep it quiet, not use something told by a friend. Surely?

Only . . . it'd make a hell of a news story. The famous Pete Newbury kidnapped as a child, the man everyone loved to love treating his real mother badly, refusing even to see her.

Oh, hell! What was he going to do?

Gerry fumbled for his mobile and rang Maggie. Her warm voice said she was out and invited him to leave a message. His mind went blank for a minute then he said, 'Gerry here. Give me a ring, Mag. It's important.'

But she didn't ring back. He checked that his battery hadn't run down, that his phone was still working. He left another message and sat at home all evening waiting, hoping, but there wasn't a squeak from Maggie.

18

On Friday morning the story hit the headlines in one of the leading tabloids as an exclusive. Pete spluttered coffee all over it in shock as he sat at the breakfast table.

Pete Newbury kidnapped as child.

A Mother's Heartbreak.

How the hell had they found out? Had his birth mother gone to the press out of revenge? No, he couldn't see her doing that. She wasn't that sort of person. He didn't know how he was so certain of that when he'd only met her once, but he was. She'd been gentle, straightforward. And he'd been — He dismissed that thought quickly.

He scanned the article. The reporter, Maggie Quinn, even told how reluctant Pete had been to see Linda Harding.

He'd never met this Maggie, so how could she have found that out? He couldn't believe what he was reading, how it had been slanted to paint him in the worst possible light. And yet . . . it was all basically true.

Was it Ilsa who'd spilled the beans? She certainly liked money, but he paid her well and . . . No, not Ilsa.

The phone rang and when he picked it up, it was another newspaper offering him money to tell his side of the story. He slammed the phone down, angry at their effrontery, then picked it up to ring his cousin.

He paused. Edward had walked out on him in disgust. He put the phone down, not wanting to be made to feel like a worm again.

What was he going to do? How much credibility would he have with *In Focus*, a people-centred programme, once viewers read this rubbish?

The journalist had done her research carefully. She'd even found some old newspaper articles about the kidnapping of Greg Harding, which came complete with photos of him as a child, one of them the photo his sister had showed him. He studied the images grimly. His birth father and mother, looking young and carefree. His sister, looking giggly and girlish. She wasn't at all like that now. She seemed tight and guarded now. He didn't understand what Edward saw in her.

What had changed that happy little girl into such a self-contained woman? Losing her brother? Or the break-up of her whole family?

He turned the page to find the image of himself at the age of three from his first *Who Am I?* segment, the image his mother had claimed wasn't a good match. Only it looked exactly like the photo of the boy who'd vanished. He turned back to the front page and the photo that showed the scar so clearly. He looked down at his arm then back at the photo. He hadn't needed to force a DNA test on his sister. It had been very clear from the start that he was the missing child.

He shivered, feeling a need for the warmth of the sunlight outside, so carried the newspaper out to the balcony and re-read the article.

Bad. It was really bad. *Star spurns own mother*, a subtitle said.

He'd seen other celebrities suddenly lose their golden touch and with it, their whole careers. He shivered at the thought of that happening to him. If his popularity plummeted, so would his income, then what would he do? He had no other talents, let alone qualifications.

He should have been more careful with his money, as Edward had advised. Clever Edward, always doing better than Pete at school, then going on to university, where he'd got a first-class degree. *He* wouldn't have made such a mess of things.

Pete buried his head in his hands and groaned.

What the hell was he going to do?

How was he going to save himself from disaster?

★   ★   ★

Edward didn't see the newspapers until he'd finished his exercise session in the pool. As he was coming out of the men's changing room, one of the neighbours he socialized with occasionally said cheerfully, 'You got out just in time, didn't you? Was that why you left?'

'What do you mean?'

'Pete Newbury.'

'What about him?'

'Ah. You haven't seen the newspapers today, then? There's a big spread in *Best of the News* about your cousin. Seems he was kidnapped as a child. Lurid stuff. But is he really refusing to see

297

his birth mother? Bit thick, that. Poor woman must have gone through hell when he vanished.'

'Thanks for telling me. I've got to go.' Edward grabbed the rest of his clothes and ran out to the foyer, picking up a newspaper from the stand and hurrying up to his flat.

He flung his damp bathers and towel aside and spread the paper out on the breakfast bar. It didn't take long to read the article and he closed his eyes for a moment in dismay as he finished it.

This journo had really got it in for Pete.

He reached for the phone, then withdrew his hand. No use ringing his cousin until he'd thought about what to say and do. He went to take a long shower, because that's where he did his best thinking.

Did he want to be involved in damage limitation? Not really.

Did he have any choice about getting involved? None at all.

Pete might not be his cousin by birth but he was like a brother by upbringing. Aunt Sue and Uncle Donald had taken Edward in when his own parents died and he owed them big time.

No, he couldn't walk away when Pete was in trouble, when his aunt was getting hurt by the flak. He'd have to try to help. Somehow.

But what would this do to his relationship with Beth?

★　★　★

Beth was on early turn, so was at her office by five-thirty that morning. She managed to get a lot of paperwork done because there were no emergencies, or at least the phone didn't ring by the designated hour, so she could only assume everyone had turned up for work on time. At seven she nipped down to the café across the road to pick up something to eat and a newspaper, looking forward to a peaceful few minutes' reading as she ate.

As she walked up to the news-stand, she found herself staring at Pete Newbury's face on one of the posters. It wasn't a happy photo, either. What had happened?

She looked at the row of newspapers. Only one seemed to be carrying the story, so she bought that, though it was a paper she didn't usually bother with. Lower down its front page was one of the old photos showing her mother pleading for news of her missing son. Inside was the TV image from the show. There was also a photo of herself.

Dear heaven, how had that information got out?

She walked slowly back to work, forgetting about food, her stomach churning with anxiety.

As she finished reading the article, she heard footsteps pound along the corridor and Sandy came in, breathless and flushed. She jabbed one finger towards the newspaper. 'You've seen it, then?'

Beth was still too shocked to do more than nod.

'I thought you might need me early.'

She forced a smile. 'I don't know what I need yet. I've only just this minute read the article.'

'It's going to upset your poor mother.'

'It's going to upset a lot of people.'

Herself included.

And what would it do to her relationship with Edward?

★ ★ ★

Linda smiled at Nat as he put his folded newspaper on the table and sat down. She was cooking him one of the fluffy omelettes he loved for breakfast. She watched him tenderly as he opened out the newspaper but didn't try to start a conversation. He hated to be disturbed when he was reading the main morning news. He took three newspapers, saying you needed several views of the world to get a fair picture.

Just as she was about to turn back to her cooking, she saw his expression change and his mouth drop open.

'What's wrong?'

He made an involuntary movement with one hand, as if to cover the newspaper, then removed his hand and gestured to it. 'You'd better come and look at this, love. Turn the gas off.'

He made room beside him on the bench seat and tapped the front page.

The headlines were enough to make her gasp and grab his arm. 'How did they find out?'

'Who knows?'

She kept hold of Nat's hand as she read the article, with its snide remarks about Pete rejecting her. She hated the way they portrayed her as such a pitiful creature. Maybe she had been pitiful when it first happened, but she wasn't now. 'They're disgusting. All that without even a word to me, and yet they're pretending to quote me.'

'I'll get on the phone to my lawyer. We're not letting them get away with it.'

'Pete might think I've done this in revenge because of him not wanting to see me.'

'No one who knows you would ever believe such a thing.'

'That's the whole point, Nat: he doesn't know me.'

His phone rang and he picked it up. 'Oh, hell! Thanks for letting me know, John. Yeah, I'll work from home today.' He slammed the phone down.

'What's the matter at the yard?' she prompted.

'John was ringing to tell me there are some reporters waiting at the gate. They know you work there and want to see you. He refused to let them inside. Smart fellow, John. Said if we came in together they might guess you're living with me and trace you that way. He deserves a bonus. Don't know what I'd do without him.'

She started studying the article again. 'What's this going to do to Pete's career?'

'Frankly, I don't give two hoots. He's a spoiled, selfish brat, even if he is forty-one years old, and he hurt you badly. It's you I care about.'

'There's Beth to consider as well, not to mention Jo and little Mikey. When the gutter press start making up tales, who knows where it will all end?'

He pulled her to him and planted a smacking great kiss on her cheek. 'I love you.'

She blinked in surprise. 'What was that for?'

'Always thinking about others. You're a wonderful, caring woman.'

She didn't think she was all that different from other women, especially when it came to her children, but his compliment cheered her. 'Let me finish cooking your omelette, though it'll have lost all its fluffiness now.'

'It'll still taste good. Afterwards we'll decide what to do.'

'Is there anything we can do to stop it?'

'There must be. But I confess I don't know what.'

'I'm not doing anything without consulting Beth.'

★ ★ ★

Beth rang Edward on his private mobile. 'Have you seen it?'

'Yes.'

'I've not phoned Mum yet. I wanted to discuss tactics with you first.'

'I've not got any tactics worked out. I'm still too angry to think clearly. Who do you think leaked the news?'

'It won't be anyone from my family.'

'I knew that already. It won't be my aunt and it certainly won't be Pete, because this threatens his career big time.'

'Does it?'

'Take my word for it, yes. He's built a reputation for being Mr Nice Guy, and most of the time he is. But this paints him as Mr Nasty.'

'It'll pass.'

'Maybe, but his programme will suffer, viewer numbers will decline and maybe there won't be another series. He was just building it up big and was ready to lease out the *Who Am I?* segment round the world. Our two computer gurus won't be so pleased, either. They were set to receive good royalties.'

It was a moment or two before he spoke again. 'I'd better go and see Pete. It's one thing to wash my hands of him when he's riding high. I can't leave him in the lurch.'

She smiled. 'No, I'm sure you can't.'

'I'll come and see you later.'

'No need.'

'I think there will be every need. If there's one thing everyone involved needs to do it's present a united front to these sods. Tell your mother Pete and I are both sorry this has happened.'

'You might be sorry. I doubt he is — except for it hurting his career.'

'You've seen the worst of him. He's not a bad guy, honest.'

'I'll have to reserve judgement on that.'

★ ★ ★

When Beth rang her mother's office, the foreman answered.

'Nat and Linda are staying home today. We've got reporters just about camping out on our doorstep here, but luckily they've not found out that Nat and Linda are together.'

'Vultures!' She rang her mother's new phone

number and Nat picked it up.

'Beth here. Can I speak to Mum?'

'Yes, of course. Where are you?'

'Still at work. I came in early today, before the news broke. I've only just found out.' There was a commotion in the outer office. 'What on earth — ? Just a minute, Nat.' She ran out, to be greeted by flashing cameras and a barrage of questions.

'Get back inside!' Sandy yelled. 'I've rung security.'

Beth put up one arm to shield her face and found she had to push past one man to get back into her own office.

'We can pay you well for an exclusive story,' he yelled, trying to thrust a business card into her hand.

She let it fall and slammed the door on him, leaning against it, sickened by the avid expression on his face. She picked up the phone again. 'I'll be with you in a minute, Nat. We've just had a media invasion here.'

A man's deep voice yelled something in the outer office and the noise subsided. There were mutters and protests, but the sound of voices gradually faded.

Sandy poked her head round the door. 'They've gone back to the corridor now. You all right?'

'Yes. I'm just talking to Mum and Nat. I'll be with you in a minute.'

★ ★ ★

'Sounds bad,' Nat said. 'Do you want me to send an escort to get you safely home?'

'I'll see how I go.'

'Here's your mum, then.'

Linda's voice was firm and sounded almost normal, to Beth's relief. 'Are you all right, Mum?'

'Yes, dear. They don't seem to realize where I am, thank goodness.'

'Then you should stay there and be thankful for it.'

'I can't do that, Beth. We have to help Pete.'

'*What?*'

'You heard perfectly well what I said.'

'Why should you help that rat?'

'Because he's my son and your brother, and this is at least partly my fault.'

'How can it be your fault?'

'I shouldn't have confronted him with other people nearby. Someone must have overheard us. Perhaps it was that receptionist. I don't know. If I'd let sleeping dogs lie, just been thankful he was alive, then it'd not have got out.'

'Mum, as far as I'm concerned, he deserves everything he gets.'

'I don't like to hear you being so harsh, darling.'

'I can't forgive him for hurting you.'

'I can.'

Silence, then Beth said, 'I can't see any way we can help him except by staying out of his way, which suits me just fine.'

'There must be something we can do. I've not worked it out yet, but I don't intend to let him be pilloried. I'll ring you back later.'

Beth put the phone down and watched as a tear plopped on to the desk beside it. She didn't know why she was crying. Her brother wasn't worth the tears.

But perhaps the situation was. Everything was in such a mess and she was sure it was going to get worse before it got better. She'd been through this media circus once before, when she was much younger. She should be able to face it better now. She was a strong modern woman.

Wasn't she?

Another tear dropped on to her desk and she fumbled for a tissue. She didn't feel at all strong today.

Her brother wasn't worth crying over, that was certain.

How could her mother be so *forgiving*?

★　★　★

It was ten o'clock by the time Edward pushed his way past the journalists into Pete's besieged office. Cameras were flashing and he was sure once they found out who he was they'd be after him as well.

A man in a security uniform barred his way, yelling over his shoulder at someone inside. 'What about this one?'

Ilsa looked up. 'You can let Edward in any time, Des. He's Pete's cousin.'

The man nodded and stepped back for a moment, before immediately taking up his position in front of the door.

'Thank goodness you're here!' Ilsa pushed her hair back from her face. 'It's been mayhem, people trying to shove their way in. I had to bring Des in to keep them out.'

Edward grinned. 'I bet they didn't get past you, even before he arrived.'

She allowed herself a near smile. 'Definitely not.'

He went to perch on the edge of her desk. 'You see a lot of what's going on, Ilsa. Have you any idea how they got hold of this information?'

She avoided his gaze and began to fiddle with the computer keyboard.

This was the last reaction he'd expected. 'Ilsa? Do you know something?'

'I don't. Well, not exactly.' She heaved a sigh. 'Gerry and I both heard you and Pete arguing about his birth mother. We couldn't help it. You were making no attempt to keep your voices down. But I swear I didn't say a word to anyone.'

'Do you think Gerry might have?'

She was still frowning. 'He doesn't seem the sort, but who else could it be?'

'Give him a ring and ask him to come here ASAP, will you? Don't say why.'

He went into Pete's office and found his cousin sitting behind the desk, staring glumly down at the newspaper.

He looked up, surprise and relief on his face as he saw Edward.

'I came to help.'

'Thanks. I can't seem to think what to do. I'm a bit upset by all this.'

'I'm not surprised. The other papers will be

307

carrying the story tomorrow and will no doubt add their own flourishes unless we do something to stop them.'

'We?'

'I'll come back to work with you temporarily, then I'll train my replacement.'

'Maybe we could come to some arrangement. I could pay you more and — '

Edward thumped the desk. 'When will you bloody well learn that this isn't about money?'

Pete's voice was sulky. 'It's what makes the world go round.'

'Were you able to buy off your sister?'

Pete hitched his shoulders and began to fiddle with his pencil.

'Or your birth mother?'

Pete shook his head.

'And you can't buy me, either. I'm coming back because I'm as near to a brother as you've got. If you spin me any lies or don't do *exactly* as I tell you, I'll leave instantly.'

Pete swallowed hard. 'Thanks. I've — been a bit of a shit, haven't I?' Silence, then, 'But what the hell *can* we do?'

'With your agreement, I'm going to visit your birth mother to see if she'll appear with you at a press conference. I'll need Beth's help as well. I don't think she'll refuse. They're both decent sorts. Maybe when this is all over you can get to know them properly.'

Pete looked sad. 'They won't want to know me now.'

'They will. They do. But first we have to stop the wild rumours. Your job is to go and see Aunt

Sue, make sure she knows what's happening. Break the news gently if she hasn't heard.'

'That mob out there will follow me if I go outside.'

'Let them follow you. They're bound to be camping out at the hospital already, trying to see your mother, but I doubt they'll have been allowed inside her wing. Don't say anything to them except 'No comment', but tell them we'll be making a press statement later.'

Pete nodded.

His docility was starting to worry Edward. 'Are you sure you're all right?'

Pete shrugged. 'I don't feel — as if I know myself any more.'

'It's not going to be easy but we'll get through it. And Pete — '

'Yeah?'

'Be kind to your birth mother. She doesn't deserve this.'

A nod was the only answer.

'Afterwards, let them follow you back to your flat. The concierge will keep them at bay and if you need to get out without being seen, he'll help you do that, I'm sure.'

'How are you going to escape pursuit when you leave here?'

'I'll use the fire stairs but we need to create a diversion. Ilsa will hold the fort at the office and contact us if anything important turns up.' When his cousin didn't move, he said more sharply, 'For heaven's sake, Pete, get up off your backside and start moving.'

'You'd break it to Mum better than me.'

309

How many times did he need to tell him? 'This time you're going to do your share of the dirty work. I've protected you for too long. From now on, you either learn to stand on your own feet or you sink. After you've seen Aunt Sue, go and wait at your flat. Do nothing else.'

'You mean I've just got to sit around while those sods destroy my reputation?'

'We have to get our act together before we do anything. Your job is to draw their attention. On second thoughts, don't say 'No comment'. Pull out all your charm. Tell them the article was wrong, but refuse to explain how. You've had enough practice at charming the press.'

Pete's face brightened a little.

'Remember, this depends on the goodwill of your mother and sister. Would it have been so hard to be kind to them?'

Pete flushed. 'I was in shock.'

'You could still have been kind. Now, let's hope the security guy can get me through to the fire door. I'll — ' He broke off as there were voices in the reception area and Ilsa tapped on the door.

'Gerry's here to see you.'

'Show him in.'

The younger man paused in the door, looking as if he hadn't slept. 'I'm sorry. It was me who let it out, Pete. I didn't do it on purpose, though. I was drunk. I'll resign. I just wanted to tell you how sorry I am.'

It was Pete who answered. 'Come in and shut the door.'

When Gerry had done that, he said, 'If you

didn't do it on purpose, there's no need to resign. I treated you badly and I'm sorry for that.'

Edward smiled at him. This was the Pete he knew and liked best. Maybe now Fran was out of the picture, they could get the old Pete back. He turned to Gerry. 'We really need you to stay here with Ilsa. I don't want her leaving on her own. All you say to the press is 'No comment now, but a statement will be made later in the day at a press conference.' That should hold them for a while.'

'I'll be happy to do that.'

'I presume you know this Maggie person who wrote the article?'

'Yes. She used to be a friend — well, more than a friend. She isn't any longer. She was there when I got drunk, after the show.'

'All right. I'll be in touch.' He squeezed Gerry's shoulder briefly and received a grateful look in return. He went out into the office to ask the security guard's help in getting out of the building.

The journalists were herded into a small waiting room and told that Mr Newbury would make a brief statement. Edward sent Pete in to them ostensibly to calm them down. While they were focused on his cousin, Edward used the fire stairs to get out of the building, leaving by the rear entrance.

He hoped his plan would work. It all depended on how kind Beth and her mother were prepared to be. They'd been shabbily treated, but surely they wouldn't be vindictive?

19

Ghita walked to the shops to pick up some fresh fruit and eggs. The little boys, who loved going out for walks, were jabbering away, pointing and asking questions.

It was as she was passing the newsagent's that she saw Pete Newbury's name on the poster and stopped to read the headlines. Oh, no! She bought a paper and read the front page as she stood beside the pram.

Pulling out her mobile, she rang Jo, but got only the answering service. She left a message then wondered if she should ring Jo's mother. No, surely Beth would have heard the news by now?

After she'd made her purchases, Ghita walked back along the street, not noticing anything, too upset about the scandal that had engulfed her kind hostess. Some things were private, not to be shouted from the rooftops, and this was one of them. Journalists like those had a lot to answer for.

When she arrived at the flats, she found a TV cameraman busy filming a reporter who was speaking earnestly and gesturing to the flats. She tried to walk past quickly, but another man stopped her.

'Do you live in these flats, ma'am?'

'Yes.'

'Then you must know Mrs Harding.'

'Who?' Ghita hoped her face wasn't betraying her. 'I've not been here long and don't know many people yet. Has something happened to this woman?'

'Watch the midday news on TV. Thanks.' He stepped back.

She hurried inside, breathing a sigh of relief when she'd closed the door of the flat on the world.

She settled the boys with one of their favourite children's DVDs, giving them a biscuit and a drink of milk, then rang Beth's office.

Sandy answered, and when Ghita explained that it was urgent she speak to Beth, the other woman said bluntly, 'If it's about that ghastly article in *Best of the News*, she knows.'

'Oh. Is there anything I can do to help?'

'Not really, thanks. If I were you, I'd stay home for the rest of the day, though, and don't say anything to the press.'

'I certainly won't.'

Ghita put the phone down with a sigh. You felt so helpless at times like this.

* * *

When Beth's personal mobile rang, it was Edward again. 'How's it going?' she asked.

'I've seen Pete and now I'd like to talk to you. Where are you?'

'Still at the office. I daren't poke my head out today.'

'Any way you can get out of the building without being followed?'

'Not without an army escort or in heavy disguise.' Then an idea occurred to her. 'Talking of disguise, perhaps there is a way.' She began to smile. 'I think I'm just going to change myself into a cleaner. I've got plenty of our uniforms here. Can you come round to the car park at the rear of the next building, Number thirty-six?'

'Yes.'

She explained to Sandy what she wanted, and soon they had her kitted out in one of the bright orange uniforms, padded underneath with other uniforms to make her seem much plumper. With a scarf on her head and Sandy's reading glasses, she was transformed.

'I'd have walked past you myself.'

Beth tried to focus and found it difficult. 'The way these glasses magnify everything, I'll probably bump into things and give myself away.'

'Take a bucket and — No, a portable vacuum cleaner would be best, strapped to your back. Why don't you vacuum your way along the hall? They'll be less suspicious if you're not in a hurry to leave.'

'Brilliant.' She gave Sandy a hug, switched on the vacuum cleaner and sallied forth.

As she got outside, the reporters came over to her.

'Do you know Beth Harding?'

'Who?'

'The woman who owns your company.'

'No, dear. I'm just a casual. I deal with my supervisor not the bigwigs. I'm only here today because someone called in sick.' She looked down the corridor in disgust. 'Who's been dropping sweet papers? Who do you think has to pick those up? No consideration, some folk.'

They moved away as she continued vacuuming and complaining about people's dirty habits. She was still grumbling as she got into the service lift.

Even in the underground car park she didn't drop her persona and continued to pick up bits of rubbish as she walked across it. At the far corner was a door to which only the lessees of suites in the building had a key. It connected to the building next door, which was under the same management. The car park there was used for overflow parking.

Only when she was through the door did she stop, lean against the other side of it and let out her tension in a long sigh.

'You all right?'

She jumped in shock because she hadn't heard him approach, then smiled at Edward. 'Yes.'

He grinned. 'Very glamorous. And haven't you put on a bit of weight lately?'

She grimaced. 'I'm getting overheated from all the padding.'

'I'd still like to kiss you,' he said suddenly.

The oxygen seemed to vanish from the air around them as they stared at one another. 'I'd better not hug you till we're out of their reach,' he said regretfully. 'Come on. I'm parked over here.'

Before they drove off, she removed her uniform and padding, then crouched down in the back of the vehicle.

'There's no need for that,' he said, amused.

'Humour me. You can't be too careful today. I don't want to lead them to my mother.'

'How's she bearing up?'

'She sounded all right on the phone, better than I'd expected, actually, but I want to see her, to be sure.'

'I want to see her too.'

'You do?'

'Yes.' He peered into the rear-view mirror. 'You should be all right to sit up now. We're not being followed. In fact, I'll pull to the side and you can get into the front.'

'I'd rather stay here till we get to my mother's. If we stop, someone might notice us.'

'Whatever. Perhaps you could tell me where to go?'

'Sorry. I wasn't thinking. Turn right at the next traffic lights and . . . '

★ ★ ★

Pete went to see his mother in hospital quite openly. He was stopped at the entrance to the private wing, where a hospital security officer seemed to be acting as a guard and questioning everyone who wanted to enter.

As he waited his turn, Pete dredged up a smile and said to the journalists, 'Look, my mother's had a stroke. I need to see her before I do anything else. And guys . . . can we leave her out of things, please?'

They nodded at that, and since he knew several of them and had found them helpful in the past, he said, 'Thanks,' with some confidence that they would co-operate.

'When are you going to talk to us, Pete?' one asked. 'Can you deny you're refusing to see your birth mother?'

'We'll be making a full statement later. For now, I just want to check that this hasn't upset the mother who brought me up.'

They started taking photos as he showed his identification to the security officer, who clearly recognised him, but still went through the ritual.

It was a relief to get the media off his back for a few moments, and Pete paused to savour the quietness of the long corridor, the lack of people nipping at his heels. Then he moved forward to the nurses' station, smile back in place.

'Hi. I'd like to see my mother, Mrs Newbury.'

They looked at him curiously but no one commented on the article.

'She's just been moved to Room Three, Mr Newbury.'

'How is she?'

'Making a good recovery. Don't upset her.'

'I'll try not to.'

He walked in the direction the nurse had indicated and found Room Three. The door was open and he could see his mother lying in bed, staring into space. His heart sank at the sight of a newspaper spread out on the bedcovers.

'Hi, Mum.'

She looked up and smiled. Her speech was a little hesitant but clear enough. 'Pete, darling. I

317

was just reading about you.' She indicated the newspaper.

'Edward's helping me deal with that rubbish. You don't need to worry about it.' He tried to take the paper away from her, but she put one hand across it to prevent him.

'I want to be involved in whatever you're doing to counteract this rubbish. This was more my fault than yours, after all. I've been thinking how it all came about, why your father went to such lengths. I'd probably have had a nervous breakdown if I hadn't managed to adopt a child, and that's the sad truth. But I'd never have stolen another mother's child like that, never.'

He sat down beside the bed since it was obvious he'd do more harm than good if he refused to discuss the matter. 'Do you think Dad knew how they got hold of me?'

'I think he must have known there was something fishy about the adoption, or he'd not have used the identity of the baby who died. But I can't believe Donald would have condoned a kidnapping. Maybe he guessed afterwards when it hit the news headlines, though, because he grew very sharp-tempered for a time.' She rubbed her forehead. 'I was too happy to have you to notice much except you, and I just went along with what he suggested, a fresh start, he said. So we moved and were very happy, both in Australia and after we came back to England.'

'You mustn't make yourself ill worrying about this.'

She gave him one of her assessing looks. 'I'd make myself ill if I tried to *avoid* thinking about it or if I was worried about you being overprotective towards me.'

'I can't let them hound you. You didn't do anything wrong.'

'A wrong was done nonetheless and I want to meet your birth mother and apologize.'

He gaped at her. 'Mum, no!'

'If you don't help me do that, then I'll do it on my own. And Pete, darling, I want *you* to apologize to her as well. You must know how much you hurt her, refusing to have anything to do with her.'

'I still don't want anything to do with her, only . . . I think Edward's in love with her daughter.'

'Your sister, you mean?' She smiled. 'It's about time Edward found someone.'

'He's not been seeing Beth for long, but from the expression on his face when he talks about her, he's pretty keen.'

'I'm glad!'

'*Her* of all women. There are plenty of others around, better looking ones, too.'

'What have looks to do with falling in love? I'm glad for him. I was beginning to despair of him finding anyone after his divorce — given the circumstances.'

'He's not exactly lacked company over the years.'

'That's not the same thing at all. And when you marry again — '

He gaped at her, caught on the back foot by that one. 'When *I* marry again! I'm not sure I'll be doing that in a hurry. I'm not even divorced yet.'

'Oh, you will marry again. You're not the sort to live alone, and anyway, who'll look after you, do your washing and cooking with Fran gone? I want you to have a proper marriage, not a pretty doll to display by your side, so this time make sure you choose someone more mature, who wants a family and who'll make a happy home for you all. I never did take to Fran.'

'But you were always pleasant with her. She really liked you.'

'As if I'd alienate my only son by being nasty to his wife!' She smiled at him. 'Stop looking so anxious, darling. I'm recovering nicely, and if my left side's a little weak, well, I can still manage to do most things. I have to take more exercise than just gardening from now on, though, and they'll keep an eye on my blood, use thinners and things like that. Believe me, I don't intend to die till you've given me some grandchildren.'

He was relieved to see her old self re-emerging to deal with this crisis. She'd been so quiet and sad since his father's death. He took hold of her hand and raised it to his lips. 'You'd better choose someone for me next time, then.'

An image of Rosa slipped into his mind, surprising him. He wasn't ready to think of that sort of thing. But she was a restful and yet stimulating woman — and one who already had a successful life in her own right, so wouldn't be hanging on his coat tails.

He stayed chatting for a few more minutes, then saw that his mother was looking tired and took his leave. He stopped at the hospital florist's on the way out to order some pink roses for her, knowing how much she loved them, then drew a deep breath and turned to face the media circus again.

'How's your mother, Pete?' a woman called.

'She's improving, thank you, but has a long way to go before she'll be fully recovered. You know what strokes are like.'

'Was it this crisis that shocked her into the stroke?'

He felt like punching that fellow right on the nose, but shook his head. 'No. Sadly, she's not been taking care of herself since my father died. We'll make sure she's better looked after from now on.'

'What about your other mother?'

'Be at the press conference later and you'll find out.'

'How much later? There's been no announcement.'

'It'll be announced when my manager has arranged everything. And now, I really must go. I have next week's show to prepare for.'

'The visit hadn't gone too badly, considering, nor had the journalists been as pushy as he'd expected. But he hoped Edward could get the press conference organized for this afternoon. The media wouldn't be kept quiet for long, and if they started speculating and guessing, who knew what they'd dream up about him next?'

He didn't want to go back to the flat, which was stupid. It was his home. He'd fought to keep it.

But he'd be alone there. He didn't like being alone.

His mother's words came back to him and he suddenly grew angry at himself. What was he, a child who needed a nanny? She was wrong. He could look after himself perfectly well. How hard could housework be? He'd do a bit of tidying up, and some washing too when he got back. He wasn't totally helpless.

But it was harder to keep the smile pinned to his face as he went through another barrier of journalists waiting outside his home.

Once inside he looked round the rooms. They were too large for one person. Sounds echoed because they weren't carpeted but tiled. The place looked more like a display house than a home.

And worst of all, he hadn't yet heard from Edward.

How long could it take to organize a press conference?

Or were his birth mother and sister refusing to play ball?

★ ★ ★

Linda paced up and down. 'Beth should be here by now.'

'She may be having to take evasive action if the press are still after her. Where do they find all these people to chase after the unfortunates who hit the news?'

'I don't know.'

'You're still worrying about *him* too, aren't you?'

322

'My son? Yes. It's no good, Nat. He may be weak like his father, and he may not have treated me well, but this could destroy his career, and I don't want to feel even vaguely responsible for that.'

'I keep telling you, it's not your fault.'

'It is, though, if only inadvertently.'

He shook his head sadly and came to plonk a kiss on her cheek. 'Let's see if there's anything about it on the TV.'

On the hourly news update Pete Newbury was mentioned again, this time pictured going into hospital to visit his mother who'd recently had a stroke.

Linda watched her son hungrily, noting again the physical resemblance to her father. She'd watched Pete on TV for years. How had she missed that likeness?

Because she'd been thinking of him as a little boy for nearly forty years, because that was all she'd really known him as. She'd told herself how old he would be as the years passed, and had even studied other young men in the street who might be that age, but the image that stayed with her was the loving little boy lifting his arms to be picked up and cuddled.

She took a deep breath. She was *not* going to cry again.

A car drew up in the drive and Beth got out, hair rumpled, wearing an odd assortment of clothing. She hurried across to the front door, followed by Edward Newbury, who looked immaculately dressed but worried.

Nat let them in while Linda put the kettle on.

She turned to greet them.

'I hope you don't mind my coming to see you, Mrs Harding?'

'No, of course not.'

'Edward helped me escape the press,' Beth said, hugging her mother. 'Are you all right? Really all right?'

'Yes, I am.'

'She's worrying about Pete,' Nat informed them. 'I keep telling her, it's herself she should be worrying about.'

'I don't have a career to lose,' Linda said, starting the coffee machine. 'Piece of cake?'

'I'm ravenous!' Beth said in a tone of surprise. 'I think I forgot to eat this morning.'

'I'll do you a proper breakfast, then. Mr Newbury?'

'Edward, please. A piece of cake would be nice but I did have breakfast.'

'My daughter misses too many meals,' Linda told him. 'You'll have to keep an eye on that.'

He realized she was treating him like an ally. 'It'll be my pleasure. I'm getting very fond of your daughter, Mrs Harding.'

'Call me Linda. And I can see that you are.'

'Is it so obvious?'

'Oh, yes. Takes one to know one.' She smiled conspiratorially at Nat.

When they were seated, Edward waited till Beth had finished some cheese on toast before taking over. 'Linda and Beth, I want to ask your help in defusing this situation. I've got Ilsa ready to call a press conference later this afternoon, but what I'd like to give them is a conference

324

with a united and amicable group of people, not a family torn apart.'

'That's all very well, but your cousin didn't even want to see my Linda before,' Nat said, positively bristling with indignation. 'He really upset her.'

'I know. There is no excuse, not really, but he was in a state of shock about the kidnapping. He didn't even know he was adopted. And his marriage had just broken up, too.'

'If it'll help him, I don't mind appearing,' Linda said.

'I do. I'm not a good enough actress to carry off the amicable bit,' Beth said. 'I feel anything but amicable towards him.'

Edward turned to look at her, his expression softening. 'I won't let him hurt you again. Couldn't you try?'

'I meant exactly what I said: I don't think I *could* do it. I'm not saying that to be awkward. I can't act, fudge things, pretend. I just can't. And that'd show.'

'You can leave most of the speaking to me,' Linda said. 'It'd be all right if she was indignant on my behalf about the misunderstandings, wouldn't it, Edward?'

'I suppose so. But I was hoping you two could sit on either side of Pete.'

'No way!' Beth glared at Edward. 'I don't want to go near him or see him ever again, if you want the truth.'

He looked at her aghast. This was the last thing he'd expected.

Linda intervened. 'What about your aunt,

325

Edward? How is she? Will she be well enough to join us?'

'No. But I'm hoping to film a statement from her.'

'And if you do all this, Pete will get away scot free.' Beth shoved her plate away and left the room, tossing 'He doesn't deserve it!' over her shoulder at them.

Linda sighed. 'She's always hated lying. And she's right about one thing: she's not good at it.'

'Then we'll have to reconcile her and Pete.'

'Do you think you can do that in time?'

'I have to.'

'Is he a good actor?'

'Usually. But he's more upset by all this than she realizes. He loves his mother dearly.' Edward looked at Linda. 'Sorry if that upsets you, but my Aunt Sue has been a good mother to him.'

'It does upset me, but at the same time I'm glad she's looked after him and loved him so much. It'd be far worse to know he'd had an unhappy childhood.' She dabbed at her eyes. 'I'm sorry. I can't help getting emotional.'

'I'm sorry that I have to ask you to do this.'

'I want to help him.'

Nat put an arm round Linda. 'Better go and see Beth now, Edward. If you can't sort things out with her, it's going to be harder to convince people that today's story was wrong.'

★ ★ ★

Edward found Beth in a spacious sunroom, silhouetted against the brightness, her whole body stiff. She hadn't noticed him, so he cleared his throat. 'Beth?'

'Go away. I'm not going to change my mind.'

'Your mother suggested I talk to you.'

'She's always been too kind for her own good. Well, this time you're pushing it too far, taking advantage of her generous nature. I *can't* forgive him for the way he spoke to me — and to her. He hurt her all over again. I'd rather not have a brother than have one like him. He turns his charm on and off like a tap. It's not *real*.'

'Don't be fooled by his charm. He's very insecure under it.'

She let out a bitter laugh. 'Oh, yes?'

'Yes. He was the same at school. He can't bear anyone not to like him. I've been wondering since I found out the truth if that was because he was torn away from everyone he loved when he was small. He doesn't seem to remember his previous life, but maybe something inside him does and is terrified of losing everything again.'

'*I* was torn away from everyone I loved, too, but no one seemed to think about that.' She raised one hand to dash away the tears. 'I was passed from one family member to another, a month here, a month there. Distant relatives or friends of my parents who didn't really want me. I was alone and grieving. My mother couldn't come to see me for months because she was ill. My father visited a few times. And that was it.'

'By the time my mother recovered, their marriage was on the rocks and Dad had moved out. He was very like Pete, you know. *Charming*.'

The way she said it was more like an insult

than a compliment, he thought. His heart ached for the lonely little girl she must have been.

'I adored my father until then. But he didn't visit very often, and when he remarried, I saw him two or three times a year at most, so I soon learned to manage without him. He'd take me out to a café or a park, and he'd always be looking at his watch.'

Edward could hear the pain ringing in her voice and wondered if she'd ever told this to anyone. He didn't dare move, not as long as she was talking. He could only hope it helped her to let the pain out.

'When I did go home again, I had to help Mum. She was still fragile. Young as I was, I looked after her more than she looked after me.'

'That must have been hard.'

Her voice was low and had a bitter edge to it. 'You don't know how hard! No one does.'

'But your mother did recover, so you must have done well.'

'Yes, she recovered. We were ticking along nicely till this happened. She'd found Nat. My business was going well. I'd met you. And then *he* had to come out of the woodwork and upset everything all over again — even my relationship with you.'

'He hasn't upset as much as you think. Your mother's coping brilliantly. She's a very strong woman. And — '

She didn't let him finish. 'Well, I'm not coping, brilliantly or otherwise. I can't do it any more. I just *can't*!'

As she burst into tears, he hurried across to

take her into his arms, and though she tried half-heartedly to push him away, he wouldn't let her. As he listened to her sobbing, felt her whole body shaking against his, tears welled in his own eyes. How long had this been bottled up? he wondered.

As she began to calm down, he kissed her forehead and cheek. 'It's been hard for you. First losing Pete and then losing your daughter on top of it all.' He guided her across to a seat.

'I'm sorry.'

'Shh now. I think you needed to get this out of your system.'

'You must think I'm weak.'

'No, I don't. And actually, I understand more than you realize, because I lost my parents when I was ten. My whole world turned upside down then. I not only lost them, but my home, my school friends. Even my cat, because my aunt is allergic to cats. But I had my aunt and uncle to help me, at least, and I soon realized how Aunt Sue loved me. And I had Pete. He was amazingly kind for a child.' Edward waited and when she said nothing, he added, 'It doesn't sound as if you had anyone. People were too focused on your mother.'

She nodded and sighed against his chest.

'Look. We'll manage the press conference without you, but I'm not leaving you on your own when you're so upset.' He reached out to brush away a tear with one fingertip. 'I'll take you home now and wait with you till Jo can come home from work to look after you.'

'No need. Ghita's there.'

'Kind as Ghita is, you need your own daughter at the moment. I'll go and tell your mother what we're doing and give her a few details of the press conference. Wash your face then meet me at the car.'

'I should speak to Mum.'

'She'll understand, believe me.'

20

Edward dropped Beth at home and she directed him to the rear entrance, where her resident's key would let her in through the dustbin and recycling area. He watched her go into the building and saw how slowly and wearily she was moving. He wanted desperately to stay with her, but had to sort out Pete's problems first.

Beth had insisted she was all right, but he found out from Ghita where Jo was working and drove there first, telling the manager that Jo's mother was ill and he'd come to take her home.

Jo came hurrying out, stopping in surprise when she saw Edward waiting for her. 'What's wrong with Mum?'

'Nothing physically, but she's very upset. She needs you.'

'Mum never seems to need anyone.'

'She puts up a good front,' he agreed, 'but believe me she needs your support now. Did you see the newspaper article?'

'Yes. Ghita rang to let me know. Horrible, isn't it? I didn't let on at work that it was Mum. It was on the midday news on TV as well. I saw it while I was eating my lunch. They showed our block of flats and Ghita walking past. What exactly happened with Mum?'

He explained about the floods of tears.

Jo stared down at her clasped hands. 'I've been there. I know how she feels.'

She spoke so quietly he had to strain to hear what she was saying.

'Ghita helped me when I was at my lowest ebb, otherwise I don't know what I might have done.'

'Then you'll understand. I think your mother's been pushing her own feelings back ever since Pete was kidnapped.'

'Do you think that's why she's always been a bit uptight and guarded?'

'I'm no psychologist, but I wouldn't be surprised. I've rarely seen anyone as upset as she was today.'

'She doesn't usually cry at all.'

'I hope your boss won't mind you leaving early.'

'Too bad if he does. But Mr Benson knows I don't take time off unnecessarily.' She walked in silence, then said, 'I'm not sure Mum will open up to me, though. She doesn't talk about her feelings, never has.'

'It'll comfort her just to have you there, I'm sure. This is my car.' Edward made no attempt to unlock the doors, standing with one hand on the top of his car. 'Look, I think she worries about upsetting you and losing another person she loves.'

Jo stared at him aghast. 'As she lost her brother!'

'Just a guess, but yes.'

'I was sorry I'd run away even a week afterwards, but I was too proud to go home. Dad could be so sarcastic. He'd never have let me forget. But there's no fear of me running away from anyone or anything again, believe me.' She put up her chin and stared at him.

'I do believe you. Tell your mother that sometime.'

'I will.'

When he'd dropped Jo off, he went to Pete's flat and ignored the journalists waiting outside, moving through them so purposefully they fell back before him.

'What's wrong, Edward?' one of them called.

'I'm just sorting out the mess that incorrect story has made of my cousin's life.'

'How is it incorrect?'

'Come to the press conference later this afternoon and find out.' He was through the doors by then and didn't look back. Some situations could only be dealt with face to face, and this was one.

He wasn't sure how Pete would react, though. That one incident, so many years ago, had marked the whole family, it seemed, Pete as well as his mother and sister. The father was conspicuous by his absence, even now, so Edward didn't intend to waste time on him. A man who'd abandoned his wife and daughter so easily and jumped straight into another relationship wasn't worth it.

Could the main players in the drama be made whole again? He'd try his hardest to help them, because they mattered very much to him.

But if Pete wasn't prepared to be kind to his birth mother, then Edward would wash his hands of his cousin's problems and concentrate on looking after Beth.

She wasn't going to face any more crises on her own if he could help it.

★ ★ ★

Jo went into the flat and found Ghita in the kitchen, cooking something and looking sad. 'Has Mum come home?'

'Yes. She said she wanted to lie down. She looked dreadful, Jo, as if she'd been crying good and hard.'

'She has.' Jo explained quickly, then made a cup of tea to take to her mother.

She tapped on the bedroom door and when there was no answer, peeped inside. Her mother was lying on the bed, staring up at the ceiling. It took her a minute or two to react to Jo's entrance.

'Sorry. I'm a bit tired.'

'You're upset, you mean. Edward came and got me from work. He didn't think you should be left alone.'

Even that didn't rouse Beth out of her lethargy. 'Well, he's wrong. What I need quite desperately is to be left to think my way through this.'

'Let me stay with you, Mum. You've never talked about what happened to you after your brother vanished. Tell me about it now.'

Beth sat up and glared at her. 'I know you mean well, and Edward means well, but I can't take any more kindness and fuss. It's *suffocating* me.'

She looked so fierce Jo set the cup of tea down

beside her and went back to the door. 'All right. If that's what you want, face it alone. But you don't need to. I'm definitely not going back to work today and I'll be here whether you want me or not.'

She went out, then poked her head back round the door to yell, 'And I won't run away again, whatever you do, so get used to that!'

★ ★ ★

Beth watched the door shut, feeling guilty about upsetting her daughter. Why could none of them realize that what she needed most was peace and quiet to pull herself together? That had always worked before. It was her way of tackling problems. She was ashamed of how she'd broken down in front of Edward. Weak, that was.

First she had to centre herself again. Somehow, ever since she'd discovered that Pete was her brother, she'd felt off balance.

She'd tried to look after her mother in this new crisis, as she always did, but she hadn't been needed. This time her mother was the strong one, and anyway Linda had Nat now.

More tears came into Beth's eyes, but she took a few deep breaths and got control of herself again. It was nice to know Edward was concerned enough about her to fetch Jo, though. He was a kind man, and foolishly she'd fallen in love with him. But if being with him meant being with her brother as well, seeing Pete regularly *and* his mother . . . then she couldn't face it. Just couldn't.

The look of scorn on Pete's face as he'd offered her money to go away and keep quiet about their relationship, the way he'd treated her mother, who was also *his* mother — that'd shown her what he really thought of them. However hard he pretended to be friendly now, she wouldn't be able to trust him.

No, she couldn't face having anything further to do with him and that was that.

A short time later she hugged another thought to herself. It was comforting that Jo had come home from work, wanting to help. She couldn't really help, no one could. But still, to know her daughter was there for her felt . . . good. It meant this horrible business hadn't driven her away.

And if Jo meant what she'd yelled as she left the bedroom, that would fill some of the emptiness after she stopped seeing Edward.

She had her daughter back, even if she'd lost the man she loved. She must cling to that. Nothing in life was ever perfect. She should know that by now.

★ ★ ★

Ghita's father was watching the television news during his lunch break at the corner shop he owned when he saw his daughter on the screen. She was going into the block of flats where Beth Harding, Pete Newbury's sister, lived. It suddenly occurred to him that Beth Harding was the mother of Ghita's neighbour Jo Harding. He snapped his fingers as he realized exactly where his daughter was living. No wonder he hadn't been able to find her.

He listened to the reporter and it just bore out what he felt about the way life ought to be organized. His sons could say what they wanted, but the old ways were best. If Pete's mother had been looking after her child properly in the first place, no one would have been able to kidnap him. A woman's place was in the home, first her family's home, then her husband's. Women still bore the children whether you'd moved to a new country or not.

But he'd been wrong to throw Ghita out when *it* happened. His wife had never forgiven him for it. And see where it had led.

He called his eldest son in, and when they showed a summary of the main news articles on the television, he pointed Ghita out to Nuriel. 'I'm going round there to find your sister and bring her back. She shouldn't be living with a woman like that.'

'What has Mrs Harding done wrong?'

'It's what she *is* — a woman running a business like a man. A woman whose mother let her son be kidnapped. What kind of an example is that for a decent young woman? No wonder her own daughter ran away from home. And now that woman's name is on everyone's tongue. How will any man want to marry Ghita if she associates with notorious people?'

Before his son could stop him, he'd hurried out of the shop.

Nuriel stood there for a moment, trying to get his head round all this. His father was so old-fashioned he'd treated Ghita unfairly over something which wasn't her fault. When he found out what had happened, Nuriel had tried to find her, but she'd vanished, been taken into a women's shelter. It had made him sad that strangers were the ones to help her, but at least it meant she was safe. And anyway, she'd have had a miserable life if she'd come home.

He and his mother worried about his father, who refused to change with the times. They lived in England now and had done for the past twenty-five years. Nuriel couldn't remember living anywhere else, and Ghita and the others had been born here. This was their home.

Why had his father gone chasing after poor Ghita? What did he think he could do, drag her back by force? The trouble was, he might even try to do that, and then *he* would be in trouble with the police.

Leaving his youngest brother in charge of the shop, Nuriel hurried upstairs to the family flat to tell his mother what had happened. 'I'm going after him.'

'No one can stop him when he gets like this,' she said sadly.

'I can try.'

'Tell Ghita I want to keep seeing her — and my grandson. He's a lovely child.'

Nuriel went to give his mother a hug. 'I will.'

★ ★ ★

Although Edward was longing to check that Beth was feeling better, time was of the essence. He went straight from the office to the hospital, armed with a video camera. If his aunt would say something conciliatory, it would help fill in the gap where he'd planned to have Beth make a statement.

Aunt Sue listened to his request and nodded. 'Of course I'll speak. But on one condition.'

'Oh?'

'Afterwards I want you to ask Mrs Harding if she'll come and see me. Beg her to, if necessary. I can't rest easy till I'm sure she understands that I didn't know about the kidnapping.'

She was looking stressed, so he agreed. 'But only on condition you rest after this and don't let yourself get agitated.' To his relief she sagged back against the pillows, nodding.

She smiled sadly. 'How can I help but feel agitated, Edward, when the press is trying to destroy my son?'

He laid his hand on hers. 'I told you I was going to sort all that out. Trust me. I shall do it. Unless we're very unlucky, by the time I'm finished, Pete will come out of this more pitied than reviled.'

'I never thought, you know . . . ' She broke off, staring blindly across the room.

'Never thought what?'

'How *he* must have felt at being taken from everything he knew. He wouldn't speak at first, cried a lot. I held him, comforted him, was glad when he'd only come to me, not Donald. I was so selfish. I tried to make him forget the past by never speaking of it. But he was three, not a baby. Of course he must have remembered things.'

339

He kept a careful eye on her, still worried, but she took a deep breath and turned back to him. 'You're right. I mustn't get agitated. It'll do no one any good if I get ill again. Tell me what you want me to say.'

It was quickly done. She spoke simply and directly. What she said moved Edward greatly, but he didn't let himself give in to his emotions. He had to hurry. It was up to him to get them all out of this safely.

Not only Pete, but the woman he loved.

★ ★ ★

Thanks to Ilsa's efficiency, the press conference was scheduled for five o'clock in one of the big hotels near the office. Edward grabbed a sandwich on the run as he and Ilsa made the final arrangements. She phoned the major newspapers and television news programmes, while he called a few other important people to let them know what was happening. He particularly didn't want the senior management at the television station to be surprised by what was going on.

He tried several times to phone Beth, but Jo said her mother was having a lie down and wasn't answering the phone. He explained to Jo what he'd arranged and she listened carefully, questioning him a couple of times.

'I'll let Mum know you called and try to make her change her mind about coming to the press conference.'

'I doubt she'll do that and I won't pressure her into it.'

'It'd help, though, if she was there, wouldn't it?'

'Yes. But she's been hurt enough so we'll manage without her.'

Jo's voice grew softer. 'You really love her, don't you?'

'Yes. I'm not sure whether she loves me, though — or should I say whether she loves me enough?'

'She'd be mad to let this come between you.'

'Only she can know whether she'll be able to face meeting Pete and his mother regularly. I can't stop seeing him, or my aunt. They're my only close family.'

'You mean you're not going to try to persuade her if she gives you the heave-ho?'

'Persuade, yes, force, no.'

She was silent for a few moments, then said, 'And on top of all else she's had to face, I ran away, so she was left on her own again. I can't believe how stupid I was, how insensitive! I knew about her brother and I still did it to her again.'

'We all learn a few things the hard way as we grow up.'

She chuckled. 'You don't look as if you've ever put a foot wrong.'

'Oh, I have. Believe me, I cringe when I think of some of the stupid things I did as a teenager. I was just lucky they didn't have serious lasting consequences.'

She surprised him by saying, 'I hope you and Mum do get together.'

'Thanks. So do I. Um — what brought that vote of confidence on?'

'Chatting to you, realizing you're being straight with me. And what's more, I think you'd make a great grandfather for Mikey.'

He was still smiling when he put the phone down. Grandfather! He'd given up hope of that when he found he couldn't father a child. It'd be wonderful to have a grandchild, possibly more than one if Jo met another guy she liked.

Ilsa looked into his office. 'Something nice happen? You're smiling for the first time today.'

'Yes. Just a small thing, but it lifts the spirits.'

★ ★ ★

At three thirty there was a knock on the door, and when Ghita answered it, she let out a cry of shock at the sight of her father.

He pushed into the flat, grabbing her arm and giving it a shake to emphasize his words. 'You, my girl, are packing your things and coming home with me now. I'm not having you staying with *that* woman for one hour longer.'

Jo rushed into the hall and saw her friend trying to pull away from her irate father, so tried to shove between them. 'Let her go, you big bully!'

'Mind your own business, you! I'm not having my daughter associating with people like you and your mother.'

'What's my mother done wrong, for heaven's sake?'

'She's a bad example for my daughter, goes out and works like a man. And *her* mother was bad too. *She* was so careless she let her son be kidnapped.'

Furious, Jo poked him in the chest. 'You're a fine one to talk. What did you do when your daughter needed help? Disowned her, that's what. If it hadn't been for the women's shelter, she'd have been begging on the streets. Some father you are!'

She grabbed Ghita's hand and yanked her away, knowing how her friend froze when faced with the man who had once dominated her life. Shoving Ghita behind her, she glared at him. 'Get out of this flat before we call the police.'

'I'm her father. I have a *right* to tell her what to do.'

Jo made a loud, scornful noise. 'Rubbish! She's twenty-four, not fourteen. Besides, as I just told you, you lost that right when you abandoned her after she was attacked. She's happy here and she'll be happy living with me, too, when we find a place of our own. But she'd never be happy with you because you don't care about her, only about yourself.'

Ghita's father gaped at her, then lunged forward, arm raised.

★　★　★

Beth woke from an uneasy doze to hear someone shouting in the hall. She lay for a moment, then jerked upright as she realized one of the voices was a man's, and that it was Jo who was yelling at him.

Had the journalists broken in?

She rolled off the bed and ran to the door, flinging it open to see a man lunging for her

343

daughter. Grabbing the nearest thing, which was one of Mikey's soft toys, she hurled it at him.

The toy was too soft to harm him, but it stopped Ghita's father in his tracks. He turned to glare at her just as someone else pushed open the front door and called, 'Father, stop this!'

The newcomer was a startlingly handsome young man, with dark hair and beautiful coffee-coloured skin.

'I beg you, don't cause trouble, Father!' he pleaded. 'These people have enough to bear.'

His father grunted but let his hand fall.

Beth looked from one person to the other. 'Let's go and sit down in the living room. We should talk about this reasonably, Mr Haddad, not come to blows.'

Ghita gestured to the door of the living room. 'Please, Father.'

'I'll come in willingly.' Nuriel moved forward.

His sister gave him a quick smile of gratitude.

His father hesitated, looked at his son and daughter, then flung up his hands, speaking in his own language.

To everyone's relief, after hesitating for what seemed a long time, he went through the door to the living room.

Beth gestured to the sofa. 'Please sit down, Mr Haddad. May we offer you some refreshment?'

The others filed into the room and took seats, but Ghita took the one furthest away from her father.

'Thank you for your hospitality, Mrs Harding,' Nuriel said, seeing that his father seemed struck dumb. 'We'd like that very much.'

344

'I'll put the kettle on,' Jo said.

For once, Ghita didn't rush to help in the kitchen. When Kaleel came across to her, she pulled him on to her knee and cuddled him close, as if protecting him.

Nuriel went across to his sister, who looked at him warily. He knelt down beside her and spoke to the child. 'Hello, Kaleel. I'm your uncle.'

She whispered in her son's ear.

He smiled at Nuriel and said, 'Hello, Uncle Nuriel,' then grew shy and hid his face against his mother.

Mikey tried to go towards them. Beth grabbed him. 'Stay with me, darling.'

He looked at her mutinously but let her pull him on to her lap.

Nuriel pulled out his mobile phone, took a photo of his sister and her child, then showed it to Kaleel, who clapped his hands in pleasure. 'I'll give a copy of this to my mother,' he said. 'She longs to know her grandson better.'

Mr Haddad closed his eyes, but tears leaked out and he wiped them away with one forearm, muttering something.

'What's he saying?' Beth whispered to Nuriel.

'He's saying he wants his family back,' he said. He turned to his sister. 'You don't need to come home to live, but you could come to visit us, surely? I'd fetch you and see you got home safely afterwards each time.'

Then she too was weeping, flinging herself into her brother's arms. 'Yes, yes! I'd love that.'

The two little boys, upset by all the fuss, began to cry as well, and by the time they'd been settled, Jo was back with a tray of refreshments.

'I'm not as good at this as Ghita,' she said conversationally. 'She's teaching me a lot, but I'll never be a good cook like she is.'

She began to pass out the cups of coffee, offering sugar and milk, then a platter of biscuits.

Mr Haddad hesitated, then took what she offered, and Nuriel breathed a sigh of relief.

Ghita stayed where she was, her son on her knee, looking occasionally at her father, an uncertain gaze in which hope was mingled with fear.

Kaleel saw where she was looking and peeped at the man, too.

'He's your grandfather,' she whispered. 'Say hello to your grandfather.'

For a moment all seemed to hang in the balance, then Mr Haddad put down his cup, held out his arms and said in a husky voice, 'Come to me, Kaleel.'

To everyone's astonishment, the little boy slid off his mother's knee and went across to the man sitting opposite, standing in front of him, staring at him as he said, 'You came to see us before.'

'Yes.' With an inarticulate murmur, Mr Haddad gathered his grandson in his arms, tears rolling down his cheeks.

Nuriel exchanged thankful glances with Ghita. 'Maybe now,' he said softly, 'we can begin to mend our family.'

Beth had been watching all this, not daring to interrupt. Impossible not to be moved by the reconciliation. Impossible not to shed a tear with them.

And, she realized suddenly, she'd learnt something important from it.

'I have to leave,' she said. 'I don't wish to offend you, Mr Haddad, but this is very important. Please stay as long as you like.'

'Where are you going, Mum?' Jo asked, coming to the door.

'I'm going to the press conference, where else?'

Jo gave her a hug. 'Oh, Mum, I'm so glad. It's the right thing to do, I know it is. Do you want me to come with you?'

Beth hugged her back. 'No. But I want you to be here when I get back.'

'You won't lose me again, Mum. We may quarrel — ' She smiled wryly and amended it to, 'We will quarrel sometimes, but I won't run away again, I promise.'

So Beth had to give her another hug.

★   ★   ★

When her mother had left, Jo turned to Ghita's father. 'I can't do it as well as your daughter, but I think we should have some more bits and pieces to eat, show you proper hospitality. It'd be nice for us all to eat together, don't you think? And apart from anything else, the boys will be getting hungry.'

'I'll help you,' Nuriel said.

Ghita stared at her brother in amazement. 'You will?'

'I have English friends. I've learned not to sit and expect to be waited on. You stay and tell

Father about Kaleel. Have you any baby photos?'

'Quite a few.'

'Please let me see them,' his father said.

Mikey tugged at the visitor's trouser leg. 'I've got a huffilump.'

'He means elephant,' Ghita said.

'I've got a teddy,' Kaleel said.

'Show me your toys.'

Mikey and Kaleel trotted off to fetch them and Ghita was left with her father.

'He's a fine boy,' he said. 'A fine grandson.'

'I'm bringing him up carefully to know what's right and wrong. Father . . . I did no wrong that night, spoke to no one, looked at no one.'

He nodded his head. 'I knew that really. Your mother said so straight away. I was . . . ashamed. It's not an easy thing for a man like me to deal with.'

She sat with head bowed.

'I shouldn't have turned you out, Ghita. I should have helped you. Your mother weeps at night still.'

'I can't come back to live with you but I'd love to come back to visit. I could bring Jo, too, perhaps? She's like a sister to me. She's protected me, helped me.'

'Then she's very welcome in our house.'

In the kitchen Nuriel was proving inept but willing. Jo got him to set out some small crackers on a plate and cut up cheese into pieces while she refilled the coffee pot.

'There.' He indicated the plate.

As they both looked at it, a piece of cheese rolled off.

'Ghita would have made it look pretty. And it looks a bit bare, don't you think? I know . . . Mum's got some olives.' She opened the fridge and offered him the jar. 'Set them out next to the cheese while I see if I can find anything else. Ghita always seems to produce several plates of things.'

She pounced on a platter of halva in the fridge and put some on a doily on a smaller plate, then grinned at Nuriel. 'That's the best I can do.'

'It's symbolic to share food. Important. No one will complain.' He frowned and bent his head for a moment. 'Will your mother be all right? I could see she'd been crying. Shouldn't you go after her?'

Jo shook her head. 'No, this is something she needs to do on her own.' She peeped into the living area. 'Let's go and rescue Ghita now.'

'Rescue?'

'They both look as if they don't know what to say and your father looks embarrassed.' As they picked up the plates, she studied Nuriel. 'How come you're not like your father?'

'I came here when I was three, grew up in England, and we lived in a small town at first where I went to the local school. That was fortunate for me. The headmaster didn't allow bullying and welcomed children of every nationality. I was very happy there, sorry when my father brought us to London and tried to live more like the old way. It was too late for me by then. I felt English. How did you meet Ghita?'

'I was living rough until I had the baby. I met Ghita in hospital and we teamed up. I got

349

depressed after the birth and she just about saved my life. I swore then that one day I'd get a home of my own for me and Mikey, and she wanted the same for her son.' She broke off and smiled at Nuriel. 'Though why I'm telling you this when I've only just met you, I can't think. Come on. Let's go and relieve Mafeking.'

She didn't explain the last comment, just sailed into the living room and offered the plate to Mr Haddad, winking at Ghita and automatically telling Mikey and Kaleel to find towels to sit on if they wanted some food.

21

Beth drove to the hotel where Jo said the press conference was going to be held. She was worried she'd miss the beginning, but hoped to get there before it ended.

Having seen the difficulties and stresses faced by Ghita and her family as they tried to reconcile with one another, she'd suddenly realized she had no right to expect things to be any easier for her. Why should Edward have to give up his relationship with his cousin, which was obviously a close one? Why should Pete do anything to hurt the woman who'd brought him up, when they clearly loved one another deeply?

What had happened had been hurtful after the years of wondering whether her brother was still alive — but the kidnapping wasn't Pete and his mother's fault. She didn't suppose anyone would find the guilty person after all this time, but there were still many years, hopefully, in which to rebuild their relationships. She hoped Pete wouldn't refuse to associate with her mother once this fuss had died down. She was going to try very hard to hold out an olive branch to him and see if she could become his sister again as well.

After all, if her mother could put the situation behind her, then perhaps Beth could too. If Ghita's father could try to reconcile with her, going against all his upbringing, then Beth could

351

at least try. She wasn't perfect. No one was. And it wouldn't be easy for her to open herself to the world again. But she thought, she really did, that Edward would understand and help her.

And that now she'd let him.

When she arrived at the hotel, she found a man standing guard at the door of the suite where the conference was being held.

'Sorry, ma'am, but my orders are that no one else is to go in.'

'I'm Pete Newbury's sister. I've been delayed. I have to be there. I'm late already.'

'They haven't started yet. Just a minute, ma'am.' He pulled out a mobile and rang someone, explaining the situation. 'They're just asking Mr Newbury about you.'

The man was burly, taller than her and as immovable as a rock, or she'd have pushed him aside. As it was, she could only wait impatiently. It seemed to be taking a long time to get an answer.

★ ★ ★

One of the security men came into the area where Edward, Pete and Linda were waiting to go out and talk to the media. He went towards Edward and bent to whisper something. Pete watched anxiously, wondering what had gone wrong now. They were already fifteen minutes late and he just wanted to get this over with. He felt too nervous to move across the room and find out what was going on.

Strange. He didn't usually get nervous before

352

a performance, and what was this but a performance? Only, it was more than a performance, it was one of the most crucial appearances he'd ever made.

His sister had refused to join them and he didn't blame her. He'd acted like a prize shit when he spoke to her.

His birth mother was sitting beside him looking slightly sad, and he wanted to say something to her but couldn't think what. She turned her head and gave him a tentative smile so he gathered up his courage in both hands. 'I'm sorry.'

'What about?'

'I'm sorry I treated you so badly. It's no excuse but I was in shock — and denial. I'm not just saying I'm sorry, either. I really mean it.'

The smile that lit her face brought a lump to his throat. He'd done so little, only said a few words, and she looked as if he'd given her the moon.

'I didn't mean to upset you,' she said, 'but I'd been waiting for years, hoping, praying that you were alive, and I just couldn't wait another minute to see you.'

'I don't remember anything from before the kidnapping, I'm afraid.'

'Why should you? You were barely three.'

He looked at her hands, clasped so tightly in her lap that the knuckles showed white. 'Are you nervous — about this press conference, I mean?'

She nodded. 'I'm not the sort to seek the limelight. I'm afraid of saying something wrong, making things worse.'

'Well, the less you say, the less likely you are to spoil anything. But it was me who nearly destroyed my career, treating you like that and treating Gerry badly, too. I need to apologize to him as well.' He gave a little shrug. 'I'm not saying I'll ever turn into a saint, mind, but I will be more careful how I treat people in future.'

'You enjoy being in the limelight, don't you?' she said wonderingly.

'I love it. Well, I do normally. Not today.'

'How strange! Your sister is a very private person, quite the opposite to you.'

He suddenly noticed that Edward was beaming at the security man. His cousin stood up and beckoned, so Pete went across to him and Linda followed.

'Beth's outside. They wouldn't let her in without an authorization. Will you fetch her?'

Pete stared at him in shock. 'Me?'

'Yes. She's changed her mind about appearing, it seems. The least you can do is apologize for how you treated her and try to make your peace with her first.'

'You'd do it better.'

Edward raised one eyebrow, stared at him and said nothing.

'I'll go and fetch her in, if you like,' Linda volunteered.

'No. Pete should do it.'

The two men locked gazes then Pete sighed and gave in. 'All right.'

Now he was not only nervous about the show, but nervous — no, make that terrified — of meeting his sister again. But when Edward

354

got that steely look in his eyes, there was no moving him.

Pete swallowed hard and followed the security man out.

★ ★ ★

He saw Beth turn round as the door opened. When he moved towards her, she looked as if she had a strong urge to flee, but she held her ground, waiting for him to come to her.

He'd never found words so difficult. He looked round the large space which seemed to be a small ballroom. On the other side of a partition wall, he could hear crowd noises. They seemed to be getting restive. 'I — um, think we need to talk before we meet the press. This isn't the best of places, but at least we've got it to ourselves. Will you listen to me?'

She nodded and gestured towards the partition. 'There sound to be a lot of people in there.' She looked even more nervous than her mother.

'Yeah. The whole circus, TV, radio, newspapers, you name it.'

'Oh dear.'

'Never mind them. They're strangers. It's the family who matter.'

She nodded.

'First I want to say how sorry I am for treating you so badly. And — well, you might like to know that I've already apologized to your mother.'

'*Our* mother.'

'I'm sorry. I've not quite got my head round that yet. It keeps surprising me. She seems nice.'

He rubbed his temple where a headache had been threatening all day.

Beth's voice was sharp. 'She *is* nice.'

'I didn't mean to suggest she wasn't.' He touched her arm briefly. 'This isn't easy, is it? If you assume there's goodwill behind what I say, even if the words are awkward, it'll help — because there is.'

'Sorry for jumping down your throat. If it's any consolation, I'm finding it hard too. And I'm not nearly as good with words as you are.'

'Why did you change your mind about appearing today?'

'I watched a family reuniting, in spite of their differences, and suddenly I wanted that too. I realized it'd be wrong to refuse to speak to you, wrong to let the media pillory you, wrong to avoid Edward because of you. I expect you weren't yourself when you spoke to me before.'

'No, I wasn't. I'd just broken up with my wife. Not that that's any excuse. It really threw me when you said you were my sister. I didn't even know I was adopted.' He closed his eyes for a moment, searching for words. 'I'm not sure I know who I am any longer. I'm a bit old for finding myself. You'd think I'd have done that by forty-one, wouldn't you?'

A scrape of laughter escaped her. 'It must run in the family. I'm completely off balance at the moment.'

'You've been crying.'

'Oh dear, does it show so clearly?'

'Yeah. Pity there isn't a make-up department here.'

'I've probably got something in my handbag. Maybe I can improve things a bit.' Beth fumbled in it, her hands shaking so much she dropped the whole bag.

He picked it up. 'Let me. Goodness, you're a tidy one. My ex used to carry the kitchen sink round in her daytime handbags. There. Is that it?' He pulled out a small pouch.

'Yes.' She tried to open the foundation and couldn't.

'Here. Let me make you up. Your hands are shaking too much. You don't have to worry, I'm used to doing this. I've spent time on the stage, though I wasn't the world's best actor.'

With swift, smoothing movements he put the make-up on, then pulled out a lipstick. 'Hold still.' When he'd finished he studied her. 'Don't cry any more.'

'Does it still show that I've been crying?'

'Not as much. Can I borrow a tissue?' He blew his nose hard. 'I'm a bit wobbly too. We're a right old pair, aren't we? Oops!' He blotted a tear that had escaped her control. 'No more tears, now.'

The door at the back of the room opened and Edward appeared, studying them anxiously then walking towards them. 'Everything all right?'

It was Beth who answered, speaking as honestly as she always did. 'It's starting to mend, I think.'

'Good. Are you ready to face them now?'

Pete looked at Beth. 'Are we?'

'Not really, but I'd like to get it over with.'

Edward smiled at them both. 'I'll speak first, OK?'

She nodded agreement.

He gave Pete a nod of approval, then turned to Beth, put a hand on each of her shoulders and kissed her on the nose. 'You'll be fine.'

When he took his hands away, she grabbed one of them and held on to it tightly as he led her to the door.

Pete followed them, looking enviously at their clasped hands.

★ ★ ★

In the waiting area Edward picked up the prepared statement. 'Shall we go and meet them?'

Pete took the statement from him and ripped it in half. 'You won't need this. I'm telling them the truth. There have been too many lies.'

Edward gaped at him. 'That's much too risky, Pete. I drew this up really carefully. We don't want to give them anything to hit you with afterwards.'

'I'll risk that.' He looked at his sister and mother. 'My whole life has been a lie. I need to clear that up and start afresh.'

'I don't know anything about dealing with the media,' Linda said, 'but I must admit I always prefer to tell the truth.'

'So do I.' Beth gave them a faint smile. 'And I'm the world's worst liar anyway.'

Edward threw up his hands. 'Go gently, then. Remember: don't tell them more than you have to.'

When they got out to the front, Edward

calmed the audience down and explained briefly what had happened to Pete as a child. He then handed over to his cousin, hoping desperately that he wouldn't blow it.

Pete turned to the expectant media. 'We're here to show you a united family front,' he began, pausing for a moment to let a ripple of surprise at this frankness die down. 'And I think I can safely say that we *are* starting to unite. But it hasn't been easy. At first I was in denial and I didn't behave well — though not nearly as badly as a certain newspaper would have you think.'

His mother patted him on the arm and he turned to smile down at her, a gesture that would touch the heart of a nation later on.

He turned back to the audience. 'My marriage had just broken up when I found out I'd been kidnapped as a child, and that my mother — who still feels like my mother and whom I love dearly — wasn't my birth mother. Can you imagine how that felt?'

More murmuring.

'Since then, I've started to get used to it. I've apologized to my birth mother and sister for trying to deny the truth,' he gestured to the two women beside him, 'and I hope we've now taken the first steps towards becoming a family. It looks as if I'm going to be in the very fortunate position of having two mothers, not to mention a sister and a niece whom I didn't know about. I hope they feel as fortunate about having me in their family as I feel about being part of it.'

He sat down and the audience burst into spontaneous applause.

Edward stood up and introduced Linda.

Her voice quavered as she started to speak and Pete reached out to hold her hand. She smiled at him gratefully and started again. 'Sorry. I'm a bit nervous. I'm not used to this sort of thing. I just wanted to say how happy I am to have found my son again after all these years, and to know he's been well loved and cared for by his other mother.' She dropped back into her seat as if her legs wouldn't hold her a minute longer.

Pete was still holding her hand, as the cameras recorded.

Edward introduced Beth, worried that the traces of weeping still showed clearly.

Her voice didn't wobble, but she sounded brusque. 'I didn't want to come today. I don't like being on show. But I wanted to support my brother and stop this stupid witch hunt. We're all human beings, with faults and virtues. No one here, least of all Pete, is a villain. We three are finding our way towards being a family again, so please . . . leave us in peace to do that. It's not easy after thirty-eight years apart.' She looked sideways and smiled at the sight of Pete comforting her mother. 'I think we're doing pretty well, though.'

She sat down with an audible sigh of relief.

Edward stood up. 'One member of the family couldn't be here today, my aunt, Pete's adoptive mother. She's had a stroke and she's still in hospital, but she did allow me to film her saying a few words on her son's behalf.' He gestured and the room went dark, then Sue appeared on a screen, looking frail, her mouth turned down a little at one side, but her words clear enough.

'I wanted to say how horrified I was to find my adopted son had been kidnapped. I'd never, ever have taken another woman's child unless it was offered willingly, which I thought Pete was. Linda, I apologize unreservedly for causing you such pain. You bore a wonderful son and I hope we can share him from now on. If you'd like to come and see me, I'll start by showing you all his childhood photos and probably boring you to tears, then we'll see if we can go on from there together. Thank you.'

Edward gestured again and the lights came on, revealing Linda dabbing at her eyes. He looked at the audience. 'There aren't many people who get such a public display of love and support. I'm quite certain Pete won't let any of them down. Thank you. We're not taking any questions. I know Pete is as upset about this media beat-up as Linda and Beth are, so I hope you'll excuse us now.'

Pete stood up and led the way out, offering his arm to his mother once they were clear of the table.

Somehow Edward managed to get next to Beth and put his arm round her shoulders, ignoring the flashing camera lights. 'You all right?'

'Better than I'd expected.'

'Thanks for coming.'

'I'm glad I did.' She looked ahead to see her mother introducing Pete to Nat. 'My brother's certainly a charmer.'

'He is. But I'm sure he meant what he said

today. He abandoned the prepared statement, after all, and tried to tell the truth. That's not something you do lightly when your whole career is at stake.'

'If he hurts her again, I'll kill him with my bare hands.'

'And if he hurts you, I'll do the same.'

She stopped walking to lay her head on his shoulder with a sigh. 'I don't think I've ever been so tired in all my life.'

'I was going to suggest we go back to my place if we all still needed to talk.'

Linda turned, having overheard this. 'No. I think we've talked enough today. Pete is going to take me to meet his mother tomorrow. Until then, I just want to go home and be quiet with Nat.'

Pete looked at Beth searchingly. 'You all right?'

She smiled. 'I'm the same as my mother. I need to sleep for a million years. It'd be nice if you came round tomorrow to meet your niece and your great-nephew, though, Pete.'

He looked at her in horror. 'I'm a *great-uncle*? For goodness' sake, don't tell anyone. I'm too young, surely!'

Suddenly they were all laughing.

★ ★ ★

As they walked out to the car, Beth turned to Edward. 'Can I come home with you?'

He beamed at her. 'I didn't dare ask.'

'I doubt I'll be much use for anything but sleeping.'

'As long as you sleep next to me, I'll not complain. Does that mean that I'm making progress with my courting?'

'Could be.' She smiled back at him. 'I need to go home first to get some clothes. I came here by taxi.'

'I have my car. I'll drive you back.'

★   ★   ★

At the flat they found Ghita and Jo sitting talking over the remains of an evening meal.

'You know Edward,' Beth said.

Jo raised one hand. 'Hi!'

Mikey, looking scrubbed and angelic in his pyjamas, turned to look at the newcomers. 'Kaleel's got a granddad and a uncle.'

'And a grandma,' Kaleel said. 'I'm going to see her tomorrow.' He nodded several times to emphasize this.

'It went well, then?' Beth asked.

Ghita smiled wearily. 'Better than we could have expected, thanks mainly to my brother Nuriel.'

'How did your press conference go, Mum?'

'The same as your meeting. Better than expected. It'll be on the TV news. But I hope it's the last one I ever have to feature in. I felt sick to my stomach with nerves.'

Edward put an arm round her shoulders. 'She did well, though. That's the main thing.'

'There's some food left if you're hungry.'

Beth flushed. 'We'll eat later. I'm just going to pack a bag. I'm staying with Edward tonight.'

Jo mimed applauding as her mother left the room and winked at Edward.

'Let's get it straight,' he said. 'I intend to marry your mother. She's not making it easy, though.'

'She's very independent. But my money's on you.'

Beth came back, still with a heightened colour, carrying a small backpack. 'I'm ready. See you tomorrow, girls.'

When they got to Edward's flat, Beth sat down with a sigh.

'I think the occasion calls for champagne, don't you?'

'Sounds lovely.'

He poured her a glass then raised his own, 'Here's to us. We got a bit lost in all the family stuff, but I think we're on track with our courtship now.'

She clinked her glass against his and took a sip. 'You've worn me down.'

He looked at her in mock dismay. '*Worn you down?* You really know how to make a man feel loved, don't you?'

He set his glass down, removed hers from her hand and pulled her into his arms. 'I love you, Beth. You know that. And I think you love me. Can't you say it?'

Slowly her face softened and she raised one hand to caress his cheek. 'I love you too. It was the thought of losing you that made me deal with my feelings today. I couldn't bear the thought of that. And seeing Ghita's family put their differences aside showed it could be done.'

She moved to kiss him, and as the kiss deepened, he said, 'What a waste of champagne! It'll go flat.'

'Mmm.'

Leaving the glasses behind, they walked into the bedroom, shedding clothes one by one, not hurrying now, relaxing together as they kissed and caressed one another.

'Your body is beautiful.'

'I'm too thin.'

'Whatever your body's like it's beautiful to me, because you're Beth. My Beth. And I love you.'

'I love you too.'

Over an hour later, he said apologetically, 'I'm sorry to disturb you, darling, but I'm ravenously hungry.'

'Do you know, I am too.'

'Bacon, eggs and slightly flat champagne do you?'

'Sounds perfect to me.' She slipped on her practical fleece dressing gown and grimaced. 'This ought to be satin and lace.'

'Stop worrying. You could be wearing sackcloth and I'd still think you looked lovely.'

As they sat eating bacon and egg sandwiches, he said suddenly, 'How about we throw a party?'

'A party?'

'Yes. For the family. A getting together party. Say in a couple of weeks. Aunt Sue should be all right to attend by then, even if she can't stay late. I think we ought to celebrate becoming a family.'

'Ghita too?'

'Ghita and her family too.'

'That'd be wonderful.'

Epilogue

Nearly two weeks later, the caterers moved into Edward's flat early in the morning and took over the kitchen for a luncheon party.

'It'll be the oddest mixture of people,' Beth worried as she got dressed for the celebration in clothes chosen by Renée.

Edward pulled her towards him. 'Stop worrying. You're not responsible for them all, only for yourself.'

She looked at him. 'I know that in my mind, but I don't feel it yet. I've had so many years worrying about Mum and Jo.'

One by one, people arrived. Ghita was very shy and had brought her brother to give her support. Jo was more confident, beaming at the sight of her mother and Edward standing with hands linked together.

'Look at Mum!' she hissed, nudging her friend.

'That's lovely.'

'Perhaps she's going to move in here permanently and let us have the flat.'

'You shouldn't be thinking things like that. Anyway, the boys would be better if they had a garden to play in. Oh, hello, Mrs Harding. That's a pretty dress.'

'New for today.' Linda smoothed it with one hand, admiring the sheen on the silk. 'Did I hear you two talking about finding somewhere to live?'

They nodded.

'Do you know anywhere?' Jo asked.

'Yes, I do. My house is standing empty and it has a garden. It seems to me you'd make perfect tenants.'

'Gran, do you mean that?'

'Of course she does!' Nat said, putting his arms round her. 'I'm not letting her leave me.'

The doorbell rang again and since Edward didn't appear to have heard it, Linda went to open it.

She stopped short at the sight of Sue Newbury in a wheelchair pushed by Pete. She'd not managed to go and see Sue yet, because the latter had been moved into a rehabilitation hospital and had been busy starting to retrain parts of her body.

'They've given Mum three hours' leave,' Pete said. 'Real bullies they are at that place.'

'I need to use the bathroom,' Sue said. 'Would you help me, Linda?'

'Yes, I'd be happy to.'

In the guest suite Sue looked at her so nervously that Linda said frankly, 'We've all decided to move on. Don't look at me as if I'm going to bite you.'

'I'd not blame you if you did.'

'It wasn't your fault, and I'd be a fool to let an old pain stop me from enjoying my son's company.' She stopped. 'Oh dear, that's going to be awkward, what to call him.'

'Son. He's son to both of us. Now, I'll just use the bathroom and then we'll rejoin the others. I'm looking forward to meeting your daughter and grandson. I've longed for grandchildren, but Pete said he didn't want any.'

'Maybe Mikey and Kaleel will change his mind about that.'

'Maybe. He's not got over the idea that he's a great-uncle yet!'

They both chuckled.

In the living room they found Pete and Edward on the floor helping Mikey and Kaleel put together a miniature plastic railway Beth had bought for them. She was sitting next to Ghita, laughing at their difficulties.

'It said for three year olds, so maybe only they can understand it. It seems to be too hard for grown men.'

'They make things differently these days from when we were children,' Pete protested.

Kaleel took the piece of plastic out of his hand and locked it neatly into the rest.

'Outdone!' he moaned.

Jo and Nuriel were standing near the big picture windows, chatting as they enjoyed the view.

'Thank you for looking after my sister,' he said.

'She looked after me most of the time. She's a lot more capable than you realize. Don't let your father bully her into returning home.'

'He'll be too busy scolding me for moving out. I can't live his way. I'm looking for a flat.'

'You'll have to take lessons in housework.'

'I can do that. And Ghita's promised to give me some cooking lessons.'

'She's a brilliant cook and always so

organized. Mum says she can find Ghita a job once Kaleel's in school.'

'Cleaning?' He grimaced.

'No. In the office. Or as a housekeeper. Though she'd have to do some office cleaning as part of her training if she worked in the office, so that she understands how things work in commercial cleaning. It's a boom business, but Mum is wanting to spend less time at work now she's with Edward.'

They turned round as Nat called out for their attention.

'Linda and I have an announcement to make.'

Everyone waited expectantly.

'We're getting married next month and you're all invited.'

As everyone crowded round to congratulate them, Edward went into the kitchen and soon afterwards a waiter brought in a tray of full champagne glasses, a few of which contained a colourless liquid.

'It seems appropriate to toast the engaged couple in the old-fashioned way. Some of the glasses contain lemonade for those who don't drink alcohol.'

When everyone had been served, including the little boys, he raised his glass. 'May I wish you every happiness, Linda and Nat.'

His words were echoed as the others raised their glasses, the little boys being helped to do the same.

Edward waited till the murmurs had died and said, 'There's one more thing. Beth is moving in with me permanently, and if I have my way, we'll be following Nat and Linda's example soon.'

Beth blushed furiously. 'Edward!'

He feigned innocence. 'What did I say? You'd not move in with me if you didn't love me.'

She went even pinker, but she was smiling. 'I do.'

'That's a big thing for Mum,' Jo whispered to her grandmother. 'She's not one for being demonstrative, is she?'

'If anyone can teach her, it's Edward.' Linda smiled and raised her glass to Sue, who was across the room. 'I can't believe how well it's turned out.'

'You all right now, Gran?' Jo asked.

'Yes. I've come to terms with the past and Nat's dragging me pell-mell into the future.'

'That's good, then. We'll look after your house carefully if you'll trust us with it.'

'I know, dear.'

★ ★ ★

When they'd all gone, Beth lay on the sofa with her head on Edward's lap. 'It went well, didn't it?'

'Yes. Your mother was lovely with Aunt Sue.'

'My mother's lovely with everyone.'

'Forgiven me now for embarrassing you today?'

'You took me by surprise.'

'I meant it. I do intend to marry you and I don't want to wait too long.'

'I can't give you children, Edward. I've had a hysterectomy.'

370

'I can't have any. It's why my marriage — my *first* marriage — broke up. But I'd love to have grandchildren if you don't mind sharing yours.'

'No, I don't mind at all. Edward — ' She paused but she had to ask it. 'Are you sure?'

'Very sure. I fell in love with you the second time I met you and that's not going to change.'

A happy sigh was his only answer. He thought he'd never seen her smile in such a relaxed, carefree way.

We do hope that you have enjoyed reading this large print book.

Did you know that all of our titles are available for purchase?

We publish a wide range of high quality large print books including:
Romances, Mysteries, Classics
General Fiction
Non Fiction and Westerns

Special interest titles available in large print are:
The Little Oxford Dictionary
Music Book
Song Book
Hymn Book
Service Book

Also available from us courtesy of Oxford University Press:
Young Readers' Dictionary
(large print edition)
Young Readers' Thesaurus
(large print edition)

For further information or a free brochure, please contact us at:
Ulverscroft Large Print Books Ltd.,
The Green, Bradgate Road, Anstey,
Leicester, LE7 7FU, England.
Tel: **(00 44) 0116 236 4325**
Fax: **(00 44) 0116 234 0205**

Other titles published by
The House of Ulverscroft:

FAREWELL TO LANCASHIRE

Anna Jacobs

Cassandra Blake has raised her three motherless sisters. The girls are the pride of their father Zachariah. When Lancashire's cotton supplies fail, due to the American Civil War, the mills fall silent and there's no work. There are stark choices: stay and risk starvation or pack up and begin again elsewhere. Cassandra has fallen in love with Reece Gregory. When he's given a chance to start a new life in Australia, he promises to send for her. Then an old feud tears the family apart. Cassandra is kidnapped and her sisters are forced to sail with a group of desperate cotton lasses to the Swan River Colony. Penniless and alone, Cassandra is determined to find them again — but there is a painful price to pay.

FREEDOM'S LAND

Anna Jacobs

Her husband was killed in the Great War, and his wife was dead. So why not join forces and build a new life for themselves in Australia? Andrew needs no persuasion: his children are motherless and he lives in a Lancashire town with no prospects. Yet for Norah, the very idea seems ridiculous . . . The government will give ex-servicemen a farm providing that they clear the land themselves. The only thing he needs is a wife to join him and time is short. But when Norah's father dies, there's nowhere for her or her daughter to go. It may be madness to follow a man she barely knows to an untamed land of heat, spiders and endless bush far from home, but it may also be the answer to all her dreams.

SAVING WILLOWBROOK

Anna Jacobs

When Ella discovers that her husband Miles plans to sell their farm without her agreement, it's the final straw: her marriage, already on the rocks, is over. Determined to save Willowbrook, and to protect her daughter Amy from a father who doesn't love her, Ella embarks on a mission to build the farm into a successful bed-and-breakfast business. But Miles, an ambitious and ruthless man, has other plans for the property development, which has been in Ella's family for centuries. And when Cameron O'Neal, a rival property consultant, arrives in the Wiltshire village and offers to help Ella, she finds herself torn between a fear of getting hurt again and a powerful attraction to a man whom both she and Amy instinctively like . . .

CHESTNUT LANE

Anna Jacobs

When novelist Sophie Carr rescues a man hiding in her garden from a group of paparazzi, she finds that her neighbour is ageing pop star Jez Winter. She's loved his music for years and knows he's had a tough time lately: an intruder having slashed his face, then a car accident putting his ability to play music at risk. Life's not been easy for Sophie either, losing her husband just as she was taking off as a novelist and having difficulties with her control freak son William and her daughter Andi, who is into recreational drugs and has lost her way in life since her father's death. And Sophie also has a secret to hide. One that makes her very wary of getting involved with Jez.